ACCEPTED

BOOK TWO OF THE BALANCE OF KERR

Kevin Steverson & Tyler Ackerman

New Mythology Press
Coinjock, NC

Chris Kennedy/New Mythology Press
1097 Waterlily Rd.
Coinjock, NC 27923
http://chriskennedypublishing.com/

Cover Design by J Caleb Design

Ordering Information:
Quantity sales. Special discounts are available on quantity purchases by corporations, associations, and others. For details, contact the "Special Sales Department" at the address above.

Accepted/Kevin Steverson & Tyler Ackerman -- 1st ed.
ISBN: 978-1648551536

We would like to both thank and dedicate this book to a man who left this world far too soon. It didn't matter that we all weren't related by blood…we accepted him and he us, like we were brothers. Thank you for that, Tommy.

There are those in this world who make everyone around them smile and feel upbeat. Those who have the ability to launch right into a conversation, taking up where you were the last time you saw each other. It didn't matter if it was a month ago. Tommy had that ability. Thank you for the conversations, Tommy.

Every once in a while someone comes along who can teach you things by just being who they are. Things like loyalty, humility, and dedication. Tommy taught others to chase their dreams, simply by watching how he did it relentlessly. Thank you for the lessons, Tommy.

Tommy was a man we wish you, the reader, had a chance to meet. We really do. It would have been life changing for you. He was a big man with an even bigger heart, and he wasn't afraid or ashamed to show it. A man who could tell another man he loved them at the end of a phone call and mean it. Tommy believed in our Creator and loved everyone accordingly. It showed.

Tommy, we know you are up there in a far better place and smiling down at us. Thanks for all the memories. We struggle with them being not enough, but we are grateful for them. We miss you and we always will. This book is for you, brother. Tommy Chayne, a true legend.

—Kevin and Tyler

Thomas Alan Herring
August 27, 1988 ~ March 22, 2021

Chapter One

The Creator proclaimed, "There will be good and there will be evil in the world. Therefore, as I have given Deities to aid you, I have given demons to tempt you. Only One can save you. Choose wisely, for the after awaits."

– second paragraph of The Book Of The One

Note: *it is widely accepted among clergy and scholars alike that the Creator, in infinite wisdom, created Deities and demons as written in The Book Of The One. The Deities are there to aid if asked, while the demons are there to tempt, allowing all thinking mortals the choice of good or evil. Right and wrong may be subjective, but the decisions one makes in life determines one's outcome in the after. What exactly the afterlife may be is fiercely debated to this day.*

Gar-Noth

The server left two mugs on the table and walked away without saying a word. Kryder glanced at Tog. He could read the unasked question on his face. When they'd first sat down, the woman had been friendly. She was a little surprised at their clothes, slight accent, and the size of Tog, but she hadn't mentioned it. Her mannerisms completely changed after she spoke to the owner of the establishment. She was silent and wouldn't look at them when she put their beers on the table.

"This isn't good," Kryder said after she walked away. He took a sip of the beer and wrinkled his nose. It was bland and watery. It sure wasn't like the beer Lucas served in the *Hobbled Goat*. He noticed his cousin's hand covered the mug in his grip across the table.

"Yeah?" Tog said. He pursed his lips at the puny mug. The last time he'd drank beer, Lucas had made sure the Half-Orc had had one more to his size. "We should have bypassed this town after we had to duck into the forest when the messenger galloped past."

"It didn't take long for word to spread," Kryder agreed. Then he whispered, "Then again, the Halls of Magic is only a half day's walk from King Westell's palace. He isn't there, but, whoever the steward is, he moves fast."

"You think their king made it to Yaylok yet?" Tog asked.

"Probably," Kryder answered. "He and more than half his forces, I'd guess. Enough to keep the citizens of Yaylok from rising up against it when they find out they now fall under his growing kingdom."

"That leaves the others to hunt down the ones who burnt the Halls to the ground," Tog surmised. He took a long sip from his mug. "You're right. Not good." He wrinkled his nose. His incisors showed slightly. If those around him hadn't already guessed he was of mixed race, they knew he was part Orc now. "Oh, you didn't mean the beer."

Kryder looked around the tavern. It was like many others they'd been in. One wall was covered by a huge fireplace, burning brightly to warm the room against the late fall weather. The stone it was made of was different from those used farther south in the next kingdom, but it was built nearly the same. Smoking lanterns were placed on small shelves on the other three walls. They gave the room the smell of burnt cheap fish oil.

About half the tables were occupied by locals and the occasional traveler. None of them were dressed quite the way they were. It was obvious by the cut of the leather traveling cloak Kryder wore that they were from the Baronies West or thereabouts. The other patrons could certainly tell they weren't from Gar-Noth.

"You can bet there's a reward or something for our capture, or worse," Kryder said. "We stick out around here."

The lighting in the room changed as the front door opened and shut. It allowed sunlight in for a brief instant. Kryder glanced over in time to see it close. Whoever had left was in a hurry. He glanced around to see if anyone else had noticed the hasty departure.

"Drink up," he said. "We need to get out of here. We're not going to be able to wait on the food. I think the owner sent someone to bring the watch."

Tog drained his mug and stood. Kryder took one last sip, but didn't finish it. He stood, tossed a few coppers on the table, put his traveling cloak on, turned, and made his way to the door and out of the tavern, with Tog right behind him. Without pausing, he turned toward the east and the road out of town heading to the coast, several days away.

After a few minutes of walking, they reached the edge of town. Without a word, he began to run. Tog ran beside him, mindful of his stride. He forced himself to slow and keep to a pace Kryder could maintain.

After about two miles and several looks back as they ran, Tog said, "Here they come. Looks like a half dozen on horses. They just rounded the bend back there."

Kryder nodded and said, between the steady, even breaths of one who ran often, "As soon as we get over this hilltop, we cut into the forest. Being able to run for hours won't do us any good when a horse is faster than we are. If they have bows, we'll take a few arrows to the back when they get close."

"Sounds good to me," Tog agreed, "because I have a bigger back, so…"

* * *

An arrow hit the tree Kryder hid behind and remained embedded. Another flew by and into the bush with a swishing sound as it tore through leaves. He dropped to his knees and peeked around the tree. He could see them, but they didn't notice him down low, where the bushes met the base of the tree. Two of the guards had bows, and five others had their swords out. The last was a little young to be part of the local guard. He did his best to hold the reins of their panicky horses.

Kryder glanced over. The huge oak tree Tog was behind was actually wide enough to provide cover for the big man. His cousin looked back at him with eyebrows raised. Kryder didn't want to make this decision, but it was the only way out of the situation.

They'd managed to travel a day further north into Gar-Noth, away from the Halls of Magic, but hadn't turned toward the coast and the port town where ships from Minth docked on occasion. The two nations were on the verge of war, but some goods still made their way back and forth, transported by brave ship owners, the merchants paying higher-than-normal costs for their transportation. The two intended to make their way to Minth the same way Kryder's mother had so long ago when she'd fled the Halls of Magic. By sea.

"Do it," Kryder said, resignation in his tone. "Take the two with bows first."

Tog nocked an arrow, drew the entire length of the massive bow, ducked around the tree, and let loose. At this short distance, the large arrow struck the guard in the chest, punctured the thin leather armor, went through the man, and buried itself in the swordsman behind him.

An arrow hit the oak tree six inches from Tog's side. Tog looked over, saw his cousin's outstretched hand, and knew a wind spell had moved the arrow in flight.

Before the guard could nock another arrow, Tog's next one punched through the man's metal-studded leather armor. It went through him and pushed the leather away from his back in a tent-like shape. He fell beside the first archer.

One of the sword-bearing guards panicked and turned to run. The sergeant grabbed his tunic from behind and tried to stop him. He used the hand holding his sword, so he only had a finger or two of his clothes. The man broke free and kept running, so Tog let him go. Instead, he shifted aim, and his arrow struck the sergeant—who was turned sideways to them—in the upper arm, causing the man to drop his shield.

Tog laid his bow and quiver beside the tree and stepped out with Kryder to meet the remaining guards. By the time he pulled his axe over his shoulder, his smaller cousin was engaged.

Kryder's daggers flashed as he fought a dizzying dance with both hands to get past his opponent's sword and defenses. Though his opponent had a small shield for protection, it was obvious he wasn't used to fighting with it. In moments, Kryder succeeded in getting around it. As the man fell, Kryder turned in time to see the last armed guard fall to a full swing of Tog's axe.

Kryder walked over to the lad. He was scared, like the horses shifting back and forth at the end of the reins in his hand, but he tried to hide it. The boy was dressed in a worn leather jerkin too large for him and had a short sword on his hip. He stared at Kryder's bloody daggers. When Tog walked over, the boy was still clearly nervous, but he held his ground. At seven feet tall, the Half-Orc was truly a giant in the young teen's eyes.

"Left you holding the reins, huh?" Kryder asked as he casually flipped a dagger.

The teen nodded quickly, unable to utter a word. His eyes followed the dagger as it ascended, spun, and came back down into Kryder's hand. Kryder glanced toward Tog, yet still caught the dagger by its handle on the next flip. He could see in his cousin's eyes the same thought he'd had. They weren't the type of men to harm an innocent. The boy might have been part of the local guard hunting them down, but they doubted he would have been there if he had another choice in life.

"Which of these horses is the best?" Tog asked as he finished strapping his quiver on. "I figure you know, since it's obvious they had you take care of them."

The boy was shaken loose from his fixation on the flipping dagger. He looked at Tog, and in a shaky voice, answered, "The dark bay. Sh…she is."

Kryder wiped both daggers clean with a piece of cloth from a pocket, sheathed them, and stepped over to the dark reddish-brown horse. Her mane, tail, and lower legs were black. She was a little taller than the others. He gave her a pat and checked the bindings on her saddle.

"Looks like she has some Minth in her," Kryder said over his shoulder as he tightened the strap on a stirrup.

The boy brightened as his fear faded. "I think so," he said. He ran his hand over his dark blonde, shoulder-length hair and pulled it away from his face to let it fall on both sides of his head.

"Maybe not her dam or sire, but somewhere in her line. Sergeant Barthan said I didn't know what I was talking about, but he doesn't…" He paused and glanced at the bodies. "*Didn't* spend time with them like I did. I sleep in the stables, so I should know."

"The stables?" Tog asked.

"I don't have a home," the teen said. He shrugged his shoulders. They could now see the clothes he wore under the old leather top were threadbare. He was also a little thin. "I get to stay in the stable as long as I take care of the horses. Today is the first day they gave me my own sword, besides during the sparring sessions. Then I get a wooden one like everyone else."

"Yeah?" Tog asked with a grin. "We learned on wooden weapons, too. Busted knuckles are the worst."

The boy grinned with him. "Not if you're the one busting them. They hated sparring with me for the last six months or so, because I tore their knuckles up. That's what they get for making messes in the stable on purpose." He reached up and patted one of the horses he still controlled with the reins in his other hand.

"What's your name," Kryder asked, "and how old are you?"

"My name is Dolner," the boy answered. "I'm sixteen. Almost seventeen."

"I'm Kryder, and this is Tog." Kryder indicated his much larger cousin. "I need this horse. I'll leave coin with you to give to the town council, mayor, or whoever actually owns the watch's horses, to pay for her and the saddle. With me on horseback, we can move much faster."

Dolner didn't bother looking at the bodies of what remained of the town's watch. "Where are you going?" he asked.

"That's something you don't need to know," Kryder answered, staring at the boy. He shifted his head and flicked his long, dark hair away from his eye. "Even if you don't intend to give our plans away, some of your king's soldiers may come looking for you, and they'll get the information out of you."

"That's the last thing you need," Tog added. "Torture. In the skirmishes, we once rescued a scout team in Gar-Noth. What was left of them, anyway. Your fingers won't grow back, you know."

"Not out of me they won't," Dolner proclaimed. "If you take two horses, I'll take one for myself, and leave this town forever. I may go to Yaylok, or north to Minth."

"With our coin, too?" Tog asked with a raised eyebrow.

Dolner shrugged. "If I see you again, I'd pay it back. I'm not giving it to the mayor, that's for sure. He's the one who decided I was free labor for the town watch." He paused, looking back toward the town. "I have to take care of his horses, with no pay for any of it."

"Well, here's the coin for the horse and the saddle," Kryder said as he handed several to the boy. "We don't take anything without paying for it. Not if it can be helped."

Kryder winked at his cousin and said, "Now if you feel the town owes you back wages, and the coin I paid—along with a horse and saddle for yourself—makes it even, then we have no say in the matter. That's on you and your dealings with the town. Speaking of which, we don't plan to come back here. You can ride with us for a while, if you want."

Dolner nodded with a serious look and tucked the coins away in a small pocket inside the belt line of his britches. It was obviously more coin than he'd ever possessed. He released the reins on all the horses but two and held a set toward Tog.

Tog raised his hands and said, "I don't need one. It's not like I'd be able to ride for long without tiring a horse. I'll run."

Dolner looked at Tog in disbelief, but dropped the reins he was offering. The horse sensed no restraint on it and moved away. He swung himself into the saddle of the lone grey horse remaining. Tog retrieved his arrows, while Kryder mounted and settled himself in. With a full grin showing his tusks, Tog started running at a pace much faster than the earlier one. His long strides ate up the distance. The two on horseback urged their horses forward to catch up to the Half-Orc.

After about ten minutes, Dolner asked, "Can we stop and eat later? I'm starving. Maybe some chicken and taters? I'll buy."

"I like him," Tog said between breaths.

Kryder laughed. "It may be a while, but we'll get something on the way. Right now we need to outrun the messengers."

* * *

"There it is," Kryder said. "I can smell the sea. And look, see those birds around the marsh? Listen. Those are the same as the ones we heard the last time we were by the sea."

"Yeah," Tog agreed. "The town looks a lot bigger than the one we visited when your mother boarded the ship. That's a city."

"I've never seen that many buildings and homes," Dolner said. He shook his head. "Until now, I've only been as far as the next village, Two Forks—the first one we cut across the fields to avoid. I've never been here."

They spent the week avoiding as many people as they could. They had to travel farther north than Kryder's mother had when she'd fled the Halls of Magic. The smaller ports didn't have any ships loading goods going to Minth. These days, it only happened in the largest ports, with many businesses desiring goods. As they traveled, Dolner slipped into villages and bought small loaves of bread, cold chicken, boiled eggs, and the occasional baked tater. Here, where the large ports were, that wasn't going to be an option.

Kryder looked at Dolner and asked, "Are you sure you want to do this? You can ride into the city or keep moving. You don't have to go with us."

"Yes, I do," the boy insisted. "Now that I know what you two did and why, I want to go with you. If there's to be war everywhere, I want to be on the right side. I don't want to be forced to fight for King Westell. I want to go to the Western Borderlands one day, but before I do, I want to do my part. It's only right."

"A warrior doesn't lead an easy life, Dolner," Tog said softly, surprising the lad. "I admire your decision. If it's to be your calling, we'll teach you more than the short sword. You already have inside you something which can't be denied. Honor."

Dolner looked down, quiet. His hair fell to the sides of his face, hanging down. When he looked up, he said, "I don't know that I have honor. I've begged for food. There were times I stole. I took eggs from barns, vegetables from the vine, and fruit. I once took a pair of britches off a line because mine were too small. There's no honor in thieving, is there?"

"There's honor in surviving," Tog countered. "When you took, did you take all?"

"No," Dolner said quickly. "I only took one egg at a time, and the barn held over a hundred birds penned up. Sometimes the chickens knocked eggs from the nest and broke them because there were so many. The britches came from behind the mayor's house. They belonged to one of his boys. There were many of them drying in the wind that day."

"The fruit and vegetables?" Kryder prodded.

"The harvest was in," Dolner explained. "They'd left a few odd-shaped ones on the ground, so I took them and ate them raw. Sometimes you can find taters after they plow the fields, load the wagons, and leave. The apples came from a pair of trees deep in the woods on the lord's lands. Most of them had fallen to the ground and were eaten by wild hogs. I built a lean-to near them but had to leave it during the rainy season when the stream rose."

"I'll not call that thieving," Tog said. "Survival is what it is. A boy growing up alone with no shelter over his head does what he must to live. And I'd say the mayor owes you more than a pair of worn britches."

"He's right," Kryder agreed. "I like to think I'm a good judge of men. You have the makings of a good one. We'll have time on the ship to work with you." Thinking of the evening before when they'd sparred, he added, "You're already better than most with that sword."

"Now we need to see if I can act." Dolner grinned. He was determined to find out all they needed to know before they entered the port city. "This jerkin is too big. I'll stand out in a crowd. I think I should leave it and my sword and look around without them. The horse, too."

"The boy has a head on his shoulders," Tog said. "I didn't think of that."

"We'll wait here, off the road," Kryder decided. "A half day. No more. If you're not back by dark, we're coming to find you."

"Ok," Dolner said. "A half day. I got it." He took the leather jerkin off and unbuckled his sword belt. He stepped over to the small stream running through the woods, knelt, and washed the dust from his hair and face. His hair would dry long before he made it to the edge of the city.

Kryder and Tog watched Dolner from the edge of the woods, until he moved out of sight past some of the first homes. They were anxious to be with him, to make sure nothing happened to him in the city. They had both grown fond of him and his endless questions, and they were often surprised when the follow up questions were well thought out. They weren't surprised at his appetite, though; the boy needed to gain some weight, and he ate like it.

*****

Chapter Two

Dolner carried himself as if he belonged. He'd learned long ago that people ignored you if you didn't stand out. Why would they notice someone acting the same way they did? After a few minutes walking inside the city limits, he noticed no one was speaking to anyone else as they passed them on the street. They weren't rude to each other; they simply didn't speak as they passed. That suited him.

He stopped at an opening between buildings where a small market filled the space. A tent was selling roasted chicken, so he bought a leg quarter. He made sure to act hesitant with the small piece of copper, like it was his only one. It would be suspicious if someone dressed the way he was had more than a copper or two.

He moved around to the other side of the market and found a table selling used clothes. He bought a shirt and a light jacket. The jacket was a little large, but they were both in much better shape than the one he was wearing. He stepped into an alley to change.

He held the chicken quarter in his teeth as he pulled the old shirt over his head. He put the warm piece on the old shirt lying on the ground while he put the others on. Next, he patted the old shirt on the chicken, soaking up grease, and used the spot to rub the top of his boots. Once he was finished, they didn't look as old and worn out. They would pick up dust, but now they didn't look as if they were fit to be thrown away, like the old shirt.

He moved toward the sounds of crying seagulls and waves meeting the shore. When the sea came within sight, he was amazed. He glanced around to make sure no one noticed a boy witnessing the view for the first time. Nobody bothered looking at him twice.

To the right, beyond a series of rocks reaching out into the water, a sandy beach stretched until it grew small in the distance. To the left of the rocks, a calm area of the sea filled the port. Between two similar rock outcroppings, three docks stretched out. Most of the large slots for ships to tie up were occupied. Great ships, small ships, and everything in between were there.

One of the docks held two warships on the end. The rest of the pier had shipping and fishing boats docked to it. There was a fish market to one side. On the other side of the street, net repairers, sail makers, and shops selling rope and tackle were set up. Dolner moved toward the area to see if he could learn anything. They needed to know which ships were headed north to Minth and which of those would take passengers. The local fishermen and their community would know. Dolner figured it was like the small market in his own town. Full of gossips.

He wandered up and down the aisles looking at the different types of fish and crabs and listening to conversations. One stall had great wooden tanks filled with life. Occasionally a long tentacled arm would come over the edge of one. The woman working it would flick it back over with the stick in her hand. Dolner shivered at the thought of eating whatever it was wriggling in the tank.

On the other side of the street he listened to an older man talk to a proprietor in front of a table with several long harpoons for sale. “I’ll need the one with the brass ring on the end so we can tie a rope that will stay attached.”

"This is the one for you," the proprietor said. He reached behind him for a harpoon in a stand. "It's not cheap, but it's worth it, I say."

"I'll take it," the old man said. "My ship isn't a fishing vessel, but we missed an opportunity coming down from Minth with a pod of Mang fish. The old harpoon's iron ring broke, and we lost it. I'll not have it happen again. Brass holds up better against the salt water. It saves coin when I can feed the entire crew for days."

"That and selling the scales fetches a good price all along the seaboard," the proprietor agreed as he wrapped the wicked barb on the end in cloth and tied a string around it. "Properly dried, they make a good blade sharpener."

The proprietor leaned in and spoke with a lower voice, "If you want to keep the horn and bring it back south with you, I'll give you a good price. You don't have to turn it over to your King's Own, you know. None's the wiser, I say."

"I bet you would," the old man said with a stern look on his face, "but you'll not buy a Mang horn from me. *Jonrig's Delight* is a Minth ship. Let there be none who says Cap'n Barl Jonrig is not a man loyal to his king and country. Now I'll have no more of this talk, or I'll take my coin and buy a harpoon elsewhere."

"No offense meant, Cap'n," the man said hurriedly. He raised his hands in mock defense. "I was just letting you know, here in Gar-Noth, the horn of the Mang can be bought and sold, that's all."

Dolner turned and moved toward the docks. Once he was close to them, he waited near a tavern. After several minutes, he saw the older man walking his way with the harpoon over one shoulder. The captain had his arm over the end, holding it down casually with his wrist as his hand dangled.

Dolner stepped into the street and looked toward the man, indicating he wished to speak to him. "Good morning, Cap'n," he said.

"It is, young man; it is indeed," Captain Jonrig said. He stopped and placed the butt of the harpoon on the cobblestones. He held on to it with two hands and leaned on it. "Though it is nigh on midday. Do you have something on your mind? Not spare coin, I hope. A lad like you should have a job of sorts or be helping your family in trade."

"No, Cap'n," Dolner said and gave him his best grin. "I don't need coin. I was hoping to spend some."

"Well, now," the captain said. "That's different. You seem to know I'm a captain. I take it you're looking for passage? If you have the coin, I think we can make room to take you to Minth. We're not stopping on the way. The lads are loading the cargo as we speak, and it's going directly to the ports in Cliff Town."

"Well, sir," Dolner said, glancing around and lowering his voice, "it's not only for me. There are two others…and two horses."

"Three of you?" the captain asked. "And two horses, you say? I don't know if I can find the room for the lot of you. The other two maybe, but horses? That means rigging my pen, ensuring an extra barrel of fresh water is on hand, hay, and the like."

Dolner was unable to hide his disappointment. He hated to part with them. "I guess we could leave the horses, but we need to be on our way as soon as possible. When will you be leaving?"

"Hold on, boy," Captain Jonrig said with a concerned look on his face. "We haven't discussed a price for passage. And why are we whispering here in the middle of the street?"

He looked around and spoke lower, "Who are the others? And you did say two? Would they be the two the messengers came riding into the city talking about and posting notices for in every tavern?"

Dolner's eyes widened, and he backed away, his eyes darting left and right. Before he could turn and run, the captain said, "Don't go, lad. I'll not be turning anyone in. If they did what the messengers claim they did, good on them, I say." The captain's eyes darted left and right to ensure no one had heard him this time.

Dolner stopped and stepped closer. "Maybe, maybe not," he said. "What would it cost for passage for three?"

"Not a copper," Captain Jonrig said, still speaking low. "You provide the hay; I can get the extra barrel of water. We leave on high tide, about two hours before dark. We can't risk waiting until tomorrow. This is not the first time passage has been booked on my ship to leave this kingdom quickly. Though I didn't know she was doing it at the time. Four sell-swords came questioning me years later."

Dolner had no idea what he was referring to. "Which is your ship, Cap'n?" he asked.

"The long pier. There." Captain Jonrig pointed. "The last ship docked; you can't miss her. Her keel runs too deep to come any closer into the bay. Besides, where she is, the wind still pushes her, and we didn't have to use a boat to come ashore."

* * *

"Are you sure you heard him say Barl Jonrig?" Kryder asked.

"I'm sure," Dolner answered. "He had grey hair and was a little taller than you. He said it's not the first time he booked a passenger looking to leave quickly."

"It isn't," Tog said. "He took Kryder's mother to Minth about twenty years ago."

"Are you sure it was him?" Dolner asked. "That was before either of you were born."

"We're sure," Kryder said. "It may have been a little more than twenty years, but we saw it less than two weeks ago. We'll have to explain on the trip. It's complicated."

"Sounds impossible to me," Dolner said. He tilted his head. "But then again, you starting a fire from your hands is, too, and I saw it with my own eyes."

"What's the plan?" Tog asked. "Word's already spread here about us. If there's a reward now, we'll never make it through the city and to the ship without the watch being called on us. If they're not the ones to see us first while on patrol."

"Well, they're looking for me and you," Kryder said. "Two men dressed differently than the locals, one large, and one the size of a normal man. That's how we'll get by."

Tog reached up and scratched the side of his face as he pondered what his cousin said. "You can be so confusing. What do you mean?"

"It's simple," Kryder said. "Dolner and I will go through the city to the ship together. I'll put my traveling cloak in my saddlebag and wear the jacket he bought. You follow behind by yourself."

"Yes," Dolner said. "That'll work. I'll take the horses into the city, buy a couple of the small bales of hay, strap them to both saddles, and bring them back here. They're kind of heavy, but I don't think it will be a problem for you. You can shove your axe head into one and carry it over your shoulder by the handle, with the other one in your free hand. We may have to tie a rope around the bale. The thin ones they tie them with will break after a while."

"Do you think it will work?" Tog asked.

"I think so," Kryder said. "Remember, we saw plenty of people loading goods on ships at the other port. No one will suspect you, by yourself and working."

Kryder and Dolner rode through the city streets with no one giving them more than a passing glance. After all, no one was looking for a man and a boy in his teens. They walked their nervous horses down the busy pier, up the gangplank, and onto the ship. The sailors were expecting them. The first mate helped move the horses into the temporary pen.

Tog followed a short time later carrying the two bales of hay as if he did it every day. He received a few stares because of his size. When he was halfway down the pier, a man noticed the bow on his back. The man quickly made his way to the shore to find the local watch.

Kryder saw the commotion at the beginning of the long pier and shouted for Tog to hurry. It wasn't far to the ship, and Tog ran up the gangplank right behind the captain they'd seen so long ago. With the captain were two sailors rolling a water barrel.

"Take in the lines and bring in the plank!" Captain Jonrig shouted. "Look lively, lads! The watch is coming, and I aim to be out of their reach."

Two of his crew sprinted down the plank to the dock and untied the big lines on both ends. Both were stout, tanned men, capable of a task they'd performed many times. It was never in the haste the captain demanded now, but they moved quickly. They ran back onboard, breathing heavily. The sails were unfurled, and the ship moved in the slight breeze as the men pulled in the gangplank.

The members of the watch ran down the pier toward them, shouting at people to get out of their way. Several were pushed into the water in their haste. The soldiers were too late. The gap between the dock and the slowly moving ship was too great to even think of attempting the leap. There weren't many places to grip below the levels of the rails, even if a soldier had managed to do it.

Kryder stood at the rail with Captain Jonrig and several others. They watched to see what the soldiers would do. Once he realized what they'd planned, Captain Jonrig shouted, "Lower some buckets! Get some water ready. They aim to set fire to us!"

The leader of the men could be heard shouting for a lit lantern. It wasn't long before some were brought from within a nearby hold. A piece of cloth was wrapped around several arrowheads and splashed with fish oil from another lantern. The ship was still within range of the men's bows.

Tog stepped up. "Do you want me to take out the archers? There appear to be only four of them."

Before Kryder could answer, Captain Jonrig looked over and shook his head. "If we can help it, I would prefer to not kill anyone. I know *Jonrig's Delight* will never dock here again, but still."

"You're right, Cap'n," Kryder agreed. "With what's coming, it'll be a long time before you touch the shores of Gar-Noth, but we have to get away. More than you know depends on it."

"If we make it to sea, you lads will have to tell me why you did what you did," the old man said. "Not that I mind that the place was burnt to the ground, but I'd like to know why you did it."

"Oh, we'll get away," Tog said, looking over at the end of the pier. "You can bet coin on it."

Four burning arrows came arcing toward them. Kryder lifted a hand and spoke words the captain had little chance of repeating, much less understanding. The gust of wind from his hand pushed the arrows up and off to the side to land hissing in the waves. It was a simple spell, but Kryder pushed his will into it to ensure the arrows didn't have a chance to hit their sails.

The crew shouted in delight and began taunting the soldiers. Three times Kryder did the same. The last thing they needed was to be without full sails when the kingdom sent ships after them.

"How long do you think it will be before they come after us?" Kryder asked.

"Several hours, at least," Captain Jonrig answered. "I doubt they have those two warships loaded with enough supplies to last days at sea. They will need water and the like. Once we break free from the bay, we'll have a lead on them. Their warships are faster, but not by much. I've seen the condition of them. The hulls haven't been scraped lately, and that will cause drag. It will take days for them to catch us. I'm hoping to outlast them."

"Which are they?" Tog asked as he looked over to the third pier. "The two on the end?"

"Yes. Those are the ones. See the four harpoon mounts on the bow? They have nasty hooks and plenty of rope. They sink them in a ship and haul it back to them with those winches. Then they board it."

"Do you have a lantern handy?" Kryder asked. He glanced at the bow in Tog's hand. "We can do to them what they tried to do to us."

"I've something better," Captain Jonrig answered with a twinkle in his eye. "See that bucket there?"

Tog walked over to the bucket he'd pointed to. It was full of pitch. One of the sailors had been using it to seal and weatherproof several boards making up the temporary horse pen. Since there were two horses, more than usual was needed. He dipped two arrowheads in it. He walked back to the rail and grinned at his cousin.

"Light me," Tog said to Kryder. "Without the big sails, they can't chase us." He turned to the captain. "What do you call them?"

"Mainsails," Captain Jonrig answered with a grin of his own. "To port!" he shouted. "Bring us closer. Our passengers have a parting gift for the king's navy."

As Kryder cast a simple sparking spell from his fingertips, Dolner said, "You don't have to, Cap'n. Watch how far those big arrows fly."

One after another, the flaming arrows arced up and came down to hit the big roll of sails at the top of both ship's largest masts. They caught fire many feet above the few sailors on the decks of the warships. Seasoned sailors would be able to put the flames out, but not before they caused enough damage to render the ships useless for some time. There would be no chase.

Kryder leaned against the railing and watched the port city grow small in the distance. Tog, standing beside him, asked, "I wonder how long we'll be at sea?"

"I don't know," Kryder answered. "Like you, it's my first time. I hope we don't get sick like my mother did."

"Sick?" Tog asked. He shook his head with a slight grin. "Not me. I have a strong stomach. I wonder how Lucas and the others are faring on their journey to the Baronies West?"

"I don't know," Kryder answered. "They should be nearing the border of Tarlok by now."

Dolner walked up after having checked on their horses. The boy had an affinity for them and a way of calming the animals. It seemed almost magical in itself. "I wonder what time we eat?" he asked.

"I like him," Tog confirmed for the tenth time in a week. He had a full grin on his face with his incisors showing. "The boy asks the right questions."

*****

Chapter Three

Tarlok

"How long before we cross?" Lucas asked.

He looked toward the back of the wagon. His daughter Julia was sound asleep. When she slept, she looked more the way he remembered her, before her mind had been burnt away. Asleep, she didn't have the confused look of one trying to understand the most basic of things. After more than a week traveling like this, she had no problem resting in the moving wagon.

In the wagon behind him, his sons Sethon and Marn rode together, covering every bit of their wagon's seat. The back was full of gear. Tents, clothes, food, and a barrel of water were among the items. Not that water would be an issue, but it was good to be prepared.

In his own wagon was a small cask designed to hold flour. Instead, it held the remains of his savings, a small fortune in coins. Over the years, his inn and tavern had provided much more than his family needed. It was nestled among other containers and boxes and would not be discovered unless someone was looking for it specifically. Julia lay on the pile of blankets on one side. Behind her, the spare team of draft horses were tied, content to follow along without having to work to pull the wagon.

Up ahead, Johan pulled back on his reins and allowed the wagons to catch up to him. He didn't have to tug much, as the well-trained horse responded quickly. Beyond him, two soldiers could be seen on horses, riding point. The other two members of Johan's squad rode behind the wagons. All four were on the horses removed from the Razor's camp. The previous owners would never need horses again.

"It's a half day from the border," Johan said. "We're to be making good time, with none questioning us this last week."

"Aye," Lucas said. "Enough merchants travel these days, so it doesn't raise suspicions. Of course, not many take the fork we took toward Tarlok. Most head toward Gar-Noth and Minth. Yer squad acts like guards for me, so no one's the wiser. I've never been this way meself, but it matches what the old man said in the last village. It won't be long before we're in Tarlok."

"I'm to be thinking you're right," the old sergeant agreed. He reached down and patted the horse he was riding on the side of his neck. "Kryder's horse is the best I've ever sat upon. Minth bred, he says. Do ye think I could get one fer meself when we get to the Baronies West?'

"I don't see why not," Lucas answered. "I'll get ye one. I've the coin to spare, with me life's savings here in the wagon."

"I may take ye up on the offer, old friend," Johan said. "I've got some coin, but ye know how the city paid. Enough fer a man to live on, but not much to spare. I'll find a way to pay ye back."

"Bah," Lucas said, waving him off. "I'll accept no such thing. I'll make it a gift at yer Day of Life celebration. How old will ye be this year, anyway?"

The grey-haired sergeant tapped his heels into the sides of the stud as he said, "Ho, now, one o' the lads needs me up front."

Lucas laughed out loud at his friend as he galloped away. It was loud enough his daughter stirred behind him, and both his sons glanced at each other in question. Marn shrugged his shoulders and urged his team to keep up with the wagon ahead.

* * *

The open fields gave way to lightly wooded, gently rolling hills. After another hour of travel, the trees grew closer and closer, until they entered a forest. The road narrowed as they headed north. The smell of evergreens mixed among the hardwoods was pleasant. It was different than the trees farther south.

Lucas watched Johan up ahead. The man moved from one side of the road to the other, sometimes riding into the openings in the trees. He knew the old sergeant was looking for a suitable place to stop for the night and camp.

Before they had crossed the border into Tarlok, they had stayed at inns and tavern boarding houses in the villages along the road. Once they made the turn into another kingdom, the road they followed had no villages to speak of. They passed several homesteads and small farms, but no collections of homes.

Lucas climbed down from the wagon and walked over to Johan, who had dismounted. "Looks to me like you found a good spot. The opening is big enough to get two wagons in, with room for all the horses, I'm to be thinking."

"Aye," Johan agreed, "though I don't like the looks of that old trail going up into the hills there." He pointed to an opening under the low hanging branches of a huge pine tree. "There's to be no reason fer it, unless some mining was happening up there."

"To be honest," Lucas said, "I didn't even notice it. I'm to be out of practice fer that sort o' thing these days. It doesn't look like a wagon or even a horse has been up that way in years. Do ye think it truly leads to a mine?"

"If it does," Johan said as he ran his hand down over his long mustache, "it means a cave. Caves spell trouble, I say. Especially up in these hills. There's Goblin lairs to be thinking of."

"Goblins?" Sethon asked as the big man walked up. "Where? Here?" He looked around and reached for the war hammer strapped to his back.

"Just show us," Marn said as he walked up with one of the other men. His war hammer was already in his hands, and he tapped the double fist-sized head into a palm.

Lucas looked over at his boys and grinned. Though a large man himself, his boys were both bigger than he was. The Orc lineage in his family showed in their size. None of them had the tell-tale incisors, but they were bigger than most men.

"You boys will get yer turn with those hammers," Lucas said. "Don't go wishing trouble on us. We have a task before us, and it's best to stay on the straight path. Once we let Baron Arnwald know what's happening down south with King Westell and his alliance with the Elves, the two of ye can get ready for a fight, as there's sure to be one to stop them."

"We could go up into the hills to check," the soldier with Marn suggested.

"We'll not go looking for a fight, Corporal Taybon," Johan said. "You and the Trant lads draw straws for the watch shifts tonight. Each of you pick a partner from the troops. I'll take the first with Lucas."

"Yes, Sergeant," the corporal said. He looked around for suitable straw material. He settled on pine needles pulled from a nearby low-hanging limb.

Shortly after midnight, the camp site was invaded, but it wasn't by Goblins. Marn was the first to notice the awful smell, but by the time he mentioned it, three trolls were in the open area and looking for the source of the meat they had smelled cooking earlier.

The trolls had grey, splotchy skin and shaggy, oily hair. They were slightly taller than a man. They would have been much taller, but they carried themselves in a hunched-over posture from spending most of their time in the depths of caves away from bright light. With long arms and hands, their fingers ended in claws strong enough to tunnel.

Knowing the trolls would not stop with the food supplies and their horses would be next, Marn shouted, "Trolls! Watch the horses!"

The soldier on guard with him ran over from the other side of the camp with his sword ready. The other soldiers and Lucas scrambled out from beneath the wagons, weapons in hand, where they had bedded to prevent dew from settling on them as they slept.

The shouts and the sound of panicked horses on tether was more than enough to shake the cobwebs from their minds. Johan had the wits to throw the last two logs they had cut from an old downed tree into the fire to brighten the area. One of the trolls near the fire threw a long, gangly arm up to block the bright light from the impact of the logs on the coals.

Johan used it to his advantage as he stepped forward and swung his longsword. The blade buried deep in the troll's side, producing a splash of dark blood as he pulled his sword free to strike again. Lucas stepped over to the other side of the tall, stooped troll and swung his studded club at the creature's knee. He ducked in time to avoid the long claws as they swept over his head. The hit with the club didn't seem to faze the cave dweller but distracted it long enough for Johan's next series of attacks to strike true and kill it.

On the other side of the fire, Marn's hammer came down and struck the troll in front of him at an angle, shattering bones in its shoulder and outstretched arm. The beast had gone for the wagon—and his sister, screaming from the back of it, where she had climbed after crawling out from underneath. Anger added strength to the blow. Like his brother, the last thing the big man would ever allow was harm to his sister if he yet breathed.

The soldier who had been on watch with him shoved his short sword through the foul-smelling beast above the waist. His momentum carried him past, causing him to lose the grip on his weapon and leaving it embedded.

He turned and drew his dagger, determined to finish it off. The troll fell to its knees while trying to reach back and pull the blade free with its good hand. The next strike from Marn's hammer crushed its skull and killed it.

Sethon and the three other soldiers had the third troll backed against the other wagon as they fought to slay it. Corporal Taybon stepped in, both hands on the hilt of his longsword, and managed to get past its flashing claws to strike deep into its neck. It continued to fight, getting a slashing blow in on one of the other soldiers. Its attempts to get at them slowed as it weakened from blood loss until it toppled over.

As abruptly as the attack on their camp had started, it was over; all involved were breathing heavily from the adrenaline rush and the exertion. Marn reached up to the back of the wagon and helped his sobbing sister to the ground. She ran straight for their father and buried her face in his chest. Lucas shushed her quietly and assured her she was safe. He motioned with his hand at the bodies.

Johan agreed and set the men to the task of removing the stinking trolls from their campsite. The guard with the cut across his shoulder and arm sat on the front of the wagon, and Johan cleaned it with a splash from one of the bottles of strong drink packed in the wagon for that purpose. The soldier grimaced and sucked his breath in through his teeth.

"Steady, Neal," Johan said. "Hold steady. I know it burns, lad."

It wasn't a deep cut, and the grizzled old sergeant determined he didn't need to sew it shut. If he had, it wouldn't be a neat job, but it was one he had performed several times in the past. Clerics, herbalists, and healers weren't always available to a squad, especially in the forward areas of a battlefield.

Most sergeants learned the basics of aiding their soldiers. Stitching minor wounds was part of the training he had received years ago. He still carried his old sewing kit with its needles, and any strong thread would do, once soaked in strong drink. He didn't really understand why it needed to be stronger than wine or beer, but he did as the herbalist demanded and always soaked the thread.

Later, as they hitched the still nervous teams to the wagons, Sethon asked, "Will we see more o' the same on this journey through Tarlok?"

"I don't think so," Johan answered as he watched him finish the task. "We're to be on the edge of Tarlok. The hunters tend not to leave. They prefer to stay deep in the forests, and they rarely leave their lands. Well, not to go to populated places. Stands to reason, any areas where beasts such as those still prey on travelers would be where most o' the hunters refuse to go themselves."

"Ye can be sure," Lucas agreed, "if the hunters knew o' the trolls, they would have sent a team to be rid o' them."

"Kind o' standoffish, those hunters," Johan said. "But ye can be sure there's none better in a fight with their bows. Well, maybe Orcs, but they wouldn't tolerate a nest o' trolls in Orcanth, either."

"I hope Kryder and Tog aren't running into the troubles we are," Lucas said. "I'm to be sure they took care o' the lord mage. If they hadn't, we probably wouldna have made it this far. I'm to be betting he would have found out about us and used some o' his magic to find us."

"The lads are probably enjoying the cruise, with smooth sailing toward Minth." Johan said.

"Tog has a huge appetite. I'll bet ye he is eating everything in their supplies, to be sure," Lucas agreed. "It will cost them all the coin I sent with them to pay for it."

* * * * *

Chapter Four

The Western Sea

Tog gripped the rail weakly and emptied his stomach once again. He was on his knees, with his head over the railing. "Ohhh," he moaned. "I'm dying. Just toss me overboard and let the waters take me." He retched again, but nothing came up.

Kryder looked over at Dolner and shrugged. The two of them had no issue at all with the rolling motion of the ship and showed no signs of sea sickness. Tog, on the other hand, had been sick since they lost sight of land. The salted flatbread seemed to offer no relief to the big man. He could keep nothing down.

"Are you sure you don't want something to eat? Maybe a bowl of the fish stew we had earlier?" Kryder asked as he winked at Dolner.

"It's good and spicy, though it's cold now," Dolner said. "Cold. Spicy. Fish. Stew."

Another moan escaped from Tog's lips. He refused to even look up. "Never again," Tog moaned. "I can never eat it again. That was the first thing that came up, and I will never forget the *second* first taste I had of it." He was quiet for a few moments. "Just throw me overboard."

"Can I have your share of the meal tonight?" Dolner asked. The boy grinned over Tog's head at Kryder. "No sense wasting it. I mean…"

* * *

Zar

Across the continent, the Elven mage Mraynith stared out the window of his tower. He glanced at his uneaten meal. *A waste of good fowl.* He looked across the city of Nayzar, the largest city in Zar. Far below in the winding streets, the common Elves went about their miserable daily lives as they moved toward the holding pens. Those unfit to become soldiers or allowed to maintain a trade performed tasks no others would. They oversaw the breeding, feeding, and care of the Goblins and Humans.

Half of the latter was all he cared about. The females, not the Human males. *Almost worthless. At least the Goblins can be driven ahead of the armies to fight before we step into the fray.*

It was an annoyance, having to keep the two separated. The Goblins tended to eat the Humans. Especially the young, though there were not many young these days. The Humans had been breeding less and less. It was as if they had figured out it was best not to produce young. Most of the females were taken before reaching maturity, never to be seen again by those in the pens.

As the emperor's mage and the most powerful mage in all of Zar, Mraynith had his choice of them as often as he wished, to ensure he stayed young and strong. His choice of the ones available to him, anyway. While the emperor and his family maintained their own stock, the nobles and leaders in the army chose from the same pens Mraynith did.

He stared into the round mirror on the other side of the room. The last two times he had attempted to extend his life, the spell had failed, unaided by the Demon who had taught it to him. He wondered again for the hundredth time why the Demon wouldn't answer him. As he gazed at the mirror, he tried to envision himself growing old like the common Elves. He shuddered at the thought.

He glanced back to his desk at the crushed stone and wondered what it was he saw when he opened the window. Instead of seeing the Human mage lord, he saw the blackened stone of a wall. There had been no sign of the man. The spell should have opened in front of his counterpart, sitting at his desk. Something was wrong, but he didn't know what it could be. The lord mage was nearly as strong in magic as he was. Perhaps he was preoccupied before heading south.

In time, he would have his answers. When spring came, he would travel with a third of the emperor's army through the great swamp into the Human kingdom of Yaylok. The land they would occupy would be given to the Elves. In return, they would march with the forces of the Human King Westell. The entire world of Kerr was theirs for the taking. Once the wars were over, he and the lord mage would rid themselves of the Human king and his own emperor. Only those with the gift of magic deserved to rule over all and, if the opportunity presented itself, he would rid himself of the lord mage, as well.

* * *

Yaylok

In Yaylok, his newest lands, King Westell of Gar-Noth put his mug down and turned to Archduke Bainhorn, the former king of Yaylok. The king was a middle-aged man, and his trimmed beard did little to hide the contempt for others clearly seen at all times on his face. He reached down and shifted the thin longsword at his side as he sat at a table covered in the finest of prepared meals.

"I will need you to oversee the execution of both those knight commanders. I will not have open contempt in my armies," he said. His tone made it clear there would be no argument. "Your armies are now mine. They will be loyal, or they will die. You will handle it personally."

"Consider it done," Bainhorn answered. He raised his cup of wine in salute. He grinned. He was delighted with himself. Now that his father was dead, and he was king…no, he was not king anymore. Since he had his father's coin and crown jewels now, he didn't even have to bother with the business of being a ruler. He was now an archduke and would be able to have his steward run things. He could live the way he had always dreamed and have little to no responsibilities.

He didn't like either of his father's choices of knight commanders, anyway. Especially the woman in charge of the cavalry. He would be glad to drop the axe himself, except it was too heavy for him. Plus, it might get blood on his clothes. He wasn't having any of that.

Satisfied with the answer, King Westell took a sip of his wine. "We only have a few months to ensure the armies merge and are ready to move north to Minth. With the Elves beside us, I will not have to fight a border war. We will march deep into their kingdom and take it."

"Then Tarlok?" the young archduke asked. "Or will you take the Baronies West?'

"The Baronies," King Westell answered. "I will save Tarlok for last. Its people are scattered far and wide in those forests. There is no proper town or city to lay siege to. I have a mind to see the Elves turn the Goblin hordes loose among the hills and trees."

Bainhorn winced at the thought of the devastation a Goblin horde would wreak if turned loose. "What about the Mountain Kingdom?" he asked. "Their mountains are right in the middle of Minth."

"We will take them, as well," Westell confirmed as he reached for his mug. "The Dwarves will either sue for peace, or my mages will bring the mountains down on their heads. I don't care if it kills scores of Goblins running through the caves fighting them at the time. That will be the Elves' problem."

"What about Orcanth?" Bainhorn asked. "Will you conquer the Orcs?"

"The Orcs will remain within their borders," Westell said dismissively with a wave of his hand. "They care not for what happens outside of their boundaries. But to answer your question, I will own Orcanth as well. In time. There are not enough of the savages to stop me, and the half-breeds are even weaker."

* * *

The Western Sea

The next morning, Tog felt weak. He was able to keep water down, though. He still looked pale, but he no longer rushed to the rails to empty his stomach. He refused to eat anything other than the crisp pieces of salted bread, much to Dolner's delight, as the boy continued to eat impressive-sized portions.

"The boy eats like he's not sure when he will eat again," Captain Jonrig remarked.

Kryder glanced over at Dolner. The boy sat with some of the crew. They had unstrapped the table tops from the walls and inserted the legs so everyone could sit for the morning meal. He smiled and nodded. "Yeah. His whole life has been that way. He's been with us for the last week or so. I think he feels assured he has a place with us now, but old habits die hard. It's as if a part of him still can't accept it."

"Seems like a good sort," the captain said. "The way he scrambles around up on the masts and up into the crow's nest, I would have thought he was raised on a ship. The lad has no fear of heights, I'll tell you. If he didn't have a place with the two of you, I've a place for him among my crew, to be sure."

"I'm sure he would appreciate the offer," Tog said, "but he wants to be a warrior. He insists on it, and I'm for helping him become one. Once we hit dry land again, that is. I can't teach him to run like a warrior on this moving stomach churner. No offense, Cap'n."

"None taken." He grinned, then turned inquisitive. "Run? You have to run to be a warrior?"

"It's what we do," Tog answered with a shrug. "How else can one get where they need to be to fight in enough time to make a difference?" He took another bite of the hard bread. "I mean, there are big horses, but none that I've seen are able to carry an Orc warrior for long. He has a way with the horses, but the boy will have to learn how to move in a hurry without one, too."

"He's right," Kryder agreed. "In Three Oaks, we all run. Human and Orc. Farmer's children, merchant's…all of them can. Obviously not as well as an Orc, but it is nothing for a boy or girl to run for several hours on an errand to one of the other villages in the Western Borderlands, or even to the Red Fist village in Orcanth. We start young."

"Might be rough on him," Captain Jonrig observed. "He has some catching up to do. The boy's nearly grown. I don't envy him."

"He ran alongside his horse a bit this last week," Tog said, "to give it a break from the weight of a rider. I could see when he was winded and his feet were sore, but there is no quit in him. He only stopped when I told him to mount up."

"He needs a better pair of boots," Kryder agreed. "His feet will stay sore until we get him some that fit. Tog is right. There is something about him, and he does have a way with animals." The three of them watched Dolner from a distance as he laughed with some of the crew. The crew accepted him as more than a paying passenger.

"Speaking of acceptance," Kryder said, "your crew seems to be at ease with one such as Tog and my use of magic. I would like to try the wind spell and see if I can direct it to the sails. We can reach our destination sooner."

"They're good men, the lot of them. A man is a man, I say. The creator made us all. It matters not if he's mixed with a little Orc blood. I would be sorely disappointed if any showed otherwise. As for the spells, as long as you don't rip the sails apart, I'm for it," the captain said, looking around at his men. He gave Tog a nod of acknowledgement.

"Now, would you mind telling me why the two of you burned the halls to the ground? I'm glad you did it, mind you, my sister's…" He paused.

"My sister's boy is burnt because they wouldn't accept him as a student. I had the ridiculous amount of coin they demanded in hand when I brought him there nigh on ten years ago. Apparently we weren't the desirable sort. Turned us away on the order of the lord mage himself, they did."

There was an anguish in his voice that couldn't be denied. The old captain paused and gathered his emotions. The next thing he said did not come out in anger. It carried the sound of prayer. Prayer with conviction. "May the lord mage rot with the demons."

Kryder decided he could tell the man what they had done and why in detail. He turned to him and said, "Cap'n, you can rest assured he burns forever, and not just for denying children the right to a normal life. He did other things that would make your own blood boil. I'll tell you of my mother…and me."

While Kryder told the captain the story, the man was amazed he had met her all those years ago. Tog interjected when appropriate, confirming his cousin's tale. In places, he picked up the tale to give Kryder a moment to gather his swirling emotions. The Half-Orc reached over, picked up a forgotten piece of tater from Kryder's plate, and ate it without realizing he was doing it.

It wasn't long before every crew member was silent and listening. None disbelieved. They had witnessed the spells cast by Kryder. A few of the older sailors, those who had been with Captain Jonrig the longest, remembered the dark-haired beauty and her large horse. It is a well-known fact that sailors are a hard lot, but even the hardest man wiped away a tear now and then.

After telling of his mother and her eventual fate, Kryder paused a moment. He looked around at the attentive faces and decided to continue. He saw no reason to keep the fact King Westell had aligned himself and his armies with others a secret. The more who knew, the easier it would be to raise the forces needed to stop them. War was headed to the kingdom of Minth.

*****

Chapter Five

"There she is!" the sailor up in the crow's nest shouted. "Minth ahead! I can see the cliffs, Cap'n!"

"Good eyes, Narvel!" Captain Jonrig shouted up. "Watch for the rock outcroppings portside so the helmsman can swing her toward shore."

"Will do, Cap'n," the man answered. The rest of the crew scrambled to the places they needed to be as the ship neared the ports of Cliff Town, prepared to lower sails and complete the other necessary tasks to ease into the busy port.

Kryder turned to Captain Jonrig. "Do you think we'll have any trouble speaking to the king?"

"No, we'll get in to see him," the man said. "The knight commander is a friend of mine from years back. I always bring him the Mang horns myself. It's a good excuse to get a really good meal on his coin." He grinned. "Seriously, he and I get together for a meal now and again, even if I don't have a horn for the king's armies."

Tog looked over at the two-foot twisted horn nestled in a box stuffed with the remainder of the hay. "So what do they do with it?"

"It is used to signal," Captain Jonrig explained. "The sharp tip is cut off, and skilled instrument makers fix a mouthpiece to it. When blown through, the sounds it can make are unique to the horns. Should two forces meet on the battlefield, there is no mistaking the Minth knight commander's intent. From the stories told though the years, the sound of the horns has saved the day on more than one occasion."

"That must be the sounds we heard during the skirmishes," Kryder said. "I wondered how Sir Narthon knew when to order us forward alongside the Minth troops."

Dolner grinned and said, "If it sounds half as good as it tasted, it's amazing."

"It is a delicacy," Captain Jonrig admitted. "Many crews never get the chance to find out. They eat the typical fish caught in nets or on lines, but the flesh of the Mang fish is denied them. Here on this ship, we don't hunt them, but if we come across a pod, we take one for food…and not to sell. There are those who make a fine living at it, but even they only hunt aggressively in season. There are times of the year it is frowned upon. Saint Minokath doesn't smile on those who take and take from his seas."

The first mate interjected, "The Lord of the Seas is not one you wish to anger." He pulled a rough leather necklace with a seashell as its pendant from his shirt. He waved his hand across, chest level, mimicking the movement of waves, and said, "He will provide, but not to those who are greedy with the sea's bounty. Some of the squalls late in summer can form in a hurry. Getting caught up in one is the end of a ship and its crew without his aid and mercy."

Tog reached up and brushed his shoulder length hair away from the side of his head, exposing an ear. Hanging from a thin iron loop was a small seashell, one of several his mother had made from her collection of shells gathered when she was a child.

He surprised both the captain and his first mate when he said, "The saints provide, as the Creator designed." He shook his head, and his hair fell back into place.

"You follow Saint Minokath?" the first mate asked. He was the ship's layman cleric, a strong believer, but not one with his own official church, only the crewmembers of his ship, and sometimes several crews, as he spoke at the docks before fleets of ships set sail.

"But you are not from Minth," Captain Jonrig said. He tilted his head sideways in confusion and asked his first mate, "Granby, are there others in your order outside of this kingdom?"

"My mother was born here," Tog explained. "Of course I follow the Lord of the Seas, and several others. My mother is a shaman of faith for several deities."

"Several?" asked Granby. "How can this be? A saint must accept one with strong faith, those who will lead in their church. I do not have a following to minister to officially, but I have been granted the blessing of a prayer spell on occasion, and I received some training from the church. I have never heard of a cleric accepted by more than one saint."

"Really?" Kryder asked. "Interesting. I never thought much about it. I have seen her cast prayer spells granted by Saint Minokath, Saint Gonthon, and by Lan."

"Saint Lanae?" Captain Jonrig asked. "The keeper of memories?"

"The very one," Kryder said. "We know her as Lan, the Bringer of Seasons. How do you think I know what happened to my mother?"

"She blessed you with the memories?" the first mate answered.

"She took them through time and showed them, herself," Dolner said, as if it was no big deal.

The sailors around them stopped what they were doing in disbelief. The first mate glanced at his captain, then looked back to Kryder and Tog. "You have met Saint Lanae? Come face to face with the Goddess of Time?"

"Yes," Kryder said. "We spent a whole night with her. It seemed to last for years. Well, not the whole night. She disappeared for a little while when she was summoned by the Creator." He shrugged his shoulders. "I mean, it wasn't like she had a choice but to answer the call."

"Yeah," Tog agreed. "She just disappeared and reappeared later."

Granby was visibly shaken. He looked around, stepped over, and sat down on a large pile of coiled rope. "The *Creator*," he whispered as he toyed with the shell on his necklace. "Saint Minokath, I ask you. Can it be?"

The shell glowed a soft blue color for a moment. He looked down at it, pursed his lips, and nodded. His face showed he had been given a sign by his god. They spoke the truth.

"Hey!" Dolner said. "I saw it glow! I thought only clerics or something could see that." He looked around, nervous. "Have I been accepted or something? I don't even know the first thing about The Book Of The One." He ran his hand through his hair, pulling it from his face. It fell back down on each side of his face. His voice lowered. "I can't even read." He looked around for his own place to sit.

With a patient smile on his face, the first mate looked more like a cleric than a sailor. He stood, walked over to Dolner, and placed his hand on his shoulder. "No, lad. That's not how it works. If you had been chosen, you would see the blue glow from my necklace all the time, but only if you had been accepted by a god."

He explained, "It's different when a prayer spell is answered. When a cleric casts a prayer spell, or a holy item manifests its power, the blue glow of the gods can be seen by all. It's not like the spells cast by someone with the gift. Only one with the gift of magic fulfilled can see the red of magic spells and enchanted items, or so I'm told." He looked over at Kryder for confirmation.

Kryder nodded.

"The blue glow of the gods is something entirely different," the layman cleric continued. "All prayer spells require a small sacrifice to work. Sometimes it's a pinch of sand, a bit of a plant, or a drop of honest sweat. There are many things it could be. It is seawater for Saint Minokath, or the bit of shell worn off by the fingers. If the one who asks is blessed with having their prayer answered, the blue glow can be seen. In infinite wisdom, our Creator deemed it so. It is to let all who observe know it has happened, to affirm the power and presence of the Creator and the deities the Creator has given us. They cannot, and will not, be denied."

Dolner's shoulders slumped. "That's a relief. I don't know if I could sit still all day to learn to read. Besides, I'm not wearing robes, that's for sure."

The first mate raised an eyebrow and motioned with his hand at his own clothes. The garb of a sailor. "Really?"

"Well, you know," Dolner said. He raised his hands and smiled in apology.

"You just think you don't have to learn to read," Tog scoffed. "Wait until you meet our grandpa and my mother."

"Oh, yeah," Kryder confirmed. He pursed his lips and nodded with a slight tilt to his head. "You're going to learn to read."

They all laughed at the look on the boy's face.

* * *

The look on Dolner's face gave away his amazement the next morning, when the three of them found themselves in the private dining hall of the king of Minth. Captain Jonrig was with them, along with his friend Sir Markain, Knight Commander of the King's Own. It was enough the boy was silent.

The knight commander was younger than the ship captain, but he was far from a young man. His mustache had more grey in it than dark brown, and his hair was speckled with the same. He still carried himself as if he was in excellent shape, moving easily in his chainmail. His tunic was the blue and white of his king's colors. A longsword was in its scabbard on his left hip. Off to the side in the room stood three squires, a woman and two men, the black patches on the shoulders of their tunics denoting their rank. A lone page stood quietly with them. Like one of the squires, she was a beautiful red head.

"I hope you don't mind," Sir Markain said, "but I brought my charges with me to observe the interaction of our king and unexpected guests. Especially those bearing news such as yours."

"Not at all, Sir Markain," Kryder said. "Baron Arnwald's knight commander often did the same when we visited his barony from the Western Borderlands. He is always looking to teach diplomacy, as well as the arts of combat and war."

"As it should be," the knight commander agreed. "How is Sir Narthon? It has been a while since we last spoke. Not since the last battle on the southern border during the skirmishes." He paused and shook his head. "It would seem I will be seeing him again sooner than I thought, if we are to stop King Westell."

"He is well," Kryder answered. "Though I suspect he would prefer to retire to his horses and turn over his duties to Lady Anise, his second."

"Ah, Lady Anise," Sir Markain observed. "The woman is a formidable knight in her own right. She fights on horseback like the animal is a part of her. Not that her skills on the ground are less than impressive, mind you, but she jousts as well as any I've ever seen."

"You should see her with an axe," Tog said. "My father's father gifted her with one made for her. It is smaller than an Orc axe, but a better quality than any I've seen outside of Orcanth. I spent weeks working with her. She took to it like an Orc warrior."

"Do female Orcs become warriors?" Sir Markain asked. "Like others, I have heard tales of the famous bows and axes, but not of exactly who used them in battle."

"Some tribes have just as many female warriors as males," Tog answered. "The Night Stalker tribe has mostly female warriors. The males in their tribe work the leather, metals, and wood. All tribes make them, to an extent, especially the arrow tips, but they make the strongest weapons, leather armor, and bracers.

"As far as women warriors, our tribe, the Red Fist, only has a few. They are scouts mostly. Quiet and deadly with a shortbow, smaller than mine." He pointed to the bow on his back with a thumb. "And their hand axes. There is nothing stopping any from becoming a warrior; it's their choice. I guess it's like every other race."

A small cough caught their attention. They glanced over at the page in the corner of the room. She had her hands on the heads of hand axes on each side of her waist. The handle of her sword could be seen over a shoulder, the tip of a shortbow over the other.

Strapped to a calf, the handle of a dagger could be seen peeking from the top of a boot. She grinned at them and then looked away.

"Nice!" Tog said. He squinted an eye, pointed at her with his hand close to his face, and gave her a knowing look of conspiracy. "There's one who will be a warrior with choices in battle."

"She is a handful," Sir Markain admitted. He looked at her fondly. "My youngest sister's daughter. Her father is a forester, managing a huge swath of the king's timberland. Lord Jolny is a good man, talented with the bow. Her mother is the knight Lady Roslin, one of my captains. She takes from both parents. It will pain me to send her to another when she is promoted to squire."

"Why can't she stay with you, sir?" Dolner asked. "I mean, I don't know much about pages, squires, and knights, but why not?" It was the first he had spoken, as he was still nervous about being in the city and around nobles. He had been stealing glances at the attractive page since they walked into the room. He was genuinely interested in her.

"That is the way it is done," Sir Markain answered, patience evident in his tone. "It has been so as far back as any remembers. It is not considered good form to take in a squire related to you. There must not be even the slightest hint of favoritism. Even King Jondal's children are assigned as squires to other knights, away from this castle, once they are promoted from the rank of a page. June has been an exceptional page and is nearing the point where I must decide who to send her to, so she can complete her training."

"June," Dolner said. "June." The last he whispered to himself, memorizing her name. He continued to stare at her, everything else in the room forgotten.

June, upon hearing her name, glanced over at the group sitting at the table. She tried to keep a straight face, but Kryder noticed her finally smile at the blond-haired boy, who was about her age. Even though he was a little thin, there was something about him. Traveling with a Half-Orc warrior and a shaman—the term Kryder preferred over mage—from the Western Borderlands. The look on her face showed she was puzzled about his background.

Tog whispered to Dolner, "Close your mouth, you're drawing flies. You can talk to her later, but watch what you say. From the looks of her, she could beat you up if you cross her. I'm just saying." He grinned at Kryder, who shook his head.

*****

Chapter Six

The doors opened on the other side of the dining hall, and King Jondal walked in with a woman in dark blue robes and a man in the lighter blue robes of Saint Minokath. Kryder and Tog recognized the cleric. They had seen him weeks earlier, though the man was now almost thirty years older. Brother Pynon was now the head of his church. They stood quickly.

"Sit, sit," King Jondal said. "There are times for formalities. Breakfast is not one of them. I get enough of that throughout the day." Behind him, several servers came in with trays of food. The king thanked the servers with a kind word. He looked over to the squires and lone page. "You four, find a seat. Let us eat."

"Markain," the king said after everyone was settled at the long table, "introduce me to these three. I know Captain Jonrig." He turned to the seafarer. "Barl, it is a pleasure to see you, good sir. Thank you for your contribution to my forces. The horns are important. I believe this is the twentieth time you have delivered one."

"Why, yes, my lord. It is," Captain Jonrig answered, clearly amazed the king knew the number.

"My lord," Sir Markain said, "allow me to introduce Lord Kryder Narvok, a shaman, and Lord Tog, son of Lur, of the Western Borderlands, and their traveling companion, Dolner."

"Lords?" King Jondal asked with a raised eyebrow. He took in Tog's obvious mixed race and their traveling clothes. He didn't bother giving their weapons a second glance. With his knight commander, three squires and an extremely capable page, it was obvious he felt he was safe. He himself was armed with a short sword on each hip, though he did not wear chainmail. Not to mention the cleric and mage with him were the most powerful spellcasters in his kingdom.

"Lords," he said again. "Do tell."

Tog stammered, so Kryder answered, "My lord, I suppose we do hold those titles, as our grandpa is Sir Jynal Narvok, Lord of the Western Borderlands. We never use them. Tog is also the son of the son of the chief of the Red Fist Tribe in Orcanth. The chief is the current Lord of the Axe, a minor noble in our Grandpa's Barony, so he holds more titles." Kryder grinned at his cousin's embarrassment.

Dolner looked sideways at them. He had not thought of them as nobility. He shrugged it off and took a bite of sausage. His eyes widened. It was spiced more than the bland food of his native kingdom. Flavorful, but not too hot.

"Indeed," King Jondal said. He gave a knowing look. "When I was young, I shied away from the titles of nobility. Content to be a page, squire, and later a knight. Prince never seemed to sit well with me, and yet...here I am." He waved an arm, indicating all around him. "King. We are who we are."

"True, my lord," the mage with him agreed. "It is the same with the gift of magic. One has no choice in the matter."

"Quite right, Bethany," the king said. "Where are my manners? Gentlemen, this is Mage Bethany and Brother..."

"Pynon," Kryder and Tog said in unison.

"You know of him?" King Jondal said. "I suppose it is to be expected, though it puzzles me. He only became the head of his order a few months ago, when Saint Minokath called his predecessor home after a life long lived." A moment of silence among them showed respect.

The king clapped his hands once and rubbed them together to break the somber moment. "So, Sir Markain tells me it is urgent I hear what you have to say, and it could not wait. I brought these two with me. Like my knight commanders, I value their input. Let us eat. Then you may tell me what you would have me know."

* * *

Later in the morning, they were all still seated at the table. "Elves?" King Jondal asked in disbelief. "King Westell has aligned himself with *Elves?* The man has truly gone mad!"

"He's something, all right," Tog agreed. "I think he's a steaming pile of…"

"Whatever he is," Kryder interrupted, "he'll pay for his part in allowing the lord mage to do what he's done right at the doorsteps of his castle. Not just for my family, but for all those lost. Those still here, but not truly. Burnt, lost forever in their minds."

Mage Bethany said, "I must admit, I find parts of your story unbelievable. I mean, what you're saying about the stones now makes sense, as none of us were ever told what had happened in the room to keep us from being burnt. I would ask to see one, but first I would see you cast a spell."

She brushed a wayward strand of hair out of an eye. "Again, I'm not saying you're not being truthful. Forgive me, but you must understand my position. You say you went to the Halls of Magic and defeated the lord mage in a battle of spells. I'm aware some races have shamans, and most are accepted by one deity or another and use prayer spells." She looked to Brother Pynon for confirmation. He agreed with a nod.

"I see you're wearing an item of magic, and I also know there are tales of some Orc shamans using actual magic, but what you claim to be able to do is so much more."

"Bethany," Pynon said, "believe them, for they have given details none could possibly know, other than those in the small home where Saint Minokath answered my humble prayers and saved a child's life. I will never forget that night. They could only know from someone who was there. Those people would be the family members. I, for one, believe them."

"I understand," Kryder said. "If someone told me this tale, I would have my doubts."

"I would be looking at them sideways," Tog admitted. "I get it. Show them, Kryder."

"Yeah," Dolner agreed. "Do some of that fire stuff." He held up his hands with his fingers crooked.

"I don't think we need a fire right now," Kryder said. He grinned at the young man. "But I *will* put a little light on the subject."

Kryder raised his hand and spoke in mage speak, a language known by few and as old as the world. Hearing the words come from him, Mage Bethany inhaled sharply, for she knew he spoke it well and with conviction. Eight balls of light appeared above them near the ceiling, ensuring there were no shadows in the corners of the large room.

"Eight," she whispered, after counting quickly. "My lord, he has cast eight spheres of light."

"Eight is good, right?" Dolner asked. He looked around. "Seems like a good number. I can't read, but I can count, and I can write numbers." He held up all his fingers, thought a moment and tucked two into his palm. He glanced at June to see if she noticed. "I get a couple backward when I write them." The last he said quietly, almost to himself.

"Eight is indeed good," King Jondal said. He looked at Kryder in a new light. "Bethany, I have only seen you cast four spheres a few times. The others were always three. Am I correct?"

"You are, my lord," she answered after finally gathering her wits. "Kryder, as a shaman, is far more powerful in his gift than I will ever be. Ever."

"Maybe," Kryder said with a shrug, "but I bet you know a lot more spells than I do. Can you teach me a few more? Maybe let me copy some? Also, I have a couple I am unsure of. Some of the words I've never pronounced."

"You defeated the lord mage," she said. "Surely you know many spells. I…I could take a look at your spellbook, if that's what you are asking." She paused before saying, "It's unusual. Most of us keep our books to ourselves. I would rather write some spells down for you to copy for yourself, just not from my book."

"Fair enough," Kryder said. He grinned. "By the way, one of the stones in my pocket is for the kingdom of Minth, so you can teach me the inscription on it. I need to be sure how to use the other stone."

He reached into his pockets and pulled two large stones from them. Once again, Mage Bethany was speechless. He held one out to her across the table. She slowly reached out for it.

Dolner interrupted the moment when he said, "Hey, do you think we could get a snack? I'm hungry again."

"The boy has a point," Tog said. He looked toward the king of Minth with a raised eyebrow. "How's the chicken and taters in this kingdom?"

Page June burst out laughing. Every head turned toward her. "What?" she asked. "That's funny. Besides, it seems as if we all need to eat well and gather our strength. War is coming, and I for one intend to be ready for it."

"She is right, my lord," Sir Markain admitted. "It's coming, and we would do well to be ready for it." He turned to Kryder. "You say from here you plan to travel north to Duke Nayer's lands? Will you consider allowing Page June to travel with you? In his duchy, in the far corner of our kingdom, lies the lands of a minor lord."

"A minor lord in title only," King Jondal said dismissively. "Lord Korth's forces make up the bulk of the kingdom's army. He is a good man, never looking to rise above his position, though he could easily. We squired together. I deem him like a brother to me, as does his duke, Nayer."

Markain nodded and said, "None better for June. I would ask Lord Korth to take her on as a squire. It is time."

"Does Lord Korth have a daughter named Pelna?" Kryder asked.

"Light colored hair," Tog added. "A mage."

"He does," Mage Bethany confirmed. "I've met her on many occasions. She's strong in her magic."

"She's good with a bow," June added. She ducked her head, embarrassed at speaking out of turn. "My lords," she added.

"I plan to ask her for help with some of my spells, too," Kryder said. "Maybe teach me some I don't know. The binding spell would be a good one."

Bethany looked at Kryder in a new light. "The binding spell was never taught to us. We all used it as a test, but we copied it from a book onto scrolls." She held up a hand with a gold band on a finger. To Kryder, and only Kryder, it glowed red softly, like his own ring.

"It was too complicated to memorize, and the instructors never allowed us to copy it to our own. How did you know about it if you never attended the Halls of Magic?"

"Goat droppings," Tog said. "Sorry, my lord," he added quickly. He looked at his cousin. "You might as well tell her the details; don't skip over how we know what happened to our parents and who took us there." He turned to Brother Pynon. "Brother, get ready for it. 'Cause we didn't need anyone in my family to tell us what happened. We were *there*."

"Wait till you hear how the spring started flowing again," Dolner added. "Oh, and the great bear!" He swiped his hand across the table, mimicking a bear paw.

* * *

It was truly time for the midday meal by the time they were finished with all the details and all the questions were answered. Brother Pynon was amazed they had interacted with a saint, allowing them to witness the miracle of that night so long ago. He decided it would be best to send a cleric with them to the corner of the kingdom and on into the desert, should they have need of prayer spells. He had a young brother in mind. He was of a minor sect in his order, and skilled in battle.

Those in his specialized sect were known as front line clerics. Each unit in the King's Own had several assigned to them. Over a hundred years ago, the head of their order decided it was needed after a long series of battles with an invading Goblin horde.

Brothers and sisters traveled in the camps of the military units. They were assigned to help heal with herbs, poultices, and healing prayer spells. Front line clerics were up front with the soldiers. The fact that they were trained to fight was an added bonus.

Mage Bethany had said several times that any spell Kryder wished to learn, if she knew it, she would write it herself in his book, in return for a future look at the tomes and scrolls from the Mages' Library…if they found it in the great northern desert.

"You must get to Lord Korth's lands as fast as possible, if you intend to go north and find the library," King Jondal said. "We'll need every advantage. Spells useful in combat would give the mages a greater chance to help us."

He turned to Captain Jonrig, who'd been silent most of the day. "Barl, I would ask you to take them by sea. It will be faster going up the coast then traveling on horseback…and running." He glanced with a question in his eyes at Tog when he heard the big man moan.

"Of course, my lord," Captain Jonrig said. "I may be too old to fight in the upcoming war, but I will do my part where I can. We can leave on the tide tomorrow. I must gather my crew."

"No," the king answered. "Give your crew their time with their families. I'm sure Kryder and Bethany will need a few days—perhaps a week. King Westell and his…allies won't move north until spring. We can spare a week."

"My lord," Knight Commander Markain said, "I'll prepare a team to send to the Baronies so you may coordinate with our own allies. If you will prepare your message and proposed plans, I'll send them as soon as possible. They won't have the speed of a ship to aid them."

"Yes," King Jondal said, "if my calculations are correct, they will arrive in Baron Arnwald's barony a week or so after..." He looked to Kryder. "Did you say his name was Lucas?"

After getting a confirming nod, he turned back. "Ask Burlan Pickswinger if he will meet me this evening and designate a small team to go with him to the Mountain Kingdom. I'm sure King Nuvalk would desire to know of this impending war at the earliest opportunity. The Dwarves have always been strong allies, and this foretells more than border skirmishes."

He turned to Tog. "Tog, will you accompany them? It is but three days journey. I feel the message will show more importance if their own representative in my court brings it back to his home with one of you. I am confident they will join us."

Tog hesitated, looking at his cousin and back to the king. He said, "I don't like caves. I prefer the sky above me, even if it's not in sight through the trees, but I will go while Kryder learns more spells. You're right. We will need all the allies we can gather."

King Jondal nodded his thanks and stared off for a moment. "Do you think the people of Tarlok will join our cause, or will they stay deep in their forest?"

* * * * *

Chapter Seven

Tarlok

Deep in the woods of Tarlok, Lucas and Johan took first watch shortly after sunset. It was a cloudless night, and the stars could be seen shining above. They were only visible because of the break in the tree limbs above, in the largest clearing in the area Johan could find to camp for the night.

"Don't make it obvious, ye know," Johan said in a low voice, "but we're being watched."

Lucas kept his face turned toward the old sergeant, but moved his eyes around, trying to see what the man was talking about. "Where?" Lucas whispered. "I'm not to be seeing anyone."

"That's because I did not wish to be seen," a voice said. Its owner stepped out of the trees into the light of the campfire. "Until I revealed myself to you." He nodded to Johan.

The man was clothed in green and brown leather. He held a bow, though no arrow was nocked. Strapped to his thigh was a long hunting knife with an antler handle. The brown- and grey-speckled fletching of several arrows peeked over a shoulder from his quiver. He whistled the call of a bird they had been hearing as they traveled through the wooded hills of Tarlok for the last several days.

Three others, a hooded man and two dark-haired women, their long hair pulled into a loose ponytail and tied with a thin strip of leather, stepped out of the woods from several directions. They were all dressed in similar fashion. Lucas wondered if all the calls they had heard previously were actual birds or these four. It didn't take long for the rest of those traveling with Lucas and Johan to come out from under the wagons where they had laid down for the night, away from the frost of the coming morning dew.

"My name is Aarn, and I have questions," the man stated.

"We have answers," Lucas said. "You won't like them, I'm to be thinking. Join us around the fire, and we'll answer what we can. What yer to be hearing will only make ye ask more."

A short while later, after hearing of their plans to travel through Tarlok to the Baronies West and the reason for it, Aarn stared across the fire at Lucas. He reached up and rubbed his chin, scratching his short beard. He glanced at one of the women with him and looked back at the big man.

"What you're saying seems like a tale, told in the night around a fire such as this," Aarn said. He indicated the fire and everyone seated around it. "A tale not to be believed, and for entertainment only. We have heard you discuss it among yourselves for the last few days. That is the reason I revealed myself to you before you got far into our lands."

One of the women spoke up, "What proof have you? Your word alone is not enough to persuade us to take you to see Rannow."

"She's right," Aarn said. "The paths through some of the valleys to his village are not known by outsiders. The turnoffs along this lone road are concealed. It is true you may pass through all of Tarlok on it, but you will see few people, and you may never see an actual village without guidance. I must have no doubts before I allow it."

Johan spoke up, "I wouldn't be making this trip at my age if it wasn't to be true. I'm not the young soldier I used to be, ye know. The Elves have allied with a tyrant, and ye would be wise to prepare yerselves for what may come. King Westell aims to rule all of Kerr. He'll not leave yer woods to ye."

Aarn smiled. "You may have years on you, but your sword still strikes swift and true. We witnessed the Trolls coming for you and your horses. They are the reason we are so close to the edge of our borders. Those three were the last of a group we pushed from a series of caves in a valley two days from this spot."

"Ye let them attack us?" Marn demanded. "What kind o'..."

Aarn raised his hand to interrupt him. "Ho, now. Rest assured, arrows were aimed at each. It was well in hand. Your group did well. You didn't need us, and I wasn't ready to reveal our presence yet. We burned the bodies after you moved on the next morning."

"Still," Marn said. He pursed his lips and said no more about it. He looked at Sethon. His nod showed he thought as his brother did.

"I got it," Lucas said. He stood and paced back and forth. "I know how I can convince you. Zane and Penae."

The woman who had spoken out tilted her head slightly and said, "Who?" She had a strange look on her face. A look of surprise.

"Zane and Penae," Lucas said. "They're hunters from Tarlok. They live in the Western Borderlands now. They have been back to Tarlok several times, and now more Tarlok hunters live in the forests near them. They have a couple of daughters who touch deer. Or deer touch, whatever it's called."

The woman looked at Aarn and back to Lucas. "Describe them."

Lucas thought a moment and described them as he had last seen them when Saint Lanae took them through time. He mentioned their clothes, weapons, and the earring with the small claw dangling in Penae's ear, including the small black bead on it. The last caused the woman to inhale sharply.

"One last question," she said. "Can you tell me the colors of the fletching on their arrows?"

"Their arrows?" Lucas asked. "I don't know, I mean I never...wait! Aye. When their arrows were pulled from the great bear and put in a pile, I noticed some o' the feathers used was black. Each of the arrows had some like yours." He pointed to the arrows showing over Aarn's shoulder. "Except for the one black feather on each o' her arrows."

The woman stood and said, "I am Tyna." She reached over her shoulder and drew one of her own arrows from her quiver. "Did it look like this?" The arrow she held had grey and brown mottled fletching, save for the one black feather.

"Aye, that's to be the look o' it," Lucas said.

"Penae is my aunt. She is of my clan, the Ravens," she said. "Her daughters are my cousins. Another from there has come to Tarlok on occasion. Can you tell me his name?"

"Aye," Lucas said. "That would be Teel, a big man who uses a bow and two long-handled hand axes. As tall as me boys, though not as stout. A runner, that one, like Orc warriors."

Tyna turned to Aarn. "He speaks the truth. I cannot deny it."

Aarn nodded and stood. "My wife is convinced, as am I. I know Teel. He is a strong hunter and a good man. Get some rest. We leave in the morning for the village of Rannow, Lead Hunter of Tarlok."

* * *

The next morning, the four hunters rode up on their horses, a roll for bedding strapped to the back of their small saddles. An extra quiver hung from each as well. Lucas helped his daughter into the wagon, while Johan ensured the fire was cold, and there was no chance of an ember causing an errant fire. Aarn nodded in appreciation.

"I ask all of you now," Aarn asked, "will you hold the way to our villages safe? You will learn of routes very few know, outside of the Hunters. If others come to us easily, we will know one of you spoke of it."

Lucas looked around at those traveling with him. Marn and Sethon both nodded grimly. He knew he didn't have to worry about his daughter ever speaking of it. Johan glared at his four soldiers. The look they returned to the old sergeant relaxed him. They were all good lads. They would never speak of it.

Lucas said, "We will honor your right to guard the ways. If others find the paths, it's not to be coming from the likes o' us."

Aarn said, "I will hold you at your word. We are a peaceful people, but know this—you will not know peace if you go back on your word. You will be hunted. We will speak of this no more."

He waved two of the hunters on. "We will lead the way. Two will ride ahead and scout." His horse fidgeted, and he turned it all the way around to face Lucas on his wagon again. "Midafternoon, we will cross a shallow creek in a valley. It runs across this road. We will turn east on it."

"Aye," Lucas said. He nodded and started the team. "East." He stopped. "Wait! Turn on the creek? As in…in the water itself?"

"Yes," the hunter confirmed. "It's shallow, and your wagons will have no issue. A half mile in the creek, around several bends and through a narrow valley, we will turn up onto a road known to very few outsiders."

He looked at Lucas in seriousness. "You would never lay eyes on it if the message you deliver were not so important."

"You wouldn't get far along it even if you somehow happened upon it," Tyna added. "Not without us with you. Another group patrols the area."

Later in the afternoon, Lucas stepped down from the wagon and led the horses into the water and deeper shade. Limbs from trees lining both banks stretched out overhead, nearly touching each other. They were nervous when they realized they weren't simply crossing a shallow creek. Marn did the same behind him.

After a few minutes, the big draft horses were plodding along as if it was something they did every day. Lucas noticed the footing below him was more even and solid than it should have been. The stones below had been placed in some spots and removed in others.

True to Aarn's word, after several bends they turned on the last and came out of the water onto another road. Tyna and the other woman waited on horseback, surrounded by four more Tarlok hunters. They were clothed nearly the same as the four already riding with them. The newcomers stayed behind as the group continued deep into the woods.

***

The Empire of Zar

Mraynith stood beside Krawnill, the Elven emperor. The emperor was seated on his throne, listening to the Human speak. The knight commander explained that the lord mage had never shown up in Yaylok. They waited a morning, then left on swift horses to come to Zar. The man pointed to two mages who had made the trip through the swamps with him and his captains. "King Westell is looking into the matter. Two of his most capable instructors came with us. They are to teach your mages any spells you do not know, as he instructed them."

Krawnill looked up and over at his personal mage. He spoke in the same language as his guests so they could follow the conversation. "Will this suffice?"

"It will, Excellency," Mraynith confirmed. "I am sure they have the spells I requested in their spell books. As to the disappearance of the lord mage, I am sure he has his reasons. I'm quite sure it is not meant as affront to you."

"No," the emperor agreed. "I'm sure you are correct. In his visits before, I sensed nothing but respect. I'm sure he will reveal himself when you, and those I send with you, stake the claims of my new land in Yaylok this spring. Besides, should he disrespect me, I would expect you to kill him."

"At your command, Excellency," Mraynith answered. He tilted his head slightly with a straight face.

The knight commander raised an eyebrow, revealing his doubts regarding the Elf mage defeating one such as the lord mage. He shrugged. Magic was not his concern. He was there to make plans with the leader of the Elven warriors coming to join ranks with his armies.

"Sir Tharyeld," the emperor said, "I will have a servant show you to the wing of my palace where you and your officers will be housed. Tomorrow you and your knight captains will meet those who will lead my warriors as they join your forces. They will be accompanied by translators. Few of them speak the Human language well enough to plan with you. As formidable as they are in the art of war, they have not the education I and my mages have in languages."

"Thank you, your excellency," Sir Tharyeld answered. "Will the meetings include those in charge of the Goblin hordes preceding us in battle?"

"Indeed," the Elven emperor answered, "as well as Dragon masters. I will send five of the beasts with my warriors. Between them and the Goblin hordes, our warriors might not be given the chance to wet their swords." He stared at the knight commander with his jet-black eyes and brushed a wisp of dark hair from his face with a pale white hand, daring him to argue.

Both eyebrows shot up on the knight commander's face. He, like many, thought the images on tapestries and the stories whispered were only stories. If there were truly Dragons on chains going before the armies, surely the campaign to conquer all of Kerr would be complete by next year at this time. He smiled and glanced at the two mages with him. They wore red robes and were two of the most powerful of the instructors at the Halls of Magic.

*****

Chapter Eight

Minth

Kryder raised his right hand and spoke the phrase he had memorized. He'd heard it on their trip with Lan to the Halls of Magic, and it was a spell in his book, though one he had been hesitant to try. The three words in the phrase he was unsure of had been explained and pronounced by Mage Bethany. He was now confident and ready to cast it.

The room plunged into darkness. It wasn't simply the darkness of night. It was deeper, without the faint glow of the cooling embers of a fire or starlight aiding one's sight. He knew this because he was still able to see, but only a light red outline of solid things. He could make out his host's desk and chair behind it, the bookshelf beside her, and the framed opening to the window. He could also see Bethany's silhouette standing by the desk, one hand on it to steady herself in the darkness.

After almost a minute, the spell faded, and normal light slowly resumed. Mage Bethany stared at him with her mouth open in surprise. She glanced around the room as it grew brighter inside.

"I have never heard of the spell of darkness lasting more than a double handful of seconds," she said. "There was a rumor the instructor who taught us the spell could cast one lasting a count of twenty, but we never witnessed it.

"We were told it was a spell created to allow one to escape," she added. "In your case, it could be used offensively. Especially for you, skilled with blades."

"Now that I can pronounce the words, there are several more spells I'll be able to use," Kryder said. "Thank you."

"You are quite welcome, and thank you for the stone," Mage Bethany said. "I've been informed we have a young lady whose mother works in the kitchen and has the increasing fevers. Her gift is showing itself. They will bring her here late this afternoon, and I will sit with her. You are welcome to be there. In fact, I think it would be best if you used a stone first. You have witnessed it and know what to expect. She will be the first the stone keeps from being burnt in Minth in over a hundred years."

"I will be there," Kryder confirmed. "King Jondal has sent messengers across the kingdom. Brother Pynon has his order preparing a place for those showing signs of the gift. Are there others strong enough to use the stone?"

"Yes," Bethany said. "Besides me, there are three other mages in residence here in the palace grounds. There are four more living in and around Cliff Town. I'm sure we can convince others in the kingdom of rotating through to take their turn with the stone late at night."

"That's good," Kryder said. "I can see where it would become exhausting, remaining available every night."

"We will all take part," she said. "I estimate only a few a month. It is not very common, you know. Some months we may have four or five; we will see. The next thing I must attend to is setting up an apprenticeship of sorts. Some will want to use their gift. Not all, but some. Once the level of their gift is determined, they will need a teacher. I think it best to have them apprentice to a mage or a magic user. There are several who didn't quite earn the term mage and the black robes in the Halls of Magic, yet would be suitable instructors in what they do know."

"I agree," Kryder said. "I taught other shamans of magic some of the spells I know that can be memorized without the aid of reading it as it's cast. Very few could learn anything other than the most basic of spells, but they did learn more of them."

"I was wondering how powerful they were," she said. "I didn't think you were the norm from that area of our world. I gather every race with the gift has different levels of power."

She paused and then continued, "I am afraid the Elven mages may be as powerful as any Human—if not more powerful—in the gift of magic."

"Maybe. We're going to find out," Kryder agreed. "All the more reason to make that trek into the desert. When I get to Lord Korth's estates, I plan to talk to some of the Gnome traders to see if they can give me some insight. The southern part of the desert is their homeland. Surely they know of it, or at least the legends."

"Good luck with that," she said with a laugh. "You know they don't reveal much of their homelands. Not the places where water can be found between towns and settlements, hidden valleys, times of year and locations the roving tribes can be found; not anything. It's as if they don't want outsiders to come in…much like the people of Tarlok."

"I know," Kryder said. "Yet they leave their lands and travel in their great wagons, trading in all the Human kingdoms and baronies. Maybe I'll bring that up, and they'll see their way clear to tell me something I can use. I'm sure Tog would agree with the tactic. I wonder if they made it to the Mountain Kingdom yet?

"It couldn't hurt," she said, referring to the Gnomes. She also answered his other question. "They should be getting close. It's been a while, but I've made the trip several times in the past."

She turned back to the task at hand. "Now, about the levitation spell. The third word is pronounced *mah-took*, not *may-took*. If the preceding word has…"

The lessons continued until they were summoned to see the young woman in fever.

* * *

The Mountain Kingdom

"They're a little hot," Dolner admitted, "but I think that's because my old ones had holes in the soles." He wiggled his toes in his new boots and shifted his new sword belt and sword. It was longer than the old one he'd kept from the town watch. Unlike the other, it and the scabbard were well made. The weapon's balance more than offset the extra length.

"You'll be glad for a pair of warm boots," June said. "I've never been, but it would seem to me it will be cold underground."

"Maybe, but it will be great!" Dolner said. "Think of it. The Mountain Kingdom."

"Great?" Tog asked. He shook his large head. "What is so great about going underground? For longer than going into a den to draw out a great bear, anyway?" He glanced over at the official representative of the Dwarven Kingdom and quickly added, "No offense, Master Pickswinger."

"None taken, my large friend, none taken," the Dwarf said as he reached up and straightened his dark curly beard with one hand. He sat in a wagon, reins in hand, nearly eye level with Tog, trotting beside him. "And please, call me Burlan." He pursed his lips and shook his head. "Everyone is always so formal."

He looked at the man riding beside him, Brother Sylif, a cleric of Saint Minokath in the Front Line Order. The cleric shrugged and continued to string small shells on a leather bracelet. Those in his small order wore bracelets instead of the traditional necklace. There wasn't always enough time to slip it off and place it in an inner pocket, so it had to be replaced more often.

His legs were crossed in the wagon seat, the collection of white and pink shells resting in the depression he pushed down into his short robe in his lap. The light blue robe covered his hardened leather vest, came to his knees, and was split on each side to allow movement. It was similar to the tunics worn by the officers in the Minth armies. Breeches could be seen tucked into his boots.

Behind him in the bed of the wagon, leaned against the back of the seat, was the long steel handle of a war hammer. It may not have been in his hand, but the leather loop attached to the end was around his arm at his elbow, ready to use at a moment's notice. The Dwarf beside him had a similar weapon—though shorter, and one end of the head had a point like a pick—lying flat in the back of the wagon.

June eased her horse up past Dolner's to ride beside Tog. "What is it with going underground, my lord? Is it your fears, or something all Orcs have a problem with?"

"Page!" exclaimed Squire Lynol. "You border on rudeness. Apologize to Lord Tog."

"No," Tog said with a laugh, "I don't consider it rude at all. And please, call me Tog. In Orcanth, if you have a question, you ask. The only time you don't is when a patrol leader or chief gives a command. No questions are asked then." After a few more strides he said, "Or of a shaman. You don't question shamans. Well, except for Kryder. I can question him. That's different."

"I ask all kinds of questions," Dolner admitted. "How else will I learn?"

"The boy has a point," Tog agreed. "Not to be rude to you—I understand you are helping with her training—I'm just saying she can ask."

Lady Avilia, the knight captain in command of their group, chimed in, "Lynol, you are correct in chastising her, but in this circumstance, we must adhere to Lord Tog, I mean *Tog's*, customs."

"Yes, ma'am," Squire Lynol said. "June, I'm sorry. I still have much to learn."

"It's all right," June said. "It's all part of it. If I were watching over me, I'd have pulled my hair out, long ago." She grinned at him. She could be a handful, but she understood where things stood in her training. "I could have worded the question better."

"Yeah," Dolner agreed. "You could have just asked him if he was afraid of the dark." He urged his horse to move away from Tog as the big man threatened to whack him over the head with his bow.

"Scavenger!" Tog said. The Half-Orc laughed. "That was pretty good, I admit. Scared of the dark. Hardly. It's knocking my head on the rocks above and having to stay crouched for so long. That's what I dread."

"You, my friend, are in for a surprise," Burlan said. "No self-respecting Dwarf would have low ceilings. They must be high above for proper air flow. I take it you have never been to a Dwarven cavern, much less the great caverns of the Mountain Kingdom itself?"

"There are none in Orcanth," Tog admitted. "None I know of, anyway."

"You are correct," Burlan said, "now. Once there was an outpost in the far reaches of Orcanth. They kept to themselves, for the most part. Over three hundred years ago, the last of them boarded great ships and sailed along the coast until they reached what is now Yaylok. That is why it is not uncommon to see them there."

"Why did they leave?" Dolner asked. "Did the Orcs make them go?"

"No," Burlan said. "Legend says it was a Dragon. It decided it liked the caverns below their mountain, and they were forced to flee to the coast. They built the ships and left. They had been tolerated by the Orc Tribal Council while they stayed within their mountains. They traded iron ore to the tribes. Once that was lost, there was nothing left for them, so they moved on. The drawings of those ships show a shallow design that would never be able to take the pounding of the seas off the coast of Minth, but they were fine for sailing within sight of land down around Zar to Yaylok in the south. I'm sure you have seen maps of Kerr. They are the reason we know all land is surrounded by seas."

"A Dragon? In Orcanth?" Tog said. "I wonder if our shaman knows the tale. You can bet I'm asking *that* when I see her next."

"I thought you said you couldn't question shamans," June said. She looked at Dolner with a 'watch this' look.

Squire Lynol laughed. He couldn't help himself. Lady Avilia slowly shook her head. Burlan nudged the cleric in jest. Dolner grinned and nodded quickly several times, motioning with his hand, urging June on.

"Two of you now," Tog groaned. "And to think I have to get back on a ship…with both of you."

* * *

Minth

"I'm glad I get to show you before we load back onto Captain Jonrig's ship," Kryder said.

"I'm glad you came when you did," Mage Bethany said. "We could have lost her otherwise."

Kryder followed her down a long hallway in a wing of the palace leading to one of the great towers. There were doors spaced evenly along both sides. All were closed, except one. He glanced in as he went by and was surprised to see young ones at play.

Some stacked small pieces of wood carved into different shapes, and others played a game of some type involving small stones on a piece of cloth laid on the floor. An older woman sat in a rocking chair, watching the room full of children. Two older youths, a boy and a girl, were in the room as well. The boy had a long wooden whistle and was showing two little ones how to blow theirs, while the red-haired girl explained the stone game.

"Whose children are they?" Kryder asked. "Are they noble children?"

Bethany glanced back at him and smiled. "No," she said. "Well, one. The others are not. Their parents work here in the palace.

Though not as many as during the day, some work during the evenings. King Jondal decided to ensure their children are cared for while they are working. The other rooms are used for schooling during the day when more children are here."

"Interesting," Kryder said. "He cares for his people."

"He is a good man," Bethany agreed. "He can't help but be so. The woman in the rocking chair is the queen mother."

"What?" Kryder asked. "You mean *his* mother?"

"The very one," answered Bethany. "She loves children. I suspect she had something to do with the idea, but it didn't take much convincing on her part. The girl with the red hair is his daughter, Princess Taliah."

"Amazing," Kryder said. "My grandpa and the Red Fist chief care for those below them. They don't consider them 'below.' The barons and baroness in the Western Baronies put their people first, as well. Not that we pay attention to other kingdoms, but isn't this type of arrangement unusual here?"

"Very," Bethany admitted. "It's not done. Most of the dukes and lords in our kingdom don't follow suit. They're not cruel to their people, but they prefer to maintain the lines between nobles and commoners. No noble in the other kingdoms would ever consider such a thing."

"The girl we are going to see?"

"Yes," she said in answer to his unasked question. "We wouldn't have known of the gift showing itself if King Jondal were like so many others." She stopped and turned to him. "In the recent past, all we've been able to do was make them comfortable, and afterward, see they were afforded what opportunities were available to the burnt. Simple jobs, with folks who understood."

Mage Bethany was a strong woman, sure of herself and her abilities. She took pride in being able to keep her emotions in check. She took a deep breath and smiled, with only a slight shimmer of not quite tears in her eyes.

"Now, this stone will enable us to save them from becoming lost within their minds. Thanks to you and your cousin." She turned away quickly and continued down the hall. "Come, we must hurry."

They entered a large room at the end of the hall. It contained several sitting areas, rows of cots, and a large fireplace on one wall. The opposite wall held racks of weapons. Swords, shields, and spears filled two racks. Scores of bows and quivers of arrows hung on another. The back wall opened to a staircase spiraling up into a dark tower. It was a ready room for guards, should the castle face a siege.

One of the cots was moved away from the rest, near the fireplace. A woman and a man knelt beside it. A girl of about fourteen years lay on it. The child's mother wiped her face with a wet cloth, handing it to the man to dip and wring out in a wooden bucket of water.

They stood quickly when they realized others had entered the room. The woman said, "Mage Bethany, we brought her as you asked." Kryder could hear the distress in her voice. She had been crying.

"I moved the cot like you told me," the man said to the mage. He wore simple clothes and riding boots. He glanced at Kryder, a question in his eyes. "Will you be able to help her? Please. We don't want to lose her. I mean, I know she will still be here, but…you know."

He stared off for a few seconds, gathering himself. "I've been told she can work with me in the stables, but some of the horses are fickle. It's not always safe around beasts bred and raised to fight."

"Yes," Kryder answered. "We'll keep her from being burnt." He stepped over to the young woman. She looked up, sweat on her face. She was scared, and it showed.

"My name is Kryder," he said softly. "What's your name?"

"Lorna," she whispered. "Are you a mage? You don't wear robes." She looked closer at him. "And you're not very old." Her voice was a little louder, her inquisitiveness getting the best of her.

"No," Kryder answered. "I'm a shaman, but that's close." He smiled at her and knelt. "Lorna, I'm going to let you sleep for a little while. When you wake up, you'll feel much better. Don't be scared; you will only feel sleepy. It won't hurt. Are you ready?"

"I…I think so," she said. Her eyes darted toward her parents.

Mage Bethany nodded to them and indicated they needed to let her know they would be there, but they should step away. The girl's mother knelt and kissed her forehead and whispered to her. Her father ruffled her hair and ensured her that they would be there when she woke.

Once they were on the other side of the room, Kryder held out his hand and spoke the words of the sleep spell. The girl closed her eyes, and her chest rose and fell evenly.

"That was fast," Bethany said.

"She wasn't resisting," Kryder said. "I didn't have to push it hard. I don't want her sleeping the night through. I'm sure her parents want to know she's safe as soon as possible." He looked over to them and whispered, "I wonder if we should have them leave the room. The sudden burst of flames may scare them. I wouldn't blame the father if he tried to stop me."

"Good point," Bethany agreed. "I can see him doing just that."

She walked over to the two of them and spoke quietly. The man nodded once and led his wife out of the room. He closed the large door after them. She moved back to Kryder's side, ensuring she wasn't between him and the fireplace.

Kryder placed a hand on the girl's forehead, held his other out with the stone in his fist, and spoke the words inscribed on the stone. He didn't have to read them, as he had memorized the short phrase. Like earlier in the day, when he'd made sure he had them right, the inscription glowed a soft red. Unlike earlier, the whole stone glowed after a moment.

It grew brighter and brighter until it looked as if it was red hot. If the girl's parents had remained in the room, they wouldn't have been able to see it. The red of magic was seen only by those with the gift fulfilled. Flames burst from the stone and struck the back wall inside the empty fireplace.

Kryder held his hand up for nearly a quarter of an hourglass before the flames lessened and slowly receded back into the stone. He felt a little weary from the use of magic, but not as much as he had expected. The stone itself was the source of the spell—he only had to trigger it—so it didn't drain him like any other spell would, had he held its use for as long.

In awe, Mage Bethany reached down and felt Lorna's forehead. "The fever is gone," she said. "It worked as you said it would. Did it pull from you?"

"Not much," Kryder answered, "but you will feel it. Make sure you don't tax yourself with other spell use on the days you need to use it."

"Agreed," Bethany said. "Now that I have seen it used myself, I'll be able to convey it better. If you don't mind, I will wake her."

"Go ahead," Kryder said. He stood and leaned back, stretching.

Bethany cast the spell to negate the spell the girl was under. Nothing happened. She looked at Kryder in horror. "She doesn't waken. What do we do? Is she injured somehow?"

Kryder thought a moment and then said, "Let me try. You may not be able to counter a spell I successfully cast."

Bethany pursed her lips, then with a nod to herself at the decision made, she reached into a pocket and pulled out her personal spell book. She flipped pages and found the one she was looking for. She held it up for Kryder to read.

He read the spell to himself, not quite whispering the pronunciations. It wasn't a long spell, but it was one he didn't have. When he was sure of it, he held a hand over the girl and spoke the words with conviction. Her eyelids fluttered open, and she focused on the two of them.

"What do you feel?" Kryder asked.

*****

Chapter Nine

The Mountain Kingdom

Dolner felt his horse slow as he pulled lightly on his reins. He urged her up again and moved to the opposite side of the wagon where the cleric sat. Once he was beside him, he watched the man make a small hole with the tip of a long, thin dirk in the last shell in his lap. He slid the dirk back into a sheath on the side of his boot, its grip at knee level.

Brother Sylif eased the thin piece of leather through it and tied a knot to keep it from sliding around, like the small knots between every shell. He then put the bracelet around his wrist and decided where he wanted to tie the ends together. The last knot he formed allowed him to slide it slightly, making it loose enough to put on and tighten back up.

"So," Dolner said, "uh, if it's around your wrist, how do you rub it, count it, or whatever to remove bits of the shell to sacrifice to Saint Minokath? Especially when you have your hands full with the big hammer?"

Brother Sylif looked up at the boy with a grin. "Well, if I'm not fighting to protect those I'm assigned to, I reach over with the other hand. If I am using my weapon and wish to ask the Lord of the Seas for his aid, the movements, while I swing, rub the shells against my wrist. But even if the bracelet breaks—and it happens—the exertion I give fighting in his name suffices."

"Oh," Dolner said. "Let me ask you something. Aren't clerics only supposed to help people? You know…preach, heal, and stuff? I've never heard of brothers and sisters fighting like warriors. I mean, I am from a small town, but still, I hear things."

"We do," Sylif answered, "but some of us have been called to fight. If the cause is just, one must fight for it. Saint Minokath himself wears chainmail not of this world. It is not only for looks, you know. The Book Of The One tells us he has fought demons face to face. You pose a good question, one that will be argued for many years; are we accepted by the gods and granted prayer spells to only heal and help, or also to fight for good, and thus lessen the healing needed?"

Dolner was quiet as he thought about what the cleric had said. Finally, he spoke again, "I think both. I mean, I can't see your bracelet glow unless you cast a prayer spell, but if other clerics, accepted by their gods, can see it all the time, why do they argue against your order? It's right there in front of their faces. You're accepted by your god. Who are they to question it?"

Sylif tilted his head slightly and said, "You show wisdom beyond your years. I would not have expected this from you. No offense, but not many your age have the ability to reason this way. And…you do act your age at times, teasing others."

"I'll say," Tog added. "Kryder and I got into all kinds of things when we were his age. I'll tell you this, he doesn't act sixteen when we spar." He held up a hand and flexed his fingers. "If he asks you to break out the wooden weapons and go a round or two with him, watch your fingers, Brother. You will need those shells on your wrist and your prayer spell to heal them."

"Yeah, well, you left a bruise the size of a fist on my hip," Dolner countered. "I was paying you back."

Tog laughed. "That'll teach you to move faster. I'm just trying to help."

"Perhaps you should consider joining my order," Sylif said. "Young, with a good head on your shoulders, strong fighting skills. There may be a reason for it."

"No thanks," Dolner said, shaking his head. He reached up with a hand and ran it from his forehead over his head, letting his hair fall away from his eyes. "Too much discipline involved with all that. Besides, I can't read." The last he whispered, leaning close to the wagon. He glanced over to see if June heard.

"I see," Brother Sylif said. "Well, reading The Book Of The One and being able to write prayer spells in your own book would be required." After a moment he looked back at the boy and said, "But there are other gods, you know."

* * *

The Eastern Sea

Far from any occupied land in the Eastern Seas was an island consisting of enormous mountain peaks. It was a desolate island, with rocks interspersed with shrubs, rising up to the mountains. At the top of one was a tower, the only structure on the island. Two beings sat at a table laden with food and drink. A pleasant breeze blew in through open widows.

Zeronic smiled at his sister. "Lanae, I saw you when our Creator called us all together. You were gone so abruptly after, I didn't get to speak. It is good to see you."

"You as well," the Goddess of Time said. "Though I suppose I should have made time."

Zeronic, the God of Wind and Change, spit out a mouthful of his wine as he laughed. "Don't do that. You almost did what is impossible. You could have choked a deity to death."

Lanae smiled at her own joke. "My apologies, big brother." She placed both her elbows on the great table. "I have come to your home to ask if you think it is time."

"Stop!" he stammered and laughed as he was about to take another sip. He shook his head as he wiped the drops from his flowing white beard. "Please, stop with the references. You know how I love a quick wit."

He put his cup down and looked off in the distance for a moment. When he looked back at her he was serious. "Yes. It is time for change."

"What will you do?" she asked.

"I am constantly monitoring the winds of Kerr, but change…now change is a different matter altogether. As the Creator wills, change happens gradually. When I am compelled to force change, it comes from the One we all owe our existence to. As with everything, I am forbidden from making a mortal do as I wish. They must have free will. In this, I will urge participants into the path of one another. What happens…happens."

"Is it truly change if it used to be, but has been cast aside and forgotten?" Lanae asked.

"It is," Zeronic confirmed. "There is no living mortal with the memory. There are old writings and rumors about it from time to time, thought to be tales only. Believe me, sister. If it comes to fruition, it will be a change." He took a sip of his wine, his eyes on his sister the whole time, daring her to interrupt him again, yet prepared if she did.

"It will be a change for me, as well," he said after swallowing. "Unlike you and most of our brothers and sisters, I have no human followers these days."

"Do you think it will happen?" Lanae asked. "Like everything else set in motion to regain the balance, even I cannot see the future in this instance."

"The Creator's will," Zeronic said with a smile. "I have my eye on a pair. If they but ask, I will accept them. If they gain the trust of another pair, they will be the first in their order in thousands of years."

"And the other pair?" Lanae asked.

The God of Wind and Change shrugged. He took another sip of his wine and said, "They have free will, as well. I have done all I am allowed."

* * *

The Mountain Kingdom

The fields stretched into the distance, allowing the gently sloping hills to give way to the mountains in the distance. It had been a while since they'd seen a town or village. The last farm had ended about a bow shot from the first hill, which led to a series of others and then the mountain range. Tog looked around and realized they were in the lands of the Mountain Kingdom, though they hadn't actually entered a mountain.

Sometime later, they rounded a bend in the narrowing valley, and Tog was surprised to see a town. The homes and shops were different than any others he had seen before. They were all made of cut stone blocks, like castles and lord's manors, only smaller. The roofs were familiar, but not the walls.

At the edge of town, like most, a group of tents and stalls indicated where the market was. Dwarves wandered among them, picking out goods and foods of various kinds. Many of the shopkeepers were Human, though there were Gnomes among them. It was nearly the opposite of what would be in a Human town.

Four Dwarves in chainmail, each with a war hammer and shield, stood in the shade of a building, watching over the market. They were ignored for the most part. Several children, both Dwarf and Human, ran by in a game of chase, then stopped and walked back slowly, staring at Tog. They followed for a while, keeping their distance and whispering among themselves.

"I bet the city watch doesn't take advantage of orphans here," Dolner remarked to no one in particular. "I'm just sayin'."

"No city watch horses to keep stabled," Tog agreed. "Well, except for draft horses, I guess."

"They are here mainly to discourage pickpockets and sneak thieves," Burlan said, nodding toward the four. "Like everywhere else, a market is ripe for the picking."

They passed through and followed a wide road leading to two huge stone pillars. The road ran between them to a great framed opening with massive doors blocked open on both sides. They stopped on one side near several pens and stables, next to a set of barracks for soldiers at the entrance to the halls of the Mountain Kingdom. More than a handful of guards stood nearby.

Burlan nodded to the six guards as they walked into the cool breeze blowing softly out of the opening. The guards looked Tog up and down but did not move to stop him. After Burlan spoke to him a few minutes, one turned and trotted away from them, down the vast tunnel, through the rows of lanterns hung on each side of the wide cavern. After a few moments, he was out of sight. Others coming from the opposite direction gave their group a wide berth.

"He will inform the king of our presence," Burlan explained. "King Nuvalk will indeed be curious. I'm sure those of Orc blood have been in these caverns, though not one with half or more. That alone is enough to raise my brother's eyebrows."

"Your brother?" Tog asked.

"Yes," Burlan answered. "Nuvalk Pickswinger is my oldest brother."

* * *

"Burlan, introduce me to those I have yet to meet," King Nuvalk said. "Something tells me this will be an interesting conversation."

Tog sat with Dolner and June on each side of him. Farther down the table sat Knight Captain Avilia, Brother Sylif, and Squire Lynol. The three of them had been to the Mountain Kingdom with Burlan several times before. Lining two walls, no less than thirty armed Dwarves stood quietly.

"Certainly," Burlan said. "This is Lord Tog of the Western Borderlands and Dolner. Page June will be accompanying them and one other as they go north to Lord Korth's lands."

"Ah, Lord Korth," the Dwarven king said. He sat next to a dark-haired, broad-shouldered Dwarf in chainmail with small plates of steel attached, and a red-bearded cleric with the image of a hammer on his tunic. "A good man, that one. The ore from deep within his lands rivals our own. The weapons, too, for that matter. Of course, Dwarven armorers work the metal, so there is that."

"I heard Dwarves make the best swords and axes," Dolner said.

King Nuvalk stroked his beard. "We do make arguably the best swords, though we don't really use them. It's the quality of the steel, and we deal with Humans enough to know what is desired by most, as far as balance and style."

He looked over at Tog. "Now axes…axes are a different matter. Sure, we can make quality steel, but the weapons themselves? The fact is, the Orcs make the finest axes on all of Kerr, to be sure. For close fighting, it's their weapon of choice, though there are tribes who use a type of spear with a blade on the end. Now for us, the war hammer and pick are prized. After all, we are a race from within mountains, and they are our daily tools. Why in the world would Dwarves use axes?"

He shook his head. "Makes no sense at all for a Dwarf to use an axe. The timber we use for support beams are cut with great saws, and that's only when we can't create a stone arch." All three of the Dwarves sitting at the table nodded in agreement.

"Now, the armor our blacksmiths make is incomparable, I say," the king continued. "Well, except for what comes from Lord Korth's lands. Then again, he employs Dwarves."

"True," agreed Mylon Shieldcrusher. He was the commander of the Dwarven armies, his beard braided and neat. "But the weapons and such coming from his lands do not make the man. And it is not the horses his land is known for. He is an outstanding leader, on the field of battle and off. He is beloved by his people, nobles, commoners, and those living there temporarily."

"Agreed," King Nuvalk said. "He is good to our people there. Is it not so, Larnick?'

The Dwarven cleric spoke up, "Yes. There is a hall dedicated to Arnwerg the Hammer on the grounds of his castle. Lord Korth has no issue with those seeking gods other than Saint Minokath. In that corner of the Minth Kingdom, there are Humans wearing the symbol of the hammer…as well as more than a few Dwarves with necklaces of shells."

"All belong to the Creator. Verily I say to you, even the saints and gods," Brother Sylif quoted from The Book Of The One.

"Quite right, Brother," Larnick said. "To deny any deity is to deny His creations."

"Well," Tog said, "I'm glad you feel that way. The reason we're here ties into armor and weapons…and Lan, Bringer of Seasons."

"And Elves," Dolner said. "Don't forget them. An army of them. They use longswords and those crazy shields with the blades coming out of them. I saw pictures of them on a big blanket-looking thing once. It was hanging in a market."

He looked around at the Dwarven guards. "Maybe I need a shield. Say, does Dwarven chainmail come in human sizes?"

*****

Chapter Ten

Tarlok

Lucas climbed down from the wagon, grateful he wasn't wearing chainmail like Johan's. He reached up and took his daughter's hand to help her down. She ducked behind him, hiding her face. There weren't many cabins visible in the lightly wooded hillside, but there were more hunters than Lucas had ever dreamed he would see in one place. At least a hundred leather-clad men and women were in the open area next to a large cabin. Watching. Waiting.

Standing in front of the door was a man dressed similarly to all the others. Beside him was a woman with long, dark hair, and, like the man beside her, there was some grey at the temples. On the opposite side was an older man wearing a string of claws as a necklace.

The man in the middle may have been dressed as the others, but he was not the same. Lucas could tell by the way he carried himself, as he stood and watched them silently, that he was their leader. The man was Rannow, the Lead Hunter of Tarlok.

Sethon took his sister's hand to comfort her, while Lucas and Johan stepped forward. Lucas had to admit to himself, he was nervous. Everyone knew of the Tarlok hunters' fighting skills. Not only were they legendary with their bows, it was also whispered they could move silently, unseen in the woods, and get close enough to use their fabled long knives to end their prey. As deadly as they were, they were not aggressive or warlike. They simply wanted to be left alone and had unique ways of enforcing it.

Rannow looked at Aarn and said, "For you to bring outsiders to my home, the situation must be dire. Even Teel came to our lands several times before I allowed Zane to introduce him to me. I can count on two hands how many others have been welcome here from the outside."

"It is," Aarn confirmed. He pursed his lips, then continued, "Rannow, I do not do this lightly. Our way of life is at stake. Those of us here, and our cousins in the Western Borderlands."

He paused a moment, looked Rannow in the eye, and continued, "No. I don't think that is right. It is not only our way of life at stake. Our very lives are, because every hunter would die fighting before we allowed our forest to be taken from us. Lucas has brought us news you must hear."

Rannow stepped forward, and he held a hand out toward Lucas. "To bring us warning of something so dire, you are welcome here. Come, follow me to the Gathering Firepit. We will feast on fresh kill, and you can tell us everything."

* * *

Minth

In the king's castle, Kryder leaned back and rubbed his stomach. "It's too bad Tog and Dolner aren't here. They would have loved the roasted wildfowl. You know, your majesty, I'm getting kind of spoiled, eating at your table each night."

"Nonsense," King Jondal said dismissively. "It is you who is spoiling me with conversation of your travels, homeland, and Orcanth. Besides, I think my cooks are enjoying themselves, looking to impress the visitor. Normally I insist on fare everyone has access to."

He waved at the remains of the fowl on the platter in the center of the table. "This must be from birds penned somewhere in the city. It is not quite the time of year to hunt them. Once the leaves turn and grasses brown, they are more easily spotted. They avoid snares, so they must be brought down with arrows. The green plumage makes them hard to see, otherwise."

"They can be taken with a sling," Kryder said. "Tog and I can both use them. We're all right with them, I guess. We miss more than a few. I've seen Aunt Katheen do it many times. She rarely misses. It's impressive."

"Indeed," King Jondal said. "Those from outside the cities and bigger towns use slings. It is not a practical weapon here in the city. Those who truly live off the land, farmers and such, are quite resourceful with them I suppose."

"You would be surprised," Kryder said. "A well-placed rock or piece of steel can render a man unconscious. It may even kill."

"Perhaps I should insist the scout teams learn to use them," Jondal mused.

"If you have members of your ranks from outside the cities, I'm sure they're already skilled," Kryder said. "Maybe they should teach others. If nothing else, it saves arrows when foraging to feed the soldiers."

"True," the king said. "We will need every arrow for the upcoming war. I have asked craftsmen to join with the armorers to help make more. Arrows for bows, and bolts for the crossbows. I will gladly dip into the kingdom's coffers to cover the loss of their normal woodworking businesses. They started two days ago."

Kryder turned to Bethany. "You wouldn't happen to have the spell to replicate objects in your book, would you? I've…seen it cast once, but the one who cast it did not have the strength to make the arrow as strong as the original."

"I do not," Mage Bethany answered, "but I know one who does. Mage Pelna has the spell. From what I hear, she uses it to aid her husband and those who fish the lakes and the sea. She makes netting and floats for them on occasion."

"Good," Kryder said. "I'll ask her about it."

"Remember," Bethany warned, "most mages do not give up their spells to strangers. You will need to convince her."

"I don't think it will be a problem," Kryder said. "Not at all."

"Speaking of convincing," King Jondal said, "I wonder what it would take to convince the Tarlok hunters to join our cause?"

"From what I know from Zane, Penae, and their daughters, the hunters will defend their forests to the last man and woman," Kryder answered.

"Yes," Jondal said as he stroked his beard. "But I wonder if they can be convinced to leave their forests and join our ranks." He leaned back. "Now those would be scouts capable of using slings. Then again, I can imagine they use their arrows sparingly and retrieve them. They never miss."

* * *

Tarlok

Rannow stood up from the log he was sitting on and paced back and forth near the fire. He turned toward Lucas and Johan. "This is dire news. Elves joining ranks with the likes of King Westell. The man has no honor. None."

He turned toward a group of six men and women. "The king of Gar-Noth is the type of man to hunt for...pleasure." He spat in the fire. Many others turned their head and did the same.

"I...we, have known men and women from all the other kingdoms and baronies over the years. Most are good people. Some, as I said before, I have welcomed into my own home." He stopped pacing.

"Such as King Westell, I would not tolerate even the passage of the open road. We all know what Elves have done in the past and are capable of doing today. They keep Goblins as...pets. They drive them before their armies as a type of shock troops, attempting to overrun their opponent, taking lives and draining resources." Everyone there knew he meant arrows.

He turned toward one of those who had been sitting on the same log as he. "Migdale, tell us of the Elves, so we may spread the word and prepare ourselves."

The shaman of Nalkon stood and stepped toward the fire so all could see and hear him. "The Elves are everything we as a people detest. They are an abomination in the eyes of Nalkon the Hunter."

He held his hand up with three fingers crooked, imitating the claws of a bird of prey. "Saint Nalkon abhors those who kill without cause or need. We all should strive to be likewise. The Book Of The One tells us, 'All living things are of the Creator.' We may only take lives when it is needed for survival, save in defense of ourselves or others. At all times, we must use all we can of the gifts given to thinking mortals, including the beasts of the land and fowl of the air."

"Hunt well. Honor the gift granted. Waste not," several voices called aloud from the hunters gathered. Others nodded solemnly.

"The Elves will give no quarter, nor will they fight with honor," the shaman continued. "As such, they are not granted the right to know their slayer. Silent arrows and stealth in the forest will be honorable for our people. There is honor in ending future threat, whether here in our forest or if..." He paused and looked over to the leader of the hunters. "If Rannow decides to take the fight to them."

Rannow looked around at the hunters gathered for the feast and to hear the news. He glanced at his wife. The confirmation to follow him anywhere and back, whatever decision he made, passed between them silently. He turned back toward Lucas and those with him.

"A ruler attempting to add to his kingdom is not our business, as long as they do not attempt to take any land or a single tree in Tarlok. It has always been so." He continued pacing. "We can prepare ourselves and our forests for the eventual invasion, it is true."

Mutterings of confirmation could be heard among the hunters. He said, "But...but in this, it is not enough. We cannot allow King Westell the rest of Kerr. He will not stop at the edge of our forest. One such as he lacks the ability to control himself. By bringing Elves into his ranks, we know he will not stop. Tarlok may be the last to fall, but it *will* fall if the entire world of Kerr is against us. We must take the fight to him."

He stopped pacing, sure of himself. "Spread the word among all the settlements and to every lone cabin. We will gather here and go forth. Every ally fighting against King Westell and his armies shall have Tarlok hunters with them. We will scout the enemy and harass those the enemy sends to spy on our allies. Those not assigned to scout will form companies to enhance the cavalries and archers of

Minth and the Baronies West. Our horses are swift, and none can shoot an arrow at a full gallop like a Tarlok hunter."

He turned to the group of six. "Tonight you will go. Spread the word. Tell every man and woman capable to help gather the ore from within the hills. Instruct the armorers to fire every forge. We need arrowheads for more than the taking of game. We need them to puncture armor. We will make more arrows than has ever been seen."

He thought a moment and said, "The elder hunters will guard our borders with those too young yet to make the journey. They will continue to teach the young and care for those burnt. Leave the swiftest of horses so they may send word if the enemy attempts to pass through our forests while we prepare.

"Lucas, take word with you: the hunters will make our way to Minth by Midwinter. I will be ready to sit at the table with King Jondal, the leaders of the Baronies West, and the others leading the fight to stop King Westell. I will send four with you. I ask that you send word to our cousins in the Western Borderlands. They will wish to join the fight, I am sure."

He turned to the shaman. "These are the paths we will take. Do you think Nalkon approves of us going forth, or would he rather we wait, prepared to defend?"

"We have but to ask the saint. He may answer, he may not. If he chooses not to, we can only do that which we feel is right."

Migdale put a hand to his claw necklace, and with his other, he gently scraped a claw over the back of his hand. It didn't draw blood, but it did make a light streak visible on his skin. He prayed silently for a sign. All present saw the claws begin to glow blue, the brightness increasing. Suddenly a huge black owl swooped into the ring of light provided by the massive fire pit. It circled once, twice, and on its third pass, Migdale held his arm out.

The great bird landed on his arm, careful not to pierce it with its claws. There was a collective gasp. The big owl's feathers were jet black, interspersed with an occasional dark grey. It turned its head nearly backward and stared at the shaman, then looked around with dark eyes as its head slowly swiveled all the way around the other direction. Lucas, like everyone there, would later swear the bird looked right into his eyes, into his very soul.

As quickly as it appeared, the owl spread its wings, and with several strong beats of its four-foot wingspan, was gone. Up into the night, one with the darkness.

There was silence. Finally, Rannow spoke, "Like the Black Owl…we hunt."

*****

Chapter Eleven

Minth

A week later, Kryder, Tog, and Dolner boarded Captain Jonrig's ship. With them was newly promoted Squire June, Brother Sylif, and four horses, two of which were familiar with the ship. Dolner and June spent some time settling the other two.

Tog handed the deer he was carrying to two of the ship's crew. They managed to get the big body through the door to the galley. The cook stuck his head out and shouted his thanks.

Tog raised a hand in reply. He whispered to Kryder, "I like fish well enough, but I need red meat after so many days of having it."

"Agreed," Kryder said. He handed his reins to Dolner.

"Besides," Tog said, "I'm hoping more familiar food will help my stomach."

"How do you do that?" June asked a few minutes later as her horse and Brother Sylif's calmed down quickly.

"What?" Dolner asked. He reached up to pat his own grey horse.

"Know what the horse is feeling," she said. "You seem to know what they are thinking. What they need."

"I don't know," he admitted. "I've always had a way with animals. I just...talk to them. Even the wild boars feeding on apple trees near my lean-to deep in the woods never gave me any trouble."

She looked at him in surprise. He continued, "I mean, I know they're dangerous, can kill you, even. A big boar has razor sharp tusks. I talked to them quietly and showed no fear."

He grinned sheepishly. "All right, I was a little afraid, but I didn't show it. Animals can sense it. Like they also knew I wasn't going to hurt them. We just sort of lived near each other." He shrugged his shoulders as if it was no big deal.

"I think that's amazing," June said. "I love animals, and they seem to like me, but I don't know if I would be comfortable around something that could kill me so readily. Warhorses can, but that's different. They are trained, and I am trained to ride them in battle. But wild boars and such? Don't get me wrong, I would go down fighting, I assure you. Them or me, I say."

Dolner looked her over, at her armor, many weapons, and the grin on her face. "I believe you," he said.

After a moment he said, "You need to teach me that trick. The one where you rolled your sword around mine, moved my arm out, and tapped my forearm with the edge of your shield. It would have left a nasty bruise if I didn't have my new chainmail."

"Your new mail shirt, you mean," she teased. "It's not even as long as my mail."

"Hey, the Dwarves didn't have one long enough for a human," Dolner said. "They modified this to fit. I kind of like it; it leaves my legs free. I don't think I will get another one when we get to Lord Korth's. Though the Dwarves there make armor for humans, I think I'll stick to this and the hardened leather I can strap on my legs."

"There is something to freedom of movement," the young squire conceded. "We will have time to spar over the next few days. I'll show you. Your new shield should be perfect for it. I like it. Narrow, yet tall enough to provide good protection for you. I can't believe how light it is."

She glanced around the open deck of the ship. "I think it will be good to move and fight while the ship sways. It's great for balance training." She looked over to the other side of the ship. "Say, why does Tog look so pale? The ship hasn't even started moving yet."

Dolner grinned. "Come on. Let's go ask him. Then we can ask him if he would like to request fish stew for dinner tonight. I'll tell him I have an in with the ship's cook and can get it made really spicy, just for him." He led her across the deck.

"If you two don't get away from me, I'll thump you both," Tog declared moments later. He shook a big fist.

"Actually," Kryder surmised, "it probably wouldn't hurt for them to spar with someone your size. They need to learn angles of attack and ways to get inside on you. Let's be honest, we all know of the Lython roaming the Great Northern Desert. What if we run into some of them before we find the first Gnome settlement?"

"You have a point," Brother Sylif said. "The lizard race is no myth. Occasionally, in the past, they ventured south out of the desert on raids. They swing great stone clubs. Getting inside their swing is the only way to get to them. Perhaps Lord Korth and his people will have more information, so we can avoid them at all cost."

"Yeah, well, I'd rather fight a handful of beings my size than spend time on a ship," Tog declared. He looked at the two youngest members of their group. "When we get under way, we'll get some training in. I'm sure June can show us all a thing or two. Kryder and I can hold our own, but you can never know enough. Brute strength will only take you so far." He walked toward the wooden weapons stowed with their gear.

Brother Sylif looked at Kryder with a question in his eyes. "Apparently there's more to Orcs than I ever thought I knew."

"Absolutely," agreed Kryder. "The misconceptions about Orc warriors have been the downfall of their enemies since time began.

The Orc warriors believe in training hard with their weapons. You won't find one unwilling to learn new fighting skills and techniques. They prefer their longbows and axes, but they can use any weapon at hand with more than average skill."

* * *

During the three-day trip, Tog didn't get sick. He claimed it was because they stayed within sight of land, and he could look over and see it remaining steady in the distance. That, the venison, and the prayer spell of the first mate when he first came on board apparently helped. The five of them, with an occasional member of the crew, sparred with their weapons.

Dolner worked hard to use his shield and sword together, learning quickly, much to June's surprise. In the beginning, she was able to tap her training sword and shield on him constantly. By the end of the second day, she had to work hard to get inside his defenses. He was a natural with it. She also tried to show him how to use her bow. *Tried.*

"You didn't even hit the board," June said. She had her hands on her hips, standing beside the target she had placed against a rail. She looked off into the water, knowing the arrow was gone forever. She looked back at him. "Much less the target I scratched on it."

Dolner grinned and shrugged his shoulders. "It feels clumsy in my hands. I don't know."

"That is pretty bad," Tog agreed. "You shoot like…well, like droppings."

"How can you take so well to a sword, but can't shoot a bow?" Kryder asked. "I mean, even I hit the target, and I rarely shoot a bow these days. That's the third arrow off the target completely."

"I've never seen anyone that bad," Tog declared. "I don't care if you have to take into account that the ship moves." He leaned closer to Kryder and whispered, "Don't let him throw any of your daggers. I wouldn't even let him throw the small knife you keep in your boot."

"Agreed," Kryder whispered back through the side of his mouth.

"I think I'll stick to a sword," Dolner said. "Sorry about the arrow…again."

"Let us hope we don't get in a situation where we need you to use a bow," June said, resigned at the loss of the arrows. "Don't worry about it. Come on, show me how you got inside my shield the last time."

Tog taught Sylif several blocking techniques. The similarities in the length of the handle of his axe and the cleric's hammer helped. In return, Sylif showed him a move where the head of the weapon is swept up at an unexpected angle from ground level, when an opponent has blocked a blow, and is prone to let his guard down for a moment.

Kryder and June threw knives, and each was impressed with the other's skill. It was an experience for both of them, as they timed the ship's movements before throwing. Kryder helped several of the deckhands improve their knife- and dagger-throwing skills. Dolner wasn't asked to throw with them.

The first mate showed him one of the small hatchets used to cut rope in an emergency. The sailor threw it with accuracy, imbedding it into a block of wood strapped to the main mast. Kryder practiced with it, liked the balance and feel, and learned to throw it accurately himself. He was surprised when Captain Jonrig gave him one to keep.

"Not to worry," Captain Jonrig said, "we've quite a few onboard. Here, take this." He handed Kryder a small leather pouch. "You won't need to keep it oiled like we do to protect it from the salt water, but you can use this on your hatchet."

Kryder felt it. "What is it, Cap'n? It feels like a tube of some sort."

"It's kept that way," the captain explained. "Open it."

Kryder opened the pouch and took out the tube. It partially unrolled, revealing three pieces rolled up together. When he spread it out, he could see it was three scales of the Mang fish. Each of them was larger than his hand spread out. One side of the first was like a fine sandpaper. He rubbed a thumb across it. He noticed the other two were rougher, one more so than the other.

"That'll put a fine edge on anything," Jonrig explained. "The men use them on their knives and the hatchets. The swords, too, not that we have to break out the cutlasses for more than sparring, but one never knows."

"I have a set," June added. She explained, "After I use my stone, I wipe them off and finish with the scales. Blades, arrow tips, all my weapons." She shrugged like it was something everyone should do.

"Now this is something I need to talk to the chief about trading for," Tog said as he held the piece Kryder handed him. "Once King Westell is stopped and things go back to normal, of course."

"I'm not against sailing all the way around the Great Northern Desert," Captain Jonrig said. "That would be the fastest way to get goods to Orcanth, I think."

Tog, thinking out loud, said, "Red Fist could trade with the White Sands tribe, and they could trade with you. That may be easiest, because except for their shamans, they don't speak Human."

"You would definitely want to trade with them first," Kryder observed. "In the last few years, an occasional ship has anchored and traded with them. I think Humans on the border of Orcanth took a little getting used to, but trade by sea was bound to happen."

"But," Kryder added, "don't sail any farther than the one pier they have. The next tribe along the coast are the Long Sticks. They keep to themselves, for the most part, except for their chief coming to tribal council meetings with his escorts."

"Yeah," Tog agreed. "Besides, I hear the coast on their lands is all cliffs and rocky outcroppings. But who knows? They don't talk much when they're at the meetings." The big man shrugged. "To each their own, I guess."

"What would they trade?" Captain Jonrig asked. "I mean, if I were to consider it?"

Tog said, "I don't know. Kryder?"

"Good question," Kryder responded. "Livestock, chickens, and turkeys are all I heard of." He looked around the ship. "I got it! Bows. Big bows. Even bigger than Tog's."

"Bows?" the captain asked. "You mean ballistae? Throws a spear like a big arrow? Our kingdom has them. So do others. Some ships have them mounted. Remember the warships we burned?"

"No, but yes," Kryder said. "So, you get big bows that can lock onto pegs. Two pegs get inserted into your railing. You already have holes along them for ropes or whatever. You could break out the bows, place them where you want them, and move them when needed. One man can pull back with two hands. They don't have to be as strong as an Orc if they use their legs to back up." He rubbed his chin and said, "Burning spears, launched much farther than any arrows another ship's archers may use."

"Turkey feathers could be used for fletching," Tog added. "Big feathers."

"If they could be moved around, even if the other ship had ballistae, we would have the advantage," Captain Jonrig said, warming to the idea. "They would be limited in the use of theirs."

"True," June agreed. She looked around the entire ship. "Even if they have a few mounted on swivels, they can't fire through masts, sails, or through any of the other stuff on deck. You could move yours to any railing as you swing your ship around them."

"Aye, Cap'n," the first mate added. "A great stack of wooden spears, wrapped in oiled cloth to stay dry, the bow strings oiled and kept from the water, and a capped bucket of pitch at the ready. I pray we never have to use them, but it's best to be prepared. You know the king of Gar-Noth will send warships up our coast, maybe even try to land soldiers on our lands."

"You're right," Captain Jonrig agreed. "King Westell will do just that. If it gets bad, every ship needs to be ready in case our king calls us."

Captain Jonrig shouted up to the sailor in the crow's nest, "Look lively up there, Narvel! A pod of Mang fish, if you please."

"Aye, Cap'n, on the lookout!" the sailor shouted as he scanned ahead.

"When you finish your business looking for the Mage's Library, we'll have the scales, treated and ready to trade. If you are gone too long, I set sail."

"You'll have time to get there and back, even with the wait while they make the bows." Kryder assured him. "We have until late spring before the enemy is at our doorstep."

"Let us pray we confront them long before they get that close," Sylif said. He made the sign with his hand imitating waves across his chest. The first mate did, as well.

* * * * *

Chapter Twelve

The pier they tied up to was nearly as large as the one in Cliff Town, where the king of Minth had his palace. Kryder realized the majority of the slips were for fishing ships. There was a busy market a short distance from the piers. There were also signs the port dealt in the horse trade. He noticed one empty space had a ramp built onto the dock. He suspected he knew what it was for but was going to ask to be sure.

Tog beat him to the question. "Why the ramp?"

"For horses," the captain answered. "Lord Korth breeds the finest Minth horses in the kingdom. Most would say the breed is the finest in the entire world."

"Every horse owner I ever ran across would agree," Kryder said.

"Without a doubt, the best warhorses on Kerr come from the corner of this kingdom," June added.

"I would agree to that also," Kryder said. "My horse is descended from an incredible horse my grandfather owned. Pure Minth, he was. Bred with a mare, three-quarters Minth, owned by Baron Arnwald. The mating produced my horse's grandsire. Years later, my mother's horse was the granddam.

"He's a little leaner than your warhorse, June," Kryder said. "But then again, it's not like I wear heavy armor and fight on him."

"Still, a good horse is a great asset, even if it isn't a warhorse," June said. "The one you ride now is not bad."

"Yeah," he agreed. "Dolner picked her from the group."

She glanced over at Dolner, standing with the four horses in the pen, soothing them. "He sure has a way with them," she said. "Even my horse took to him right away, and she's kind of ornery with strangers. I expected her to nip his hand when he reached to rub her nose the first time. It surprised me."

"The boy talks to them like they're human," Tog said. "Seems kind of strange to me, but it works for him."

"I asked him how he did it," June said. "He couldn't really explain it."

"Perhaps it's a blessing," Brother Sylif suggested. "Though I know not which deity such a thing comes from."

"Well," Kryder said, "let's help him get them down the plank. We need to make our way to Lord Korth's castle. The king said it's near those mountains in the distance." He pointed to several. They weren't as tall as the ones in the Mountain Kingdom, but they were more than hills.

* * *

The next morning, they were led into the dining hall by a sentry. It wasn't as large as the king's, but it was fair-sized room, with a large fireplace dominating one wall, and several rows of tables. Two people were waiting for them when they came through the door. One was wearing a green and blue tunic, the colors of his duke, whose estates were some distance away. Some said Lord Korth could have become a duke or created a small kingdom for himself. It was something he never desired. He was loyal to his duke and their king.

"Brother Sylif," Lord Korth said. "It is good to see you again."

"You as well, my lord," Sylif said. "The king sends his regards, as well as this message." He held out a rolled parchment. "Before you read it, may I introduce my companions?"

"Certainly, you may," Lord Korth said. He ran his hand over his short hair, now more silver grey than blond. "Sit down, everyone; please be seated. I am curious as to why you requested an audience with me and asked to have my daughter present." He turned to indicate his daughter Pelna, dressed in comfortable clothes and riding boots. Her dark blue cloak, its hood pushed back on her shoulders, was the only indication she was a mage.

Kryder couldn't help but stare. Though twenty years older than when he had seen her on their trip into the past, there was no doubt he was looking at his mother's friend and constant companion while she had attended the Halls of Magic.

She was obviously older now, but her blond hair and the pleasant look on her face was unchanged. Her eyes were different, though. They were the same color but seemed to hold a look he couldn't describe. It was if she was upset about something. There were no indications it was them or the summons this morning. *Maybe it's something that happened last night*, he thought. He noticed a soft red glow. She still wore the steel ring they'd seen her enchant on their trip back in time.

After everyone was settled, Brother Sylif made the introductions. "Allow me to introduce Lords Kryder Narvok and Tog, son of Lur, both of the Western Borderlands, and their companion Dolner."

"I've heard two of your names," Lord Korth said, "but I didn't know your titles. I have never had the pleasure of meeting you. Reports from the border skirmishes mentioned you two several times. That was fine work, retrieving the captured scout team with a squad of Baron Arnwald's soldiers. I read that you led them. Perhaps you would recount it for me over a dinner when we have less pressing matters than what may be in this message." He held up the rolled parchment.

"We would be more than happy to," Kryder said, "though, after you read it and we tell you more, we may all realize the time for that will be hard fought for."

"Yeah," Tog agreed. "We're all going to be too busy to pass stories after a good meal and a beer. Well, maybe if we told them while eating. Turning down a good meal would be foolish. Speaking of meals, why are we meeting between meals?"

"It's half past midmorning snack, if you ask me," Dolner said.

Lord Korth laughed out loud and signaled with a raised hand toward the open kitchen doorway. A cook stepped into the hall, ducked back in, and a moment later, another woman came out, dressed differently than any cook Kryder had seen.

"I thought you would be in there," Lord Korth said with a chuckle.

"Old habits," the woman admitted. "I'm perfecting a new recipe for someone special." She clapped her dusty hands, sending small puffs of flour into the air.

"My wife, Lady Manessa," he explained. "She comes from a family of bakers with recipes of what could only be described as magic pastries, they disappear so." He turned back to her. "A midmorning snack if you don't mind, my love?"

"I'm sure the ladies won't mind. I'll help," she answered. She grinned and ducked back into the kitchen.

Out of the corner of his eye, Kryder noticed a subtle shift in Pelna's demeanor. She quickly gathered herself, attempting to hide whatever was bothering her. Kryder wondered again what it could be.

Sylif said, "Let me also introduce Squire June, daughter of Lord Jolny and Lady Roslyn."

"My lord," June said. She handed over her own piece of rolled parchment.

"Ah," Lord Korth said. "I thought you looked familiar. It has been a while since I saw you last. It was when your mother was promoted to knight captain, before you were a page. I see you are in a plain tunic and do not wear the colors of your uncle, yet you now have the rank of squire. Tell me, who are you training under?"

June glanced at the parchment in his hand. Korth saw the movement of her eyes and said, "Ah, I see. If this is what I suspect it is, I just happen to have an opening."

"Thank you, my lord," June said with a sincere smile.

Across the table from her, Pelna couldn't help but smile, despite whatever might be troubling her. She brushed her hair out of her face, reminding Kryder of the times he had seen her do it. "If I remember correctly," she said, "you were the young lady with the ability to shoot an arrow as well as any on the range that day, despite your age and size."

"I do remember that," Lord Korth added. "I see you still carry a bow, as well as a host of other weapons. From the looks of you, King Jondal and Knight Commander Markain have sent me a confident, capable squire. I am honored by their trust."

He paused a moment and continued, "I am also willing to bet good coin…you are a bit headstrong and more or less a handful."

June's face reddened. "My lord, I…"

"No, no," Lord Korth said, holding up a hand to stop her from continuing. "It is not a bad trait in my eyes. Not at all. Perhaps that is why they chose me, as opposed to any other. I have experience with young ladies with unbreakable willpower and a fierce independence."

Pelna's face turned a little red as she raised a hand and said, "Guilty." June grinned with her this time.

"I am remiss," Lord Korth said. "Let me introduce my daughter to everyone. This is Pelna, my only daughter."

Kryder reached down and turned his mother's ring around his finger several times. "Pelna," he said, "you are the reason we came to your corner of the kingdom."

"Me?" she asked. "What reason would you have for seeking me out?" She paused a moment studying him. "You seem familiar. Have we met? It's like I've seen your face somewhere. I think it's your eyes."

Her own eyes locked on to the ring he still toyed with on his finger. "Are you a magic user or a mage, perhaps? You are too young to have attended the Halls when I did. Your attire tells me no more than that you come from the Baronies West, and perhaps beyond." She glanced at Tog.

"No," Kryder said, "we have not met. Tog and I have seen you before, but you haven't seen us."

Pelna tilted her head slightly, perplexed. Lord Korth unrolled the parchment from King Jondal. He read it quickly and glanced up at Kryder.

"Our king gives you his highest recommendations and instructs me listen to all you have to say, including his instructions conveyed by you. He goes so far as to say, those he holds counsel with are in agreement with his trust in you and what you will tell me." He reached up and ran his hand over his hair again. Kryder was beginning to see where Pelna had picked up the habit.

"You say you have seen my daughter before, but she could not see you. Along with this message, I have to admit, I am doubly curious. Please, tell us how you know Pelna and what is so urgent that the king himself sends a message with you."

"Might as well spill it all," Tog said. He looked at Dolner, pointing a finger. "And you…don't embellish it. We don't need you reenacting me getting shocked to my knees."

"It is a good part," June said in Dolner's defense. Dolner pursed his lips and nodded with a slight tilt to his head. Tog closed his eyes and slowly shook his big head.

"Pelna," Kryder said, "I'm not a mage; I'm a shaman. I did not attend the Halls of Magic, though Tog and I paid two visits there. The second time, we were physically there, and when we left it…we left it burning."

Pelna's eyes widened at hearing this. "Burning? As in destroyed?" A look of satisfaction came over her face. "I hope the lord mage was caught up in it." The last came out with a venom that surprised all but her father. "For a couple of reasons," she added. Lord Korth placed a hand on her arm, comforting her.

"Part of him was," Dolner volunteered. He made a slashing motion across his stomach.

"Wait," Pelna said. "You say you're a shaman? Like a cleric?"

"No," Kryder said, "I'm a shaman of magic."

"Magic?" she asked.

"Show her," Tog suggested. "She's going to ask you to. Might as well light it up."

"My lord, if you don't mind," Kryder asked, "I'll cast a simple spell."

Lord Korth glanced at his daughter, and after receiving a confirming nod, said, "Please."

Kryder lifted a hand and spoke in the language only one other in the room understood. The look on her face as he began expressed that she knew he spoke it well. Above them, near the ceiling, eight balls of light floated, the same as the other times he'd cast it. The lord's eyes widened, and Pelna put a hand to her mouth, stifling her gasp of surprise.

"Eight," Pelna counted, after she gathered her wits. "Eight."

"Yes," Kryder agreed. "You cast three. Like my mother did."

Pelna's head snapped toward him. She looked at Kryder in a new light. "How do you know? Who was your mother..." Her voice trailed off, and her mouth widened as she remembered where she'd seen eyes like his.

She whispered in a shaky voice, "Zalana?"

She cried a little later as the story unfolded, and she heard of her friend's fate. Though most of the others sitting at the table had heard it before or were actually there, it was an emotional moment. The story continued as Kryder told all.

*****

Chapter Thirteen

"Elves," Lord Korth said. He slammed a fist onto the table. "Not only do we have to contend with the forces of Gar-Noth and now Yaylok, we must also contend with Elven warriors and the Goblins they will surely drive before them."

He looked at Tog as the big man enjoyed several different fruit-filled small cakes. "You were right, my new friend. We will have time for little else than preparing for war. I have much to do. I need to meet with my officers as soon as possible. Coordination must be made with the mines, the Dwarven blacksmiths, armorers, leather workers for saddles, and the Gnomes' rovers to transport and ensure the kingdom's armies are supplied. I need a good count of available horses now, and the number ready to be trained immediately."

He stood, pacing as he continued, "The leaders of the militia need to be involved. Spring will be upon us before we know it. Excess horses must be sent to the other duchies, and to the King's Own, along with weapons and armor. It's a good thing we are still well prepared from the skirmishes on the border, or the kingdom would be far worse off."

He stopped and looked at June. "Squire June, I apologize, but I will be considerably busy as I start the preparations. I am afraid I will not be able to spend the time training you properly for quite a while. You may be little more than a courier for the time being."

"I understand, my lord," June said. She tilted her head slightly, and a mischievous look showed in her eyes. "Perhaps I could accompany them into the desert in the meanwhile."

"Until we know more, I have no idea how long it will take to find the Library of Mages, if we find it at all," Kryder said. "If time becomes an issue, we will return in time to join the fight."

"Her bow and sword would be welcome," Tog added. "Otherwise, it will be the four of us. Besides, I need her to help occupy this one." He indicated Dolner with his head. "Then again, the two of them together on this trip could mean more of a headache than it's worth."

"I can find no fault in her going with you, Tog," Lord Korth said after a moment's thought. "After all, an Orc warrior would be a good instructor for her. It is always good to learn new fighting techniques from allies. You are a noble of the Western Borderlands and can teach her of diplomacy among the tribes of Orcanth as well."

"Wait. What?" Tog asked, his hand in midair with a fruit-filled muffin in it. "Droppings!" He grinned sheepishly. "My apologies, Lord Korth. I'll do my best. But these two together…"

Lord Korth nodded his thanks and looked over toward Pelna and smiled. "Now, because my daughter is holding her tongue to the best of her abilities, and I feel the same way, she will now tell you what has been troubling our household of late."

"The stone. Please?" Pelna asked. "Let me see it for myself."

Kryder reached into his pocket, took out the stone, and handed it to her. She took it as if it was a delicate object, capable of shattering into hundreds of pieces if mishandled. Tears fell from her face as they flowed freely now, released by hope.

"My own son has been having fevers, showing all the signs," she whispered. "My husband is a mage as well, so I always knew Levy had the gift. Somehow, deep inside, I knew. The last week or so, what I feared would happen showed itself."

She pursed her lips in anger. "For years now, the Halls of Magic have been denying entrance to any from Minth." Her eyes filled with tears again. "Up until moments ago, I…*we* feared we would lose him to the depths of a burnt mind."

"I will send all who show the signs to Cliff Town and the stone you left there," Lord Korth added, "in the future. My grandson does not have time to get there before it is too late. I thank Saint Minokath you have a stone here with you."

"It would seem," Brother Sylif said, "the Lord of the Seas and several other saints were involved with it."

"Can't argue with that," Tog agreed. He shoved an entire pastry into his mouth.

Dolner stared sadly at the empty plate after watching the last one disappear. Like magic.

* * *

After saving Pelna's son with the magic of the stone, she spent several days with Kryder. She allowed him to copy her duplicating spell and the spell of weaving into his spell book. He, in turn, gave her the spell to negate another caster's spell before it faded, learned from Mage Bethany.

It was much different than the shield spell used when a caster was attempting to attack with one. The others in her book were the same as the ones in his mother's, and now his. It was a tribute to how close they had been while attending the Halls of Magic together. She asked if she could hold it.

A tear came to Pelna's eye as she traced the flowing script of her friend from so long ago, written in the book he now possessed. "I hate that we were unable to keep in touch," she said as her finger followed it. "I have missed her so through the years."

"She spoke of you often," Kryder reassured her. "She missed you, too."

"Well," Pelna said. She wiped the tear away and realized she needed more than her hand. She used her sleeve. "At least I got to meet you."

She sniffed again and wiped her face with the edge of her cloak. "It seems I have cried, of late, more than I have in years. Thank you again for what you did for our son. My husband wanted me to let you know, it meant everything. He would have come himself to thank you once more, but he leads the inland fleet as they harvest fish to dry for the armies."

"A well-fed warrior is strong warrior," Kryder said, quoting an old Orc saying.

"Yes," she agreed. "Even now, Levy is with him on the boat on Lake Tarnla. His father is teaching him the spells used among the fleet to move the ships and keep the fishermen and women safe. If I know him, he is also teaching defense spells and a few to subdue an opponent."

"It doesn't hurt to know them," Kryder said. "When we taught him the spell to send sparks, the boy's hands threw flames a foot away. That's a good start, I would say. Let's hope one as inexperienced as he in the gift doesn't have to use it to fight another. Speaking of which, let me try to create some arrows now. Which one was the original? I can't tell. Some things are not as they seem."

* * *

A week later, the five of them were ready to depart. Lord Korth had introduced them to a Gnome rover specializing in the trade of weapons and armor. They also met his wife. They were to travel with him and two of his wagons into the Great Northern Desert. Driving another wagon loaded with goods were his two sons. The other wagons belonging to him stayed back with extended members of his family, preparing to move goods all over the kingdom.

"Master Sandwinkle," Kryder said, "we are ready when you are. Thank you again for agreeing to take us to your village. I understand it was not an easy decision."

The small figure holding the reins reached up and twirled the end of a long, silver moustache. "No it was not, my new friend. It was not at all. As you know, I go home several times a year, for...various reasons. It was not yet time to make the trip, but we are faced with something unforeseen. This is an issue that will not simply go away."

"Yeah," Tog agreed. "King Westell won't stop at the edge of Minth. You can bet a handful of coin he will want the desert, too."

"Precisely," the old rover agreed. "Those of us who trade in the green lands know a little more of the politics down here. My family has been roving and trading down here for many generations. Those who choose to stay home in the sands will have no choice in the matter."

"Do you really think you can convince your tribal leaders to join us in the fight?" Dolner asked.

"Pfft," Sandwinkle dismissed with a wave of his hand. "I'll tell you a secret, boy, one not many know outside of Lord Korth and King Jondal." He looked around as if to gauge who was listening. He shrugged. "The world will know soon enough, I suppose."

He looked at the small Gnome beside him. She was only about four feet tall, a hand shorter than her husband, and slim like most of her race. Moonlitdune smiled, reached up, and tucked her long, silver-grey hair behind an ear, showing the thick hooped earring on one side. "Tell them, dearest. Now more than ever, you must not hide the knowledge from the world."

"Agreed," Sandwinkle said. He looked over at Dolner, but addressed all five of those traveling with his two huge wagons. "I am the Lord of the Dunes."

Sylif stammered, "Wait, what? You…you're the Lord of the Dunes?"

"Yes."

"The Sultan of Sands?"

"Of course."

"The Master of the Mirage?"

"Guilty."

"The Owner of the Oasis?"

"Indeed."

"The Seeker of Shade?"

"Always."

"The Eternal Edge?"

"How many titles does he have?" June whispered, louder than she should have.

"Many," Sandwinkle said with a wink of his eye. "But that last is not a title. It refers to the blades my family has forged. They take years to perfect and are held in high esteem."

He pointed to Kryder and said, "You, my friend, possess one. I can see the hilt. Your dagger is at least two hundred years old. Our family records indicate the last one traded was then."

He looked at June, smiled, and said, "I am also known as the Retainer of Records."

"My lord," Sylif said, "I am pleased to have met you."

"You met me before, Brother Sylif," Sandwinkle said dismissively. "Don't be ridiculous. You just know a little more about me now."

"True, my lord," Sylif said. "Still, I..."

"Say no more," Sandwinkle said. "I am still me, a rover looking to strike a bargain. But since we are giving away all the secrets around here..." He looked over to his mate and said, "Your turn, dearest. Show the good cleric."

Moonlitdune reached over to the wide armband on her wrist and slid several thin gold bracelets up her arm, freeing the red leather. She unsnapped the outer layer, revealing a large turquoise stone. It was a vivid shade of color with small red lines running through it at random. They seemed to shimmer.

For Kryder, Tog, Dolner, and June, it was a beautiful piece of jewelry unlike any of them had seen. It appeared as if it was worth a king's ransom, but meant no more to them. To Brother Sylif, an accepted cleric of Saint Minokath, the stone glowed a soft blue, indicating she was accepted by a deity.

"Sister," Sylif said. "May your god shine on you like the emblem you wear."

"Thank you, Brother," she said. "And to you the same."

Kryder glanced back and forth to the two clerics. "You follow Saint Minokath, Brother Sylif. Who do you follow, my lady?"

"I am accepted by Zeronic, The God of Wind and Change," she answered with a smile. "In the desert, the wind is all powerful, changing our very surroundings, covering the tracks of our wagons, and bringing the scent of water to our burden beasts." She indicated the large-humped camels hitched to the big wagon.

She looked at Kryder, as she now knew he was a shaman with a gift rivaling any mage in the world. "It would seem change is before us, also."

Tog reached up and scratched the side of his face. "My mother taught us the names of many of the saints in The Book Of The One. I don't remember that one. No offense, sister."

"None is taken," Moonlitdune said. "Not much is written of him, other than a few lines mentioning him. One would have to study some of the older chapters, those not copied to the latest versions. Most of the book has been written for Humans, and is in your language. It has been said there are chapters in Gnomish in the older copies. My copy is like Brother Sylif's and does not contain them. The parts I am referring to have been passed down through spoken tales."

"As well as several in Dwarven," Brother Sylif agreed. "Brother Pynon has an ancient copy passed down through generations. He once told me there are several chapters in the back in a couple of different languages. One he has no idea of, and Saint Minokath has not gifted him the ability to read them. I daresay no one alive can read them."

"I would like to look at it," the Gnomish cleric said. "Would that be possible?"

"I'm sure it is," Brother Sylif answered. "Perhaps it can happen before spring."

Everyone was quiet for a moment, thinking of what was to come. Sandwinkle looked over to the other wagon and broke the silence, "My sons indicate they are ready. We will move out shortly. Tomorrow, late in the day, we will come through the last valley in the hills. The scrubs and brush will give way to the Great Northern Desert. Once we reach the edge, we will attach the sand paddles to each wagon wheel."

"You say we'll travel for a week before we reach your village. I didn't know you were a cleric, my lady. Do you mind if I ask a few questions about your saint?" Dolner asked.

"Not at all," Moonlitdune said with a laugh. "Though saint is not what we say; it is what most Humans call a god. The Book Of The One tells us not to hide our faith. I don't among our people. The stone only remains covered because there are those with sticky fingers in the green lands. Sneak thieves and the like. I'll be more than happy to speak to you of Zeronic. I can sense you are genuinely interested."

"I am," Dolner agreed. "I especially like the part about not reading it. The Book Of The One, I mean."

"One thing you should know," she said, her voice becoming serious, "Zeronic only seems to allow the winds to do as they will; in truth, he controls them. Rest assured, within the chaos of a windstorm, there is a pattern…a path, if you will, known only to him and those he has accepted and chooses to show."

"A method to the madness," Dolner said. He nodded. "I can appreciate that."

"I have never heard it put quite that way," the high cleric of Zeronic said with a curious look on her face.

Dolner nodded and looked over at June. "Hey, June, your horse doesn't like the bit so tight, and it's uneven by one slot. It hurts her mouth on the right side."

Moonlitdune looked at him in a new light as he eased his horse away from her side of the wagon toward his friend. She continued to glance over at the boy every now and then for the next few hours of the trip, a question visible on her face—one she was hesitant to ask her god, much less the boy. After all, the questions she had were based on whispers of legend. Legends she had dismissed long ago. She adjusted the cloth attached to the wagon above her to avoid getting burned during the journey.

* * *

The Duchy of Yaylok, a Gar-Noth Holding

King Westell threw his half empty goblet of wine at the mage in front of him. It bounced off the man, and the wine splashed across his chest and blended with the red robes to create a darker shade of red. "What do you mean the Halls of Magic has burned? Where is the lord mage? Did the messenger say they searched the rubble?"

"Yes, my king," the nervous mage said. "Your steward had it searched thoroughly. They found…well, they found *some* of the lord mage."

"Some?" King Westell demanded. He stood up and stepped toward the mage. "What does *some* mean?"

"My king," the mage answered, "he has been cut through. Only the remains of his lower half were found. What was left of his body was near a stone wall, and untouched by the flames." He hesitated a moment and added for emphasis, "He was sliced in two."

King Westell stared at the man in disbelief. He turned to the knight captain of his personal guards, who was standing near a wall. He was dressed in black armor, with the emblem of a white swan on his tunic. "What type of weapon cleaves a man in half? A greatsword? A large axe?"

"Perhaps, my lord," he answered honestly, "but I doubt it. Robes are far from armor, but they would hinder a sword blade somewhat. It would take a large man to wield an axe so, hacking several times with great strength. If the legends are true, an Orc might, with an exceptional weapon, but I doubt Orcs have come to your kingdom."

He turned to the mage. "What did the cuts look like? Did the messenger give details?"

"That's just it," the mage answered, "there was no evidence of hacking. The messenger was very sure of this fact. The robes and body were cut clean. In one slice, it appears."

The mage paused again, but continued, knowing he must. "I must also inform you, my lord, of information gleaned from several of the servants questioned. A Half-Orc in leather armor *was* seen, and there was another man, dressed as one from the Western Baronies.

"This one was witnessed casting spells. The last came from a guard who survived for two days after the incident, shot through by a large arrow. He crawled out to the center of a courtyard to avoid the fires."

"The guard was reliable?" King Westell asked. He sat back down on his latest acquired throne.

"The man was questioned by the steward's magic user," the mage answered. "As you know, my lord, she is not a mage, not even strong enough to fight with her magic, but she is in possession of a truth stone. And, by all accounts, she's loyal to you."

King Westell rested his head in his hand, the elbow on the arm of his seat. He slowly stroked his goatee with the other. "Yes. I know her well. She is the reason my steward ensures those below me do not cheat me out of taxes from their lands. You are correct. If she says the guard was speaking the truth, he was."

He took a deep breath and sighed. "Mordith, you are now the lord mage. From what your predecessor told me, you were the most powerful instructor. After I own all of Kerr, you will rebuild the Halls of Magic."

Lord Mage Mordith ducked his head and said, "Thank you, my lord, but there is more."

"More?" King Westell asked, slouching in his seat, his hips sliding forward slightly. "What more could there possibly be when the place is nothing but charred rubble?"

"Several…shall we say, items," Mordith said, "cannot be found. Without them and the accompanying spells, I cannot keep those who come with the gift of magic from becoming burnt."

"Sounds to me like you better figure out a way to find them," King Westell suggested as he sat forward. "At present count, I have 43 mages and magic users capable of fighting with my armies." He waved a hand in dismissal. "Yes, I know, some of the minor lords can cast a few spells, too. Some of these people will die in battle. I *will* have more in the future."

"Yes, my king," answered Mordith. He ducked his head and turned to leave.

King Westell stopped him. "You will also find out how your predecessor never aged while I grew grey hair around my temples. A spell, a potion, or praying to whatever deity or demon the man worshipped, I care not. Find out. I am not risking all to rule the world, only to die of old age before I am able to enjoy it."

The new lord mage looked over his shoulder and said, "There are rumors, my king, of bargains made, with sacrifices." Mordith turned around and faced his king. "I will be the lord mage, I will fight for you, and I will lead the other mages to do the same, but there are some things I am not comfortable with. Perhaps you should feel the same."

King Westell stared at the mage. To openly deny him something after having been given the keys to the Halls of Magic was bold. He opened his mouth to demand the knight captain of his personal guard kill him, then he stopped. Mordith's eyes showed no fear. Not in this decision.

King Westell wasn't sure whether it was confidence in his abilities to defend himself, and perhaps kill him and the guards, or if the man was resigned to his fate regarding his stance. Either way, he would be one to watch in the future. Perhaps to deal with when he least expected.

"Go," King Westell said. "See to your mages so they will be ready when we move on Minth in the spring."

The new lord mage left the room. King Westell turned toward two men waiting for him. "Well?"

"We found one of them spreading the message about rebelling. He was in a tavern with a large group listening to his every word, my king," one said.

"And?" King Westell asked. His eyes showed the gleeful expectation of what he hoped to hear.

"We slipped out and had the men bar the front and back door, sire," the other said. "We even nailed the shutters closed on the two windows. It was a place with no upper floor, as it was not an inn."

"We burned it all to the ground, my king," the first continued. "None escaped."

"Good," King Westell said with a smile. "I hope the tavern owner's family was inside with them all, too."

*****

Chapter Fourteen

Tarlok

Lucas tied the reins to the back of the other wagon. It was times like this he wished he was back in his tavern. Brandishing his club, he shouted at the young soldier sitting on his horse and holding the reins of the team hitched to his son's wagon, "Neal, whatever ye do, yer not to be letting them break and run. Keep them back here and the Goblins away from me daughter!"

He ran past him to catch up to Sethon and Marn. He passed the other horses tied to trees on the side of the narrow road. Up ahead, Johan and his other three soldiers, the four hunters, and his sons formed two lines in the road. Beyond them, a group of Goblins hesitated, while a large one yelled and slapped at those in the rear.

"They have us at least three to one, I'm to be thinking," Johan said.

"It looks like it," Aarn agreed. "This clan has been a problem for a while. I've never heard of this many accosting those who travel the road. They may be getting desperate, as we've been whittling away at them. We're no longer in Tarlok, but we've yet to enter the Western Baronies. Up ahead a few miles, is beginning of the canyons where their caves are."

"Well, they have us between these hills, now," Lucas said as he caught up to them. "We cannae go around, for sure. Not that they are to be letting us."

"No," Aarn agreed. "We'll have to fight through. The big one is trying to rally them. From the looks of it, they didn't expect us to dismount and fight them, but that's the only way. To try to ride past is suicide with those ropes strung behind them."

Marn tapped the large head of his war hammer in his palm. "One thing is on our side in this. They're not to be hitting us on the flank. They can no more get up those steep embankments than we can."

"We can't go far uphill," Aarn agreed, "but we can get high enough to rain arrows on them as they charge." He looked to his wife and the other two hunters. "We'll take this side, you the other." They scrambled up the banks and settled, sitting with feet against trees to brace themselves on the steep hillside, and arrows within easy reach.

"Hey!" Johan shouted. "I'm not to be getting any younger, ye know. Let's be done with it!"

Up ahead, the large Goblin had no idea what the Human was shouting, but he recognized a challenge. He wasn't having it. He screamed and shoved his underlings until they started moving. It became a full-fledged charge as they came screaming and waving short swords, axes, and small spears. Once started, they were no longer fearful of the group ahead of them. They should have been.

The Tarlok hunters rained arrows on the small horde as they charged. By the time they were close enough to engage, half their number lay in the road, arrows sticking from them like quills from a porcupine. The brothers led the men in the fight as they rushed forward, hammers high.

Marn swept across and smashed two Goblins into a third, causing them all to go down. He slammed his hammer down again and again before they could untangle themselves. Sethon struck a shield held out in a feeble attempt by a four-foot Goblin. Not only did it bend the shield, it shattered the arm holding it and knocked the slimy beast to the ground. It was dead with the next strike.

Johan dodged a warped spear thrust forward at him and took off the arm holding it with his longsword. He stepped past it to the next, while Lucas finished off the screaming creature with his studded club. Behind them, the hunters abandoned their spots once the two groups were intermingled, making it difficult to avoid their fellow Humans with arrows. They stepped in with long knives and an occasional hand axe.

The three young soldiers gave a good accounting of themselves, until one stumbled over a fallen Goblin. Two quickly jumped on him, hacking with ragged short swords before they were killed. The soldier didn't survive. In his anger, Johan was like a madman, his sword moving like a streak of silver as he fought, ignoring his years.

The last of them, the leader of the Goblins, attempted to fight the enraged man with a rusty longsword held in two hands by the foul monster. It was no match for the seasoned soldier, and the engagement ended with the Goblin's head rolling in the dirt.

Johan leaned on his sword, the tip in the road as he took deep breaths. The others had no way of knowing, but his chest was pounding and his vision tunneling. He saw both stars and black spots swimming across his sight. Though he wished it, he was far from a young man, and his body let him know more and more these days.

"Are ye all right?" Lucas asked, breathing deeply himself. "Ye look pale, old friend."

"Aye," Johan said, straightening with a grimace. "Sometimes the anger gets me, and I put more into it than need be." He took several more deep breaths and looked over as two of his soldiers pulled their friend from the fallen bodies of the Goblins. "We'll need to be burying young Edger. The lad deserved better than to die by the likes o' these."

"He chose the life, Sergeant," Corporal Taybon consoled him. "I'm to be sure the Creator welcomed him. He was a good soldier and a good man."

"Aye," Johan agreed. "He's always been the sort I'd not assume was going to be hot for all eternity. Still."

* * *

Great Northern Desert

Tog looked over at Kryder and grinned. It was hot, but he didn't mind the heat. It was drier than he was used to, but it was far better than the direction the weather was turning this time of year when they left Yaylok.

"Maybe I should run ahead," Tog said. "Walking at this pace, I'm getting out of shape."

"Yeah," Kryder agreed. "I probably should, too. The wagons don't move fast do they?"

"At least we don't have to push because one of them got stuck in the sand," Tog said. "Those paddles work."

"Yeah," Kryder said. "For the most part, the road we followed up until now was pretty firm, except for a few drifts. Now there is no road at all."

"Nothing but sand as far as the eye can see," Dolner agreed as he eased his horse up beside Kryder's. "The heat's not so bad, as long as you drink plenty, I guess. It is kind of boring, though."

"It's not hot at night," June said. "I thought I was going to freeze last night."

"It was chilly," agreed Brother Sylif. "Tonight, I'll take off the mail before I get into my blanket. It holds the cold."

"Leather is the way to go," Tog declared, tapping his chest.

"Leather doesn't provide enough protection," Dolner countered.

"Don't let them hit you," Tog said with a grin.

"There's that," June agreed. "Sometimes you have to get in close, though." She dropped her reins and threw a few punches, ducking her head left and right as if sparing on the back of her horse.

Dolner called out to Sandwinkle, "Um, Lord Sandy Shade of the Oasis?" He whispered to June, "Is that right? There are so many titles." He turned back before she could answer. "Do you think we can have a fire tonight?"

Sandwinkle stood up in the seat of the wagon, still holding the reins. "That is not a title I hold. But…I will take it!" He stood straighter and proclaimed, "Behold! Henceforth, I shall also be known as Lord Sandy Shade of the Oasis!"

Both of his sons looked over, grinned, and shook their heads. His wife said, "Sit down, dearest. You have enough titles as it is. Even I can no longer keep up."

Sandwinkle bowed in several directions to the empty dunes surrounding them, then sat back down. He looked over at Dolner and said, "We cannot light a fire on this part of the trip. There have been patrols by rogue Lython in this area in the past. A fire would be seen for some distance. Even if we rest between dunes, the glow may be noticed. Tomorrow's eve we will be able to."

"We will be much closer to our village," Moonlitdune explained. "Our own patrols will keep us safe."

"Do you have problems with the...what did you call them? Lython?" Tog asked.

"Not lately," Sandwinkle said, now serious. "A few years ago they grew bold enough to attack a village but were held off. In turn, several of the tribal leaders banded together and wiped out the raiding party."

"How did you do it?" Sylif asked. "I mean no disrespect, my lord, but your race is small in stature. You've not the broad shoulders and strength of Dwarves. The Lython race are nigh as large as Orcs and have the whipping tails of lizards."

"Plus they have those big rock clubs," Dolner added, swinging his arm overhead as if he was smashing something.

"No disrespect taken, my good brother," Sandwinkle said. "We are small. But...we are fast and deadly accurate with our daggers and knives."

He reached under his seat and pulled out a crossbow. Only it was like no crossbow the others had seen. There was no bolt, nor channel to rest one. The thick string ran through the center of the weapon, a portion hidden inside. He pulled a small handle on the side, showing the arms bend as it was partially cocked. He eased it back. Next, he twisted a piece on the end of the stock, revealing a compartment containing a stack of handleless knife blades. He closed it and showed them three vertical slots where it was loaded from the front.

He put it away and opened both sides of his vest. It was lined with four throwing knives. "Death of a thousand cuts, my friend," he said. He patted a dagger at his side; the visible part of its handle looked vaguely like Kryder's. "A thousand cuts."

Kryder nodded. He had already noticed the tell-tale bulge of a knife handle in one of the Gnome rover's boots. His eyes widened and he stared openmouthed as Moonlitdune reached with both hands behind her head, yawned, and arched as if to stretch, only to bring them down quickly, holding two small, thin, curved daggers. There was no doubt they were razor sharp.

"Impressive," June said. "I like it."

"The sands are big enough to allow our races to survive without constant conflict," Moonlitdune explained as she slid them back into their sheaths below the neckline of her dress, between her shoulder blades.

"Later," she continued, "a meeting was held with several of their leaders and it was explained. The raiding party was from a group of younger ones who decided the old ways were no longer enough. The remainder of them moved on, farther into the desert, and were not heard from again. We have had peace between us since."

"Well," Sandwinkle said, "except for the occasional attack on our wagons. Even the Lython we trade with do not light fires in this area in case their own attack them."

"How were you able to meet with them?" June asked. "Did they send a representative? I'm to begin learning of diplomacy."

"They sent a signal," Moonlitdune said, "in a manner of speaking. One of their shamans was blessed with a prayer spell. It's the same spell my order uses. When I saw the shooting star rise into the night sky, I knew. After a moment's discussion with others in my order, I decided to send one up, myself."

"She insisted we go halfway to its origin," Sandwinkle explained. "A group of us met with their leaders."

"They worship Saint…I mean, Zeronic?" Dolner asked.

"Indeed they do, much to my delight," Moonlitdune answered. "He is known as Zeron the Dune Shifter to them, but it is the same deity given to us all by the Creator."

"In infinite wisdom," Brother Sylif said. He then quoted from The Book Of The One, "All thinking mortals have been given deities, with whom I entrust the world."

"Exactly," Moonlitdune said with a nod. "Yet there are those who would do otherwise."

* * *

Zar

In the lower chambers below his Elven tower, well beyond the swamps bordering the lands of men, Mraynith threw his bloody dagger across the room. He kicked at the body of the young woman, disgusted.

"Take this away," he demanded.

Several lesser mages scrambled to gather the remains of the Human and do his bidding. Once again, the life-stealing sacrifice and prayer spell hadn't worked. As a follower of a demon and a mage, he was a rare one, able to cast both magic spells and prayer spells, though he had rarely cast any other than the one to gain life. Lately he sensed nothing when he spoke to Lethrall. It was as if there was a great hole where the demon prince's presence had been.

Perhaps I should look to other demons, he thought. He glanced up. Eight globes of light still floated near the ceiling. That was plenty to read by. He stepped over to a stand and thumbed through his thin copy of The Book Of The One. At one time, it had been its normal thickness. Someone in his family, long before him, had ripped out pages thought unnecessary. That left very little, other than where demons were mentioned, their descriptions, and stories.

"I am the One. All is of My creation. Below me, as I have given you deities, I have given you demons. Choose wisely, for only One can truly save you," he muttered, reading out loud. *I wonder which one? Hmmm, Slavonne, the Dark Prince of Pride. Interesting.*

*****

Chapter Fifteen

The endless dunes slowly gave way to low rock formations with gullies between them. Eventually, dark mountains became visible in the distance. There was no vegetation, other than the occasional scraggly bushes and tall cactuses. Once or twice, Kryder saw movement on a small ledge and in the shadows. Skittering, dirt-colored bugs, hand-sized lizards, and the occasional snake hunting them provided the only other signs of life.

"There is a little more to see than sand, I guess," Dolner remarked, "but it's still hot."

"Looks like we're headed toward those mountains," Tog said. "I don't see any trees from here. I wonder where the wood comes for making their wagons?"

Overhearing him, Sandwinkle answered, "It comes from the green lands down south. We bargain for them. Mine are made by a wonderful craftsman and his three sons in the Baronies West."

"How did you get there if you didn't have a wagon?" Dolner asked, ever curious about things.

"A camel," Sandwinkle answered. "When you're small, you can settle in between the two humps of a sturdy breed. It's actually quite comfortable. They're not fast, but they're resilient. They're a little different than the ones bred to pull wagons."

"We will camp for the night when we reach the base of the closest mountain," his wife said. "There is a well, and we should be safe with our backs to the cliffs. We'll light a fire and cook instead of eating dried food."

"Sounds good," Tog said.

"I could eat something other than dried fish," June agreed. "That gets old in a hurry."

"I rather like it," Brother Sylif said. "It beats what I ate the first year I was in seminary. A bowl of mush for two of the daily meals. That wasn't good. Not even a little bit."

"Hold up," Dolner demanded. "Not only do you have to learn to read, but you eat like a prisoner? For the whole first year? Thanks, but no thanks." He looked to Moonlitdune. "Tell me some more about Zeronic. Did you eat good when you were in cleric school, or whatever?"

Moonlitdune laughed out loud. "One does not attend a seminary in my order. You learn what you can of Zeronic and show faith in him. If he picks you from among his followers and accepts you, you become a cleric and are granted prayer spells as he sees fit. He will provide a way for you to continue to learn and grow. I must warn you, if he accepts you, be prepared for change. Not only is he the God of Winds, he is also the God of Change."

"Wind and Change," Dolner said. "Got it. Not that I want to ask him to accept me; I'm just curious."

* * *

Later in the afternoon, the wagons stopped near the base of a cliff that went up for at least eighty feet before the first ledge. To one side, a waterfall two-hands-width wide fell the distance to a small pool. The rock-lined pool was several feet deep in the center, and, on one edge, a small stream flowed away. It fed several stunted trees and bushes and a decent span of grass before it disappeared into the sands and rock beyond.

The camels were delighted to share their normal stop with the horses, as long as none of the animals staked out could reach each other. "They like it," June said as she brushed her horse's flank.

"Yeah, I'm sure they were tired of the dry hay we've been giving them," Dolner said, "and water from a barrel. I'd never have believed there was this much green this deep in the desert."

"There are valleys within these mountains where there's more," Sandwinkle said as he walked up. "That's one of the things we protect from outsiders, and why we don't talk of it. Everyone thinks we simply rove around the desert, moving our villages when we do." He winked. "I mean, we do have a few wagons moving around, more as scouts than anything else, to maintain the image.

"There are hillsides with trees, though the wood from them is not suitable to build with," the leader of the Gnomes continued. He indicated the short, stunted trees. "They grow quickly and make excellent firewood, and there are several uses for the ash, but you cannot build homes and wagons with it. That's one of the reasons we ventured to the south thousands of years ago."

"Why did they choose the south?" Kryder asked as he settled against a wagon wheel near the fire. "How did they know to go that direction?"

Moonlitdune answered for her husband, "Because the map shows the lands south of us. It's all colored in green, except for the large lakes and rivers. Oh, and mountains. Those are colored in greys and white."

"I've seen tapestries of our world," Sylif concurred. "That's how they look, as well. The king has one, and several of the counts. It's become a status symbol to have one."

"The tapestry I'm referring to is several thousand years old," Moonlitdune said. She shrugged as if it was no big deal.

"Thousands?" Sylif asked. "How is it still hanging?"

"We don't know," Sandwinkle admitted. "It's hung on the wall of the meeting house in our village far longer than anyone knows. It does not fade or sag, or have tears in it. It covers an entire wall."

"I would like to see it," Kryder said. "It may be preserved with magic, though I have no idea what spell could do that. There are so many I don't know."

"I will take you to it," Sandwinkle said. "When we…"

He didn't have a chance to finish the sentence, as one of his sons shouted, "Raiders!"

The raiders came around the bend in the trail—ten large, lizard-like creatures with tall bodies shaped more like men than monsters, save for their tails. They were mottled in brown and green, and had elongated faces with sharp teeth.

Six of them ran quickly toward the wagons, with rock clubs held high. Four others rode squat beasts, which looked like large lizards. They were without tails and moved in a fast but lumbering gate. The Lythons riding the beasts held spears made of twisted shafts with sharp rock tips fixed to them. They swung wide to come in from a different direction than those running.

Sandwinkle and one of his sons climbed into the wagon seats, grabbed their blade launchers, and loaded them quickly. By the time Sandwinkle was able to aim at one of the riders, his son had already loosed three blades in one shot at the leader. The distance was still too far for an accurate shot, but two of the blades embedded in the Lython's thigh, and one hit and bounced off the beast it was riding. Once it was closer, Sandwinkle's three blades hit the same rider in the chest, toppling it from the lizard. With no one controlling it, it veered into the path of the rider closest to it as the rider flung its spear.

The spear flew surprisingly straight as it arced up and down, but it was off its mark and embedded in the side of the wagon near Moonlitdune. She reached up and pulled it back and forth, up and down to dislodge it. Its owner toppled moments later from atop his lizard with a large arrow embedded nearly to the fletching in its chest.

Kryder shouted to June, "Take out the riders with arrows! Don't let them get close!" He knew Tog was already doing it. He stepped forward with his hand held high and spoke words of magic. Several darts of light left his outstretched fingers and struck the next rider. The raider screamed and rolled off the panicked lizard, clutching at the burned holes in his stomach. The beast darted in another direction, away from the bright lights flashing in the shadows of the mountains.

The fourth rider pulled up to turn away, but it was too late. An arrow, much smaller than the one that had taken out the other raider, hit him in his neck. He dropped his reins and clutched at it, but another of June's arrows slammed into him, and he slowly slid off his mount.

Sylif stepped forward with his hammer held high to meet the six remaining Lythons, now too close for arrows, from the other side of the campfire. Dolner was beside him, shield and sword ready. They were quickly joined by Sandwinkle's other son. He held the spear his mother had pulled from the wagon.

Ignoring the small Gnome with the spear, the two leading raiders moved toward the men. One attempted to block the falling hammer strike with its stone club, only to have it nearly knocked from its hands as chips flew. Sylif continued the mighty swing as he spun all the way around, aiming waist high below the outstretched club. His long-handled hammer caught the surprised attacker in the ribs, and several gave way. Sylif quickly finished it with an overhand blow as it bent over, gasping.

Dolner did his best to get inside the wide swing of his opponent's stone club. He ducked and stepped forward, only to be shoved back as the Lython kicked out, striking his shield. Shield up, he tried to block the next swing, only to have the shield's straps over his forearm tear loose from the crushing blow. His arm went numb, but it allowed him to move forward and shove the tip of his blade into the raider's stomach.

He fumbled for his knife with the other hand but was unable to draw it. Unsure of what to do next, he dove to the side, maintaining a strong grip on the sword hilt with his good hand. The movement twisted the sword in the raider's guts, killing him.

The third raider knocked the near-useless spear from the grip of the small Gnome in front of it and raised his club high over its head. The club fell from his hands, and he looked down to see Tog's axe buried in his chest. Without slowing as he leaped the fire, Tog drew his long dagger.

June passed him as she ran to Dolner's side. Her blade flashed in the light from the fire and the fading sunlight as she danced circles around the next raider. While it had reach on her, it never managed to land a blow. She, in turn, couldn't strike a killing blow herself. The nicks and cuts were telling, as her opponent slowed in their fight, until she was finally able to get close and end it.

Kryder shouted a command using his ring, and one of the Lythons' movements slowed. It was filled shortly after with blades from both launchers, allowing Kryder to release his hold.

The last two raiders were easily dispatched by Sylif and Tog, via hammer and the stone club Tog had picked up to replace his axe. The confusion on the face of the Lython facing one as large as Tog bearing a stone club as well was evident before it died from a blow to its head.

"Well," Sandwinkle said, "that was unexpected. They haven't raided this area in years."

"Something must have stirred them," Moonlitdune said as she examined Dolner's arm. She looked up at Sylif and said, "Broken."

Dolner flinched away from her probing fingers. "Ahh, that hurt. A lot."

"In two places, it seems," Sylif agreed. "We're in your lands, sister. I defer to you and your god." He bowed his head slightly and stepped back.

"Don't be a baby," June said. "It can't be that bad." She grinned.

"It wasn't when it was numb," Dolner said. "Now it feels like a horse is standing on it and won't move. Speaking of which, are they all right?" He looked beyond, trying to see in the dim light beyond the burning fire.

"Yeah," Kryder said. "They broke loose of their pickets and ran off at the beginning. A couple of camels did, too, but Sandwinkle says they'll come back because of the water and grass. They'll smell it from a great distance."

"I hope so," Dolner said. "Out there in the desert…maybe I should go look for them." He tried to pull away from the small Gnome holding his arm.

"No," Moonlitdune said, her tone brooking no argument, "not until you're healed, and even then, you'll need to rest it for a day or so as it will be sore."

"It'll take weeks to heal," Dolner argued. "One of the men in our watch broke his in a fall once. It was nearly a month before he could grip a blade again."

"That's because he didn't know a high priestess of Zeronic," she stated. "Now hold still."

Dolner did as he was asked. She reached down, pulled a few pieces of grass, and held them in her palm. She blew softly on them until they fluttered out of her hand to land on his swelling forearm and wrist. She closed her eyes and prayed. Time stopped for her.

* * *

Moonlitdune found herself in a room she had only been to a few times in her life. She inhaled sharply as her god turned away from the wide-open window overlooking his island home and the beautiful sunset. The wind moved his beard slightly, and his smile nearly rendered her speechless.

"Moonlitdune! Now how did I know you would call out to me this evening?" Zeronic asked.

"Su...surely you jest, my Lord," she stammered. Gathering her wits, she said, "You know all."

"Ahh," Zeronic said as he reached for a glass of wine. "A slight misconception, but understandable. Yes, I know all our Creator has seen fit to share of his plans. But there are some things that must play out. Things our Creator has not told even his own chosen deities."

"In infinite wisdom," Moonlitdune said as she bowed her head slightly.

"Indeed," Zeronic said as he held his glass up in salute to the Creator.

She looked up at Zeronic. "May I ask why you summoned me as I prayed for healing? I have done so many times in the past. The other times you brought me here were when you accepted me, and then again when I was made high priestess. I am humbled and honored to be here again, yet still curious."

"Admirable traits," Zeronic said, "all of these."

The God of Wind and Change walked across the room to a small box on the table. He opened it and removed something. He stepped over and held out his hand.

"Take these keys," he said. "The young man whom you pray for may very well be part of our Creator's plans."

He opened his palm, showing gold keys. "Do not give these to him until you know the time is right."

Moonlitdune took the keys and looked at one. The top was shaped round, like most keys were, its center filled with a stone like the one on her wrist. The bottom was shaped into two small Dragon wings. She had no idea what type of lock it might fit.

"These stones are your symbol," she said. "Only my race and the Lython bear your symbol. Humans have their own deities."

"Things…change," the God of Wind and Change said. He stared off, looking at something no mortal could see.

Moonlitdune was silent as she pondered what he might be seeing. After several minutes, she asked quietly, "How will I know when it is time?"

"You will know, my child," Zeronic assured her. "You will know."

* * * * *

Chapter Sixteen

The Western Baronies

Lucas climbed down off the wagon and stretched. It was good to know that he would sleep in a bed tonight. The last three days had been the easiest of the journey. The roads in Arnwald's barony were well maintained. There were places where it was obvious small stones had been brought in to cover where a stream or creek would flood the road during rainy season, but for the most part, the hard-packed dirt was easily manageable for a wagon.

Johan walked over, leading Kryder's horse. "It's plain this baron spends his coin on his land, it is. Roads through the countryside in better shape than the roads me and the lads walked every evening in the city, to be sure."

"Aye," Lucas agreed. "He's one to be looking out fer his people. The trade is easier when ye can get the crops to town with no worries."

"Not tae mention, he can be moving his troops around in a hurry, should the need arise," Johan added, ever the soldier.

"Aye!" Lucas laughed. "There is that."

"The road may have been less bumpy than others," Sethon complained, "but me back is still screaming at me. I'm glad to be off the wagon. Do ye want me to get us some rooms?"

"Take this coin and see can ye get enough fer all o' us," Lucas said. "We may have to go to different inns."

"We can bed down on the outskirts," Aarn called out. He stood a short distance away with his wife and the two hunters they'd first encountered.

"I'm sure ye could," Lucas said, "but ye accompanied us here, and I'd like yer first night in a town to be something to remember. A bed stuffed with feathers is what I aim to provide ye, if only for one night. Rest assured, there will be plenty o' nights o' sleeping under the stars again. War is coming, and we'll all go to meet it."

Tyna placed a hand on Aarn's bicep. He glanced at her and smiled. "One night, then. More than that, and my wife may decide I need to spend half a year hunting fowl to stuff our own mattress back in our cabin. And you know what? I would without question. So let's all try to save me the trouble."

Chall, the other male hunter with them, looked at his own wife with big eyes. She elbowed him. All knew a day—or even a month—in a modern town, with more people than they had ever seen together, wouldn't change the hunters.

* * *

The next midmorning, Lucas sat at the same table Jynal had sat at years before when he spoke of moving his family to the Western Borderlands. Arnwald was still the baron, though he was much older than when Lucas had seen him on the trip with Saint Lanae, Kryder, and Tog. He finished telling Baron Arnwald of the impending war.

Baron Arnwald looked to his cousin. "Narthon, please tell me you're as skeptical as I am."

Sir Narthon shifted in his chair and adjusted the front of his yellow and black tunic. "Arn, you know as well as I, we sent Kryder and Tog down to Yaylok to gather information. We knew King Westell had his greedy eyes on that kingdom next. Now we know they're invading Minth next."

"But Elves?" Arnwald asked. "The madman allies with the *Elves*?"

"It's not hard to believe," Narthon said. "Hard to imagine…but now that I've been told, it's not hard to believe."

"It's not that I don't believe you, you understand," Arnwald said, turning back to Lucas and Johan. "It's just that I don't *want* to believe it. The entire world will be at war, it seems."

"Rannow believes," Lucas said. "He prepares the hunters as we speak."

"Greed and tyranny can never be satisfied, my lord," Johan added. "It has to be destroyed for it to stop. A truth as old as time, it is."

"I'll not argue that," Arnwald said. "I've the tapestries on yon wall to prove it. I wonder, do the Elves still control the Dragons depicted?"

"Saint Lanae never told us," Lucas answered.

"What?" Arnwald asked, sitting upright. "The *goddess* Saint Lanae?"

"Aye, the very one," Lucas said. "There's much more to the story of Kryder, Tog, and meself, to be sure. I wanted to get the parts out about the coming war afore I told ye, err you think me daft and not believe the rest o' it."

Lucas turned to Sir Narthon. "Before I tell the tale o' that night, I want to ask ye a question, Sir Narthon."

"Ask. I will do my best to answer, though I have no idea what it may be, good sir," Narthon said. He gave his cousin a questioning look.

"Does your sister, Lady Shynae, still tend to her gardens?" Lucas asked.

"Why...yes. Yes, she does," Narthon answered. "Not as easily as she once did. She is much older than I am, you know. Well, you couldn't know, but she is. I've had her flower gardens raised into boxes waist high so she doesn't have to bend to reach them."

"That's good," Lucas said, relieved. "I was afraid she joined my wife, tending flowers in the after. It's been many actual years since I saw your sister."

"Saw her?" Narthon asked. "What are you playing at, man? I would know if she had met you before, as she resides with my family on our estate."

"It's the truth," Lucas said, raising his hands. "You can call her and ask her to bring her truth stone, like ye did when ye met Jynal."

"How do you know that?" Arnwald asked. "I remember it, but not clearly. It was nigh on thirty years ago. Long before my grey hair."

"She also threatened to wipe her hands on your new tunic. That was when the image o' her new roses were used for it," Lucas said as he folded his arms. "Sure as I'm sitting here, it was."

Baron Arnwald looked over to the large banner hanging from one of the great beams in the hall. The yellow and black banner with the emblem of a spiked gauntlet holding a red rose moved slightly in the breeze from the open shutters on both sides of the room. Lucas saw the memories come rushing back to the baron in the expression on his face.

"That *was* when I had the look of the rose changed to match the new ones she was able to produce then," he said. He looked at his cousin. "We don't need her and the truth stone for this. We need to listen to this man and believe him. Tell us, Lucas."

* * *

"Tis hard to believe, but the details are undeniable, cousin," Narthon said, sitting back in his chair with his arms dangling on both sides. "Saint Lanae herself. Amazing."

"Yes," agreed Arnwald. "There are parts of the story that hurt me like it was about my own mother, and she has been departed many years now. I'm glad the lord mage will get his, I'll not deny."

"Nor I," his cousin agreed. "The man wouldn't know honor if it walked up and punched him in the face with a spiked gauntlet. We'll need to look into preparing the troops for a long season."

"You're right," Baron Arnwald said. "Go. Start the preparations."

"At once, my lord," Sir Narthon agreed. He stood to go, nodded at Lucas, and left the hall in a hurry.

"My lord, not that it's to be any o' my business," Lucas said, "but that went from cousin to formal in the blink of an eye, it did."

"Rest assured, we are as close as any brothers," Arnwald said, "but we both know when affairs of the barony hold sway. It is a reoccurrence of many years, as lads, even."

Arnwald looked to a tapestry of the world hanging from a wall. Lucas could see the man thinking hard. After a few moments, he spoke, "Not only will we need to gather the forces, the horses, arrows, supplies, everything, I'll also need to send word to the two orders here in the barony."

He stood and paced as he spoke, mostly to himself, "Both Saint Gonthon and Saint Harnette, the Keeper of Flames. We'll need their clerics. The local healers will need to decide among themselves who will follow my army, and who will stay to tend those here. An army on the move is a complicated thing. We will grow as we move through each barony, as their forces join. I suspect the other barons and baronesses will vote to have Sir Narthon lead the armies as knight commander. They did the same recently, though on a much smaller scale. This time, all who are able to fight will go."

"My lord, I'm to leave two of the hunters with you as scouts," Lucas said. "Others will join them, as Rannow has vowed to be in Minth by Midwinter with all he has available, both to scout for all armies, and to form several archer companies, on foot and ahorse."

"Good. This is news of the best kind," Arnwald said. "The way they move, swiftly and silently, is legendary. And their bows? If the stories are true, they can launch three arrows to a normal man's one. A whole army of them? It has never been seen." He paused and said, "Speaking of which. I must send word to all magic users, and the one mage in my barony. They are needed as well. I suspect there will be magic fighting magic, as well."

Lucas stood. "By your leave, my lord, I'll be going. I must continue on to the Western Borderlands…and perhaps beyond."

"To Orcanth?" Baron Arnwald asked. "Do Kryder and Tog think they'll help? An Orcish army has not been seen…well, in centuries. Tribal skirmishes have occurred, but nothing larger."

"I don't know," Lucas said. "And they didn't ask me to go to them specifically, but I aim to. I've the right."

"Do you now?" Arnwald asked. He looked at the size of Lucas in a new light. "You might at that, if they accept you."

"Red Fist has, though the rest of the tribe is not to be knowing, yet."

"I would suggest stopping in Three Oaks and speaking with Lord Jynal before crossing their border," he said while looking directly at Johan. "Otherwise you might not get very far."

"I'll not be filled with big Orc arrows if it can be prevented," Johan agreed. "That's not something a blade can stop, no matter how good ye are with it."

"That's the plan," Lucas said. "Holding the mark o' me tribe or not, that would be foolish."

"I wonder how Kryder and Tog are getting along?" Arnwald asked as he stood with them. "You say they're going into the Northern Desert to look for the library after they deal with the lord mage and warn the king of Minth? I don't envy them. That's a place one could get lost and be gone forever."

* * *

"Are you all right?" Kryder asked. "For a moment there, you stared off and were...well, gone."

"Zeronic called me to him," Moonlitdune said. "It was not the first time, but it has happened only rarely."

"I understand," Kryder said. "The gods do as they will, and we have no choice in the matter, though I suspect you did not argue the journey."

"No," she said. "I did not." She looked at Dolner, released his arm, and asked, "How does it feel?"

"What? I was listening to you two talk about actually meeting a god," Dolner said, waving his arms about as he spoke. "Do you hear yourselves? You both act like it's nothing out of the ordinary. That's insane. It's something out of a story. I wouldn't know what to do, how to act. I would probably stand and stare with my mouth open."

Moonlitdune smiled. "Dolner, they aren't fairy tales. They are real, and they watch over us as the Creator designed."

"In infinite wisdom," Sylif said. "They are real, boy. As real as that arm you're waving around as if it wasn't broken near in two moments ago."

Dolner stopped moving and looked down at his arm. He wiggled his fingers, then made a fist. "It feels fine. It feels like there was never anything wrong with it. Amazing."

"Yes," the high priestess of Zeronic said. "Amazing. You can thank Zeronic for it."

"I do. I mean, I don't really know him, but I thank him for it. I mean, it's not like I can thank him personally, but you say he hears us. Besides, like I said, I wouldn't know what to say to him if I did meet him, which I'll never do, but you know."

Moonlitdune simply smiled, nodded, and felt for the keys in the pocket on her dress. Her god had told her to wait until she knew the time was right. She trusted in him to let her know. She walked away to help her sons clear a wagon so they could take the bodies away from the campsite, out into the desert where the vultures could get them.

* * *

Before midmorning, the scavengers of the desert noticed the bodies. Others noticed the birds circling. Perhaps their problem had been solved for them—or made worse. A decision was made, and the direction of the hunting party turned toward the wheeling vultures in the cloudless blue sky.

*****

Chapter Seventeen

"We have a problem," June said. She dismounted her horse; both were obviously winded. "A big problem."

"What?" Kryder asked. "What's wrong?" He looked around the campsite as Sandwinkle's sons finished loading the wagon they'd used to move the bodies.

"More Lythons are coming. A lot more, and they're riding those lizards. They might even have the ones who ran off after the fight. All I know is, there are more of them. I saw them when I finally caught my horse. They may have seen me."

Sandwinkle scrambled to the top of his wagon and stood on the roof. He held a small tube up to his eye, turned it slightly with his other hand, and stared. "She's right. More come, but I think we'll be all right. They're moving in a single column and don't look as if they plan to attack. They're stopped where we dropped the bodies."

"What do we do?" Tog asked, taking his bow off his shoulder. "Get ready, or wait?"

"If he says they won't attack, then we wait," Kryder said. "If there are as many as June says, I don't know if we could fight them all off, anyway."

"I don't like it," Dolner said. "I hope he's right, though. I don't even have a decent shield anymore. The shield held up but the leather straps snapped. There needs to be a better way to hold one." He moved his arm back and forth and flexed his fingers. "At least it's not sore."

Instead of moving on, they waited in the shade of the cliffs near the water. Kryder glanced over to Sandwinkle and his wife for the hundredth time. They sat near the pool of cool water, content to sip tea and engage in quiet conversation. Their sons, busying themselves with the wagons and teams of camels, did not seemed worried, either.

"Maybe these are the Lythons they know and not part of the group of raiders," Tog suggested. He leaned back against a large boulder and put his hands behind his head. "If they aren't worried, there's no sense in us being worried. This is their home; they would know."

"I trust them," Sylif said as he braided several thin pieces of leather to make a necklace. "If not, Saint Minokath will protect us."

"This far from the sea?" Dolner asked. "Really?"

"We are surrounded by seas," Sylif said with a grin. "They may be weeks—months away even—from us right here in this very spot, but, rest assured, we are surrounded."

"Being surrounded is what I'm worried about," Dolner muttered.

When the horses got restless and pulled on their tethers, they knew the Lythons were close. The horses remembered the scent and the chaos of the last encounter. Shortly after, the first few rode over the nearest dune, and down into the wadi leading to them. Many more followed.

Sandwinkle had his sons move the wagons so the Lythons could get to the water easily. Several of them dismounted, handed their reins to another, and walked over. Kryder noticed one had a necklace of small, rough stones exactly like the stone on Moonlitdune's bracelet.

A large Lython hissed in his own language and placed a fist against his chest, bumping his hardened leather vest. The one wearing the necklace translated, "Hrafarth, chief of all Lythons, gives greeting to Speaker for Zeron and those with her."

Hrafarth turned to Sandwinkle, bumped his fist to his chest again, and spoke.

The shaman continued, "He say no disrespect to Sultan of Sands, but Priestess get greeting first. As it should be."

"Indeed," Sandwinkle said. "I would be offended, otherwise. My wife is my priority; it will be the same for all I encounter, lest I defend her honor to the death." Sandwinkle winked at Kryder and the rest when he knew it wouldn't be noticed.

The Lython shaman translated his answer to Hrafarth. The big chief grinned in a strange, face-altering way and nodded vigorously. He agreed. It was then that Kryder realized there were no female Lythons with the large group.

The greeting to Moonlitdune first wasn't because of her status as the high priestess. It was because she was female. When Hrafarth noticed June, his eyes widened. He ducked his head low with his fist to his chest and murmured.

"Chief say very sorry, not greet you before greeting Seeker of Shades," the shaman said. "Ask forgiveness."

"Of course," June said. "I understand he may never have encountered a woman in armor with a sword at her hip. I am not offended, and I am honored by his concern. Please tell him if he encounters others like me, we have chosen the sword or bow, and expect treatment as a fellow warrior, not deferential treatment, unless rank or nobility warrants such. I do not claim nobility. I claim the status of one learning the arts of war…and politics, though grudgingly."

"Is much to say. I will tell him," the shaman said. "Before I do, I say Zeron's blessings on you for not make chief more embarrass." He turned and began explaining to the chief.

When the shaman finished explaining and answered a few questions from the chief, Hrafarth popped his fist to his chest and then pointed to her. He pointed to his eyes, raised his stone-tipped spear, and said one word.

"Chief say...warrior," the shaman translated.

June closed her fist, put it to her chest, and dipped her head slightly. June didn't understand them, but the grin on Hrafarth's face let everyone know his honor had been maintained, and he saw her as equal. Others with him held up their own weapons and hissed appreciatively.

* * *

Dolner, having listened to both sides of the greeting and the interaction afterward, couldn't help himself. Ever curious, he'd noticed the same thing Kryder had. There were no females in the group, and he wondered if they were forbidden to be warriors in their race, or if they stayed wherever the Lythons called home for other reasons. He wasn't really sure what he wanted to know, he only knew he had to ask.

"Hrafarth, I notice there are no women in your group, and I see you agree with Sandwinkle about putting them first," Dolner asked. "Your race doesn't have female warriors. As you can tell by June's presence, we Humans do. Now, I'm not saying you're wrong about that, 'cause I would hate to insult you. Or your mate...wife? Not sure what the term is. Anyway, is it a traditional thing, or maybe...?"

Dolner trailed off when he noticed everyone staring at him, Kryder, Tog, June, Sylif, the Gnomes, and all the Lythons in hearing distance. *Everyone* was staring at him. "What? I was only asking a question."

Moonlitdune walked over to him and looked at him with her head tilted slightly. "Dolner, where did you learn to speak Lython? I only know a few words, and those are short and simple. I have never heard another speak the hiss of the Lizard people."

"What do you...Oh," Dolner said as he realized he was speaking in their language. "OH!"

"Human, you speak to me in the language of the Dragons," Hrafarth said, stepping forward. "I have never heard another race do this." The chief turned to his shaman. "Nifarthan. How is this so? Has this ever happened?"

"It...it is written," Nifarthan said. "I have read the ancient etchings. There are images. Many centuries ago, some Humans spoke the language of Dragons. They were the Riders."

Hrafarth stepped back in surprise. "Truly? Could this one be a Rider? One of legends?" He looked at Dolner differently and slammed his fist to his chest. "Greetings, Rider of Wind. You honor us all. After Priestess, you deserve greeting before all warriors." He glanced at June with a nod.

"Whaaat?" Dolner said. "Rider? Me? I'm sure I have no idea what you're talking about. I mean, yes I'm speaking your language, but there's probably a good reason for it."

Kryder stood beside his much larger cousin and tried to figure out what was going on. Between the surprise of hearing Dolner hiss in the language of the Lythons, what Moonlitdune had said, and now the continuing conversation, which neither he nor any of his companions could understand, he was as bewildered as he'd ever been in his life.

"Hold it," he finally said. "Will someone tell me what's going on?"

"I'd like to know, too," Tog said. "Goat droppings, this is confusing. One minute we're attacked by Lythons...the next morning, Dolner is asking questions like he always does, but in their language. This is insane."

"Crazy," June said. "My boyfriend is…" She stopped when she noticed Dolner now staring at her, along with the other companions. "I mean…I. You know what I mean!" She turned red and stared off with her arms folded in front of her.

Dolner looked over at Kryder and Tog with his eyes wide. He broke into a grin. Tog looked down and shook his head. "The boy is lost. At his age, no less. Sad."

"It is a gift from Zeronic," Moonlitdune said. She rubbed the large stone on her bracelet. "The winds blow in change, directly from him." She slipped her hand into her pocket and felt the keys, again.

Dolner turned back to the Lythons and began speaking again in their language. He still had questions, and they hadn't answered one yet.

"So, anyway, back to my question…"

* * *

Western Sea

On the edge of a great cliff, on an island a day's sail from the edge of the mountainous coast of northeast Orcanth, Wryle stretched his great wings, enjoying the warmth of the sun. He turned his long neck and watched his mate, Lyna, shift uncomfortably.

He asked the question, knowing the answer before he did, "Do we fly now and follow the sun?"

"It is time, my beloved," Lyna said as she stretched her own wings. "The occasion is upon us."

Wryle watched as her deep red coloring slowly shifted and faded, turning first a purple hue, and finishing in a sky blue, nearly matching the cloudless expanse above them. He knew he would have to invoke the change as well.

"You know I dislike changing colors," he said gruffly. "I am of the flames, and all should know."

"Yes, beloved," she said. It was an argument they'd had for many years, though the reason this time was the first. "You are of the flames, and your red coloring is what first attracted me to you, but as when you hunt, you must blend in to be successful."

"Bah," he said dismissively. "It is not as if I am changing to the black of night, or even the mottled greens of a forest. I must be blue so no one or nothing sees me flying high above."

"Would you rather others know of our flight and destination?" she asked as she moved her large head closer to his to look him in the eye. "We go to the traditional birthplace of our kind so I can lay the eggs I carry. You know how I feel about it."

"I know," he said, lowering his head in defeat. "You want them to hatch the old way, which has not been done for decades. Centuries even. Why now?"

"I…I am compelled," Lyra answered. She sat back and held a foreleg in front of her. The wide red band and ring of turquoise stones interlaced with red lines at random caught the light. She reached over with a claw and touched them, her digits as delicate as any other being's on the planet.

"I'll not question Zeronic," he said. "It is said he could swallow me in one bite."

"The God of Wind and Change does not eat mortals," she scolded. "He provides the wind and currents for us to soar above the ground. He allows us to change our colors. Without these things, our race would have perished long ago. With his gifts, we took to remote islands and high mountains and other places out of reach of most other races…especially the Elves."

"Elves!" Wryle roared. He let loose a burst of flame in anger. It blossomed against the wall of the cliff, throwing off immense heat.

He snapped his mouth shut and glanced toward his mate. Anger smoldered in his eyes. "Elves took eggs from the very place we go. That is why it was abandoned as a hatching site."

"Yes," she said. "All know. But the Elves have not left their home in decades. They no longer cross the lands and go into the desert. The Lythons would attack them and fight to the death."

"They should have stopped them last time," he said. He snorted in dismissal.

"No," she said gently. "You do not believe that. You know as well as I, there were too many of them. Only now, in the last few hundred years, have the Lythons who survived their injuries in that battle grown enough in population to have separate tribes where they are not living in constant fear of extinction."

"I know," Wryle admitted. "The Elves made their way to their villages and slaughtered the females and young, as well. Very few were able to hide."

"It was an atrocity," she said. "An entire race, nearly extinguished."

"They deserved better," he admitted. "They were content to stay within their desert mountains. They never invaded others. We lived in peace as neighbors, and they guarded our nests. Perhaps…perhaps we are the reason for their near demise."

He stared off. "No. I cannot deny it. We *are* the reason. The Elves came looking to capture some of us. They did it by stealing the eggs."

He looked at his mate and asked, "Do we not put them at risk once again? What will the others say?"

"I have spoken to Nylant, of the mist, and Gryndald, of the lightning. Each agrees. Those of the flame must take back our ancient home. If we are successful, the others will go back to theirs."

"So the Trio of Speakers are in agreement," Wryle said in amazement. "It must truly be from Zeronic, then, for those two to get along."

"They are. We of the flame must lead by example. We are the largest flock, and if I am being honest, the most aggressive. If you and I succeed, we will lead the rest."

"Of course we are the most aggressive!" Wryle said. "We are of the flame. But, if I'm being honest as well, there are several Blues and Greens whom I would consider my equal. We may be different, but we are also the same. Perhaps you are right. It is time the rest of Kerr is reminded we exist."

"As I said, I have been compelled."

The huge Dragon shifted his colors. He went from a brilliant reddish orange all the way to a sky blue like his mate. "I would still prefer to be myself," he muttered.

Lyna rubbed her head against his jawline and down his neck. "I know, dear. Thank you." She stepped off the cliff, caught the updraft, and spiraled up into the sky, blending in. She was determined to go to the birthplace of her ancestors and could not be swayed.

With a sigh, Wryle followed shortly after. His mate might blend into the sky in color, but the heat from her body was still outlined in his vision. Loud roars from other cliffs of their isle and the neighboring islands followed them into the sky as the others watched them leave.

*****

Chapter Eighteen

"Are you sure your way lies to the west?" Baron Arnwald asked. "I'll be the first to admit, I would relish the thought of an army of Orcs fighting beside Humans against the Elves and King Westell's forces, but I fear you leave to make journey to the Western Borderlands and beyond for naught."

Lucas shook his head. "I have to try. You said yourself, the forces of Gar-Noth and Yaylok alone outnumber the armies Minth, the Tarlok hunters, and the Baronies West can field by many. Even with the help of the Dwarves from the Mountain Kingdom, the odds are still greatly stacked against us. "

"Add the Elves to the mix, and the balance shifts even more," Johan added.

"We need them," Lucas said, "or those of us left alive will be under the rule of King Westell and his growing empire."

"Go. Go with my thanks," Arnwald said. "For trying, at the very least. If you succeed, all the better."

Lucas climbed onto the wagon's seat beside his daughter. He looked over at the teamsters of the three wagons accompanying them. Two wagons were bound for the vast orchards a few days closer to them than Three Oaks. They were loaded with hobbled lambs for trade. The other wagon was loaded with crates of young turkeys, new breeding stock for several farmers. The cages were piled high, yet lashed securely. They were all protesting loudly.

"It's not to be a quiet trip, I assure ye," Johan said. He shifted in the saddle as Kryder's horse fidgeted.

"No," called the team master as he started his horses moving, "but it is honest trade. I don't envy you having to fight for a living. I admire you, though. I've not the courage for it."

"Yet you travel for a week into a land scarcely populated, with no guard to speak of, except you and the other two drivers and yer bows. I'd not discount yer courage, if I were you," Johan said as he pulled even with the wagon.

"Perhaps," the man said, rubbing his chin. "I never looked at it that way. As sure as I'm sitting on this seat, I'd kill a handful of brigands before I'd let them take a single thing from these wagons. My sons are the same." He looked over toward one of the other wagons. "Come to think of it, Brandle would try to run the few who escaped down if I didn't stop him."

"Courage," Johan declared. He urged his horse forward to speak with his three soldiers as they rode ahead, leaving the trader to his thoughts.

They traveled a well-worn road through the barony until a wide stretch of grasslands ended at a canyon stretching in both directions as far as they could see. The two hunters led the way down on horseback, Johan and his soldiers close behind them. Johan had already determined they needed to be far ahead in case there was an issue with a wagon.

The lead driver eased his team onto the reinforced trail with confidence. Lucas and Marn urged their nervous teams to do the same. Having a wagon ahead to follow, all were on the way to bottom before long.

After crossing a shallow creek several times, they passed a group of guards near a large mine site. Several shacks and a barn had been built near the site Lucas had seen in his journey through time with Kryder and Tog, but he recognized it still. The guards weren't surprised to see them. He smiled when he realized he had heard roosters crowing long before they rounded the bend and came within sight. Goats still ran free with the chickens.

They continued on with no incident. A few days later, they stopped in Waypoint. The town had sprung up over the ruins of a previous one and was growing steadily. The wild orchards had been trimmed back and other trees planted. The trade from here, deeper into the Western Borderlands, into Orcanth, and back behind them into the baronies had helped it to grow.

Several times Lucas saw an Orc, but he didn't get the chance to speak to one, as they were always busy loading a cart to be pulled by hand or working a trade. He decided after the second encounter to wait until he spoke with Jynal before attempting it.

"I'm to be having no idea which tribes they're from, and whether there's a feud with the Red Fist, or any other thing that could cause trouble," Lucas explained. "I just don't know."

"I don't blame ye," Johan said. "It's best to be cautious, to be sure."

"I could help," the teamster said, "but only if I see the one or two I deal with and know. Sometimes it's hard to understand them, you know. It's not often you run into one who's fluent in the language of men." He shrugged. "It seems to get better every year, though."

Tyna turned to Aarn and said, "I find it strange that we do not receive a second glance. Most of the time, people outside our lands watch us like stalking a deer. Here, they have no concern."

"That's because our cousins move about freely here. We're not a mystery," Aarn said. "A scattering of hunter cabins will be the next settlement we reach, if I remember correctly. It's been a while since Zane was back in Tarlok and spoke of it."

Before they moved on from Waypoint, Lucas and Johan met with the mayor. "Once we speak with Lord Jynal, expect a messenger," Lucas said.

"If what you say is true—and I've no reason to doubt you," the man said, "I'll have the watch sergeant get his soldiers ready. We've the normal watch, and a group who meets every other month or so, to sharpen their skills with bow and sling, and to practice sword work."

"They'll be needed," Johan said. "If King Westell has his way, he'll march his army through here as well. It's best to stop them long before."

"True," the mayor said. He ran a hand across his bald head. "I think I'll have a word with Philden and his two apprentices. It's arrowheads we'll need. The kind to puncture armor. It's time his apprentices worked their own forges for a bit. We've a carpenter or two, and several who whittle their own arrows. It's time they all went to work."

He continued, "You know, we don't have any real armor, but there are a few who have worn it in the past. We'll see what we can come up with. By my count, we can provide Lord Jynal with about twenty soldiers, and a hundred or so militia, give or take. It's not much, but we'll do our part."

"If the militia are all archers, that's a fine contribution," Johan said.

"Most are," the mayor said. "More than half of them have good bows, traded from the Orcs. I've heard the bows they trade to Humans are the ones their women use. It doesn't matter. They're made well, and stronger than what we make."

"They're bigger and stronger," Aarn said. "Stands to reason. We've a few of them in Tarlok, brought in by Teel and others. The Orcs make a fine bow." He held his out to show them. "The arrows I made myself, but the bow is from Orcanth, and I'm not ashamed to say it surpasses my other by a longshot, made for a woman or not."

They left the town and turned on the well-worn path toward Three Oaks. "The wind is up a bit today," Marn said.

"Aye," his brother agreed. "It's not as cool up this way, so it feels good to me."

Lucas called out from the other wagon, "Around these parts, they believe Saint Lanae brings the season's changes."

Johan, riding beside him said, "Aye, and it would take a god to bring it about. Change is coming, lads. Change is coming."

* * *

Northern Desert

Kryder glanced at Dolner again. The boy had changed, yet he remained the same. He was still amazed by Dolner's ability to converse with the Lython in their own language. He turned back to the chief after Dolner and their shaman translated for him.

Hrafarth spoke and waited for his words to be translated. Dolner said, "He says yes. Those were the last of the group who have been causing all the trouble. Not only have they been attacking caravans, and even slipped into Minth and the Baronies, they've attempted to climb the sacred cliffs…whatever those are."

"Sacred?" Kryder asked. "Is it something to do with Zeronic or another deity, or is it tradition?"

The shaman answered, "No, not tradition. Is home of Dragons."

"Dragons?" Tog asked. "Nobody has seen Dragons in years. There are rumors on the far side of Orcanth, but nothing else, really."

"They've been seen in Orcanth," Kryder confirmed. "The shamans talk about it. I'm sure they haven't disappeared entirely from Kerr; they just stay away from others. I mean, the cattle and occasional goat or sheep disappears from Three Oaks. It can't all be great cats, bears, or wolves."

"True," Tog admitted. "Any of those would leave tracks and the remains of the kill after they feed."

"No sign of Dragons here in many years," the shaman said. He turned and told the chief what he'd said. The chief nodded and spoke at length.

"Oh," Dolner said. "He said over a hundred years ago…probably a lot more, Elves came into the desert and attacked them at the sacred cliffs. The Lython fought them to the last warrior, but there were too many Elves. They were slaughtered."

The Lython within listening distance stopped what they were doing and were silent. All knew the tale of their past and that it had almost ended their race. Several moved their tails back and forth in anger.

"After the Elves defeated them, Elves made their way to the top of the cliffs and took the eggs from the nests," Dolner said.

"That's where the Elves got the Dragons we hear of in the stories and see in the tapestries," Kryder said. "Red ones."

"It is," the shaman said. "Then before leave, they raid villages. They kill all. Female, hatchlings, young. All."

"What!" Tog said. He stood up. "They truly have no honor. I knew they were evil, but that…that's as bad as it gets."

"How did your race survive?" Kryder asked. "They killed the warriors and they killed everyone else. How?"

The shaman remained silent. He looked toward his chief. Dolner decided to translate for Kryder again. The chief was silent, like the shaman. Finally, the decision could be seen on his face. He answered.

Dolner's eyes widened. He said, "The etchings say a few of the warriors were wounded, and should have died, but did not. Out of all villages, they missed two females and eight younglings, who were deep in some canyons searching for berries. But…but the real miracle was, once they took the eggs, they didn't go beyond the mountains into the Red. They left and went back to Zar."

"The Red?" Kryder asked.

"Yes," the shaman said. "Chief has decided it can be told. Beyond the mountains lies small mountains, hills. The dirt is colored different than here. Is red. In the hills is ancient fortress. Lython guard fortress like guarded sacred cliffs. Were fifty warriors there. Also was group of shamans learning to use prayer spell. All female."

"So the Lython race was nearly wiped out?" Sylif asked. "This is not something widely known."

"Only women were shamans?" June asked.

"Yes," the shaman answered. "I am first male Lython accepted by Zeron. I go with warriors. Pray for healing. Hunt rebels. Hunt food. Some game dangerous. Will attack."

"So that's why they don't have any females with them," June said. "They're kept safe, away from danger. I understand now."

"More precious than water. Almost end Lython long ago, but for new hatchlings the next season."

"A few were able to continue their race," Kryder said. "Thank the Creator."

Sylif, Moonlitdune, and the shaman felt a shiver at Kryder's words. None noticed the same reaction in the others, so they thought nothing of it, because the day was cooling as the evening came on.

"Yes," Dolner said. "He says there were less than a hundred left. It's hard for him to talk about. I can hear it in his voice."

Kryder paused, staring off, realizing what the fortress could be. "Tell him we've been looking for the fortress. I think it's the Mage's Library."

"And when you tell him," Tog said, "tell him why we need to get there. And tell him the Elves are coming again. Tell him we'll be part of the armies fighting those honorless cowards."

The shaman's eyes widened. He'd understood almost everything Tog had said. When Dolner explained in detail, the chief of the Lython stood. His tail whipped back and forth behind him, and he spoke rapidly.

"He says he will take us to the fortress himself. We'll go past the Sacred Cliffs to get there. He's ready to leave now."

"We're ready," Kryder said. "But we should probably wait until first light." He turned to Sandwinkle. "Will you continue with us?

Moonlitdune answered for him, "Of course we will. Change is upon us."

"You heard her," the Sultan of Sands said. He shrugged and smiled.

*****

Chapter Nineteen

The next morning, the three wagons followed the Lython warriors until the trail split. From there, the Gnome wagons went on to the village with the brothers. Sandwinkle's wagon was tied to the last. As a precaution, he made sure to get his crossbow. Hrafarth nodded in approval. The small Gnome and his wife rode Kryder's horse together.

"Are you sure?" Moonlitdune asked.

Kryder smiled and said, "The walk will do me good."

"He needs it," Tog agreed. "He's getting lazy, up on a horse all the time. To be honest, I wish we would move faster so we could run."

"I don't know if that's a good idea," Sylif said. "These trails, going up hills and down through these gullies, are sure to break a horse's ankle. The Lython have no problem with it, though."

"This is their home," Kryder said. "I have to admit, watching them cling sideways to some of these boulders is a bit unnerving. I can see now why the riders slide their feet into the stirrups and tighten the strap on their thighs."

After stopping once near a small stream for lunch, the group continued on. Occasionally Kryder glimpsed a tall mountain in the distance when they came to a wide opening. He wasn't sure, but he thought he saw small clouds above it, as if it was smoking.

"Is it just me, or is that mountain smoking?" he asked.

"It is," Moonlitdune answered. "It is warmed from deep beneath us."

"What?" Tog asked. "Like the Goblin caves bordering Zar?"

"Yes, but there are no Goblins," Sandwinkle assured him. "If there ever were, they were all killed by the Dragons."

"But you said the Dragons haven't been seen here for hundreds of years," Dolner said.

"True," the Gnome said, "but any Goblins would have to cross the desert and make their way through these canyons and mountains to get there. I can assure you, between my people and the Lython, no Goblins roam these lands."

"Look," June said, pointing. "Way up there. What are those? Goats?"

Dolner asked the nearest Lython what they were. "He says they're skandids. When I asked what that was, he described them as goats, able to scale cliffs and steep walls. He says they're bigger than their mounts and use their horns and hooves to attack. They're extremely territorial and aggressive."

"Ask him how they taste," Tog said. He saw the look on Kryder's face. "What?'

"He says they taste great," Dolner said. "They hunt them several times a year."

"See," Tog said. "It doesn't hurt to ask. Some goat and taters would be good right about now."

"It's no wonder they need a shaman with them," Sylif remarked. "A goat that big attacking its hunters could be dangerous. Someone would need the healing of a prayer spell, to be sure. If it didn't kill them outright."

* * *

They rode into a surprisingly green valley with a river running along one side of it. From what Kryder could tell, it never ran dry. There were deep pools and small rapids scattered along it until it wound out of sight behind more hills.

It flowed alongside a steep cliff going up more than a hundred feet before the angle lessened into a rocky mountainside, interspersed with the occasional scraggly tree and patches of green. Up near the top, an opening was visible. A small stream of smoke escaped from it.

"Look!" June shouted. She was loud enough that everyone in the procession looked up.

Kryder inhaled sharply. Two huge forms could be seen against the backdrop of the mountain. They were both the color blue, like the sky, but were now easily visible against the greys, browns, and green of the mountain.

"Dragons!" Dolner shouted. "Something is wrong. Look."

One of the Dragons was struggling and slowly circling downward. They watched as the larger of the two tried to help the other. It flew beneath it, and with mighty flaps of its great wings, tried to prevent it from dropping farther down the mountainside. It was no use. The smaller one, its tail limp, landed roughly on the mountainside above the cliffs. Its color shifted from blue to a brilliant red. Even at this distance, they could see it was exhausted.

The larger one roared in frustration, the sound echoing off the land around them, and landed beside it. Its color changed to red, as well. Its great head dipped, nuzzling the weakened one.

"Something is wrong with it," Dolner said. He turned and spoke to the Lython chief and shaman. He waited for their answer before translating.

"They say the etchings show the Dragons sometimes stayed in the caves up top. That was where they laid their eggs, and the natural heat rising up kept them warm in the nests. They don't know anything else about them."

"I know one thing," Tog said. "I'm glad they haven't noticed us. My bow and axe won't do much good against Dragon fire."

"I've got to get up there," Dolner declared.

"What?" Kryder asked. "Are you insane? You are *not* going up there."

"No, you're not," June said. "What are you going to do? Help her lay eggs or something? Even I know you don't get near a wounded wild animal. The big one would swallow you whole."

"Kryder, I need to get up there. I can help," Dolner pleaded.

"Help?' Kryder asked. "What can you do?"

"I don't know. Talk to them. See if I can help."

"Hey, June," Tog said, "your boyfriend *is* crazy."

"It's not wise," Sylif said. "Even the attempt could get you killed. What would you do? Bandage it? I don't even know if a prayer spell would work."

"We've got to do something. Look at how the larger one nudges the smaller one. I've seen it before in other animals," Dolner said. "The big one knows the small one is in trouble."

The shaman said, "Chief say we must move on. Leave the Dragons before they see us. Many years ago we guard caves for Dragons. No more."

"No," Moonlitdune said, "it is too late for that. The big one has looked right at us several times. It knows we are down here. Brother Sylif is right, not even prayer…"

Moonlitdune shuddered and nearly fell out of the saddle. Tog ran over and grabbed her as she slipped from Sandwinkle's grasp. He eased her to the ground.

The leader of the Gnomes leapt off the horse to her side. "Are you all right? What is it?"

The priestess took a deep breath and composed herself. "I…I have been compelled."

Sylif stepped over. He, of all of them, knew what she meant. Her god had given her knowledge. He waited to hear what it was.

"Dolner," she said. "Come here."

Dolner dismounted, followed closely by June. "Is there something you can do?" Dolner asked. "Can I help?"

"You can," she said. She glanced at the bracelet on her wrist. The stone glowed softly for all to see. "Take these." She handed him the two keys.

"What are these?" Dolner asked, turning them over in his hand. "They're not heavy. Hey, they have a stone in them like yours."

"I know," Moonlitdune said. Her stone faded.

"It is stone of Zeron," proclaimed the shaman.

"What do I do with them?" Dolner asked. He noticed June admiring them. He handed her one to look at closely.

"It's beautiful," June said. "It looks like it has wings on it, and there's a hole at the top. I wonder if it's supposed to go on a necklace?"

Moonlitdune turned to Kryder. "Dolner must go to the Dragon. I have been shown; it must happen."

Kryder pursed his lips and looked down. He knew he couldn't say no. He and Tog had been in the presence of a god before. When they compelled, there was no choice. He looked up, determined.

"You're not really going to get him up there are you?" Tog asked. "You're as crazy as he is. He'll be killed. I mean, I know about compelling because of my mama, but still."

"It has to happen," Kryder said.

"Madness," Sylif said. "But it must be. I agree. How will you do it?"

"Levitation," Kryder said. "Now that I'm sure of the spell, I can move him…to the top of the cliff, at least."

"You cast magic?" the shaman asked.

"Yes," Kryder answered. "I'm a shaman." The Lython's eyes widened.

"All right!" Dolner said. He rubbed his hands together. "Make me fly."

"Uh, you're not going up there by yourself," June said. "Don't even think about it. Kryder, send me with him."

"I don't know if I can," Kryder admitted. "I've only cast it for myself a few times. Two people? I just don't know."

"Try," June implored. She stepped over and wrapped her arms around Dolner. "Don't get any big ideas. You haven't even met my father…yet."

"Your father?" Dolner asked, putting his arms around her. He leaned his head back and looked at her nervously. "I mean, we have plenty of time before all that kind of stuff."

"Oh, you *are* going to meet him," she said. "*And* my brothers."

"Great," Dolner muttered. "Brothers. Send us up, Kryder. Maybe I'll get eaten."

June elbowed him. He grinned and said, "Kinda hard to hug you with your armor on."

"This is not a hug," she said. "Well, maybe it is. Whatever. We're ready."

Kryder raised a hand and concentrated on what he was about to do. He didn't notice the Lython take a step back. The shaman had hurriedly explained that Kryder was a shaman of magic, something they feared, because the etchings had described the Elves using it to get to the eggs.

Kryder spoke the words with conviction and pushed into the spell. Slowly, Dolner and June rose. The higher up they got, and the further away from Kryder they were, the harder it was to concentrate. His hand started trembling as he held it out. When they were even with the top of the cliff, he moved his arm, sliding them over the lip. After they were a safe distance from the ledge, he released the spell and dropped to his knees, breathing heavily.

Tog rushed to his side. "Are you all right?"

"Yeah," Kryder said. "I'll be fine. The spell was for making the caster levitate. I changed a few words, hoping it would work. I guess it did. I was able to lift them and not me."

"You created a new spell?" Sylif said. "Amazing. I was under the impression it took mages years of studying to do that."

"I don't know," Kryder said with a shrug. "I'm a shaman, not a mage."

He looked up and saw Dolner and June picking their way up the mountain carefully. "Now we wait and see what happens."

*****

Chapter Twenty

Wryle roared in anguish, the sound echoing off the mountains and hillsides for miles. He brought his great head closer to his mate's. "If I bring you prey, will you gain the strength to make it to the caves?"

"No, beloved," Lyna said. "I fear I won't regain my strength in time. The eggs come."

"Here? Now?" Wryle asked. "If you have them here, they will perish. You must have them where it is warm. I knew we should have stayed on the island, where the sun warms the sand all day."

"We could not," she said. "I was compelled."

"If Zeronic wanted you to have them here, why did he not give you the strength to make it all the way to the caves?" he demanded. "We were so close."

"I know not. I do not question him," she answered. "You should not, either."

"Can you pray for healing?" he asked, his tone properly chastised. "The way you prayed for Manvell's broken wing?

"I cannot," she answered. "Prayer spells are gifts. One does not ask for themselves."

"Can I?" he implored.

"You must be accepted by Zeronic to be granted prayer spells," she said softly. "He hears your prayers, but some things he cannot change. All things are foretold."

"But I..." Wryle lifted his head and inhaled deeply through his nostrils. "I smell something. The meal I offered may come to us." He rose up, looking for the source.

"There!" he said with a snarl. "Two...Humans come to us. How did they get up here this quickly? How dare they approach!"

* * *

"We are going to die," June said. "The big one looked right at us. He probably smelled us. Well, you, not me."

"Hey!" Dolner said.

"I'm just saying, you could use a bath. We all could, I guess." She grinned nervously.

"Let me do the talking," Dolner said as they continued, slowly now.

"Talking?" June asked. "Look, I know you talk to the horses like they understand you, but a horse can't bite you in two and swallow the pieces. You need to come up with something better than that. I came up here to keep you from getting eaten. It's looking like it will happen anyway.

She looked down at her hand. "And here, I'm still holding the key. Take it."

"Hold it," Dolner said, "I don't want us making any sudden moves."

"What about running away?" June asked as she moved forward with him. "Is that sudden?"

* * *

"The arrogance!" Wryle said. "To keep moving toward us when they both looked me in the eye. It is a challenge!"

He crouched, wings spread, ready to leap into the air, land on the other side of his mate, and meet them. Anger and fear smoldered in his eyes. Anger at the challenge, and fear for his mate. "I smell steel. They come to attack!"

"Wait!" Lyna shouted.

Surprised, he checked his leap. He tilted his head so he could see their approach and look at her at the same time. "Why?" the great Dragon rumbled. "Why?"

"His hand," Lyna said. "I caught a glimpse of a stone. I must see what is in his hand."

"Then I will bring his hand to you." He snapped his jaws shut in emphasis.

"No, beloved," she said softly. "You will wait."

* * *

Dolner stopped abruptly. June looked around wildly. "What? What is it? Is it time to run? There's nowhere to run. I knew I should've had my bow ready."

"No," Dolner said. "I heard the hurt one say, 'wait.' At least I think I heard it."

"What? I heard a hiss and teeth snap. I didn't hear one speak. Don't tell me you can understand Dragons, too."

"It's almost the same language the Lython speak. At least it sounded close to me," Dolner said as he started moving again.

"Great. Makes perfect sense," June said. "You can understand Dragons. Why not? Can I draw my sword now?"

"No."

Dolner stopped short of actually approaching the two beasts. They both stared at him. The smaller one was breathing much faster than the larger. Something was definitely wrong with it.

Throwing caution to the wind, he asked, "Are you hurt?"

The large Dragon reared back, a look of what could only be surprise on its scaled face. The smaller one tilted its head and looked at him in puzzlement.

"You speak our language, Human," a decidedly feminine voice said. She paused, surprised. "And I answered you in yours. How is this so?"

"I don't know," Dolner said. He took a step closer.

"That is far enough, Human," the larger one hissed in a deep voice.

"Look," Dolner said, "we're not here to hurt you. I don't know how I speak your language. I understood the Lython, too. Moonlitdune said it was a gift."

"A gift?" the female Dragon asked. "Only a god could bestow such a gift."

"That's what she said. She said it was from Zeronic, but I don't know. And then she gave me the keys and everything. Look, I only want to help. I have to."

"Zeronic?" the smaller Dragon said. "Know you the God of Wind and Change?"

"I do," Dolner said, surprised as much as the Dragons had been when he heard his own language. He shifted the key to his other hand and ran his hand from his forehead back, letting his hair fall to both sides.

"I mean, I know *of* him. I'd like to know more, really I would. It seems he's the one god I don't have to learn how to read to follow." He glanced at June.

"I know you can't read," she said. She elbowed him. "It's not a deal breaker."

"Wait, what deal?" Dolner asked. "Never mind. You can explain later. I'm so confused right now." He heard the female translate what he'd said. He turned back to the Dragons and was surprised to see what could only be described as a smile on the largest one's face.

"Human," he said, "your mate will confound you until the end of your time on this world. Such is the fate of a male."

"Wait! What? No...," Dolner sputtered.

The smaller Dragon attempted to rise, but couldn't. After several deep breaths, she asked, "What are you called?"

"My name is Dolner. My g...this is June. We really do want to help," Dolner said.

"Dolner. I am called Lyna. My mate is Wryle." She sighed. She continued to speak in the Human language. "I am afraid you cannot help. I pushed myself beyond my endurance. I cannot fly and will not be able to reach the caves above. I fear my eggs will come here on the mountainside. They will perish."

"Can you wait? Maybe hold them in?" Dolner asked.

June elbowed him again. "She can't stop birth, any more than a woman can. My mother's sister had a child in a wagon once. The healer was gone to a farm, so they tried to get to the next town."

"There has to be something we can do," Dolner said. He pointed to the red bracelet, blending neatly with her scales. "Wait, is that a bracelet? Why do you wear a bracelet? A Dragon with a bracelet? Seems strange to me."

"Strange?" Lyna said. She chuckled despite her discomfort. "Hearing my own language from a Human is *strange*. Learning I know the Human language is even stranger."

She reached up and turned the wide band so the stone showed. "This is why."

"Zeronic!" Dolner said. "That's the stone of a cleric of Zeronic."

"I do not know the word you used," Lyna said, "but yes, it is the symbol of Zeronic. I am the Speaker of Zeronic for those of the Flame. How do you know the stone?"

"It's like this one," Dolner said, holding out the key and pointing to the stone.

"A Rider's key," Wryle hissed. "Where did you get that? They are but legends, passed down in the telling. My sire told me of them years ago."

"That's the second time someone has said Rider. What is a Rider?" Dolner asked.

"Legend has it Humans and Dragons worked together in the past," Lyna said. "More than that, I do not know." She shuddered and groaned.

Without thinking about it, Dolner stepped up and put his hand on her flank. Her scales were warm to the touch, yet hard like armor. "Are you sure there's nothing I can do?"

"Unless you can pray for strength…no." She sighed. "I fear I cannot wait much longer."

"I can do that," Dolner said. He nodded to himself. "June, help me."

"Help you what?" June asked, reaching out and putting her hand on his. "We aren't clerics or shamans or anything. What can we do?"

"We can ask," Dolner said.

Dolner closed his eyes, gripped the key in his other hand tightly, his thumb sliding over the stone, and said, "Zeronic. Will you hear me? I am no cleric, but I have need. Will you give strength to Lyna?" He felt June squeeze his hand tightly.

* * *

An Island in the Eastern Sea

Dolner gasped and looked around. June's grip on his hand tightened so much, it hurt. They were standing in a large room with an opening the length of one wall, facing out over a mountainside leading down to the shore and the sea. Standing in the middle of the opening was a bearded old man. He turned and smiled at them. They both knew they faced an Immortal.

"Ah, Dolner, my boy," Zeronic said. "So good of you to call on me today. June my dear, I see your faith in your b…well, in Dolner, has brought you here as well." He winked.

The two of them stood, open-mouthed. Finally Dolner said, "Where are we?'

"Why, you are in my home, of course," Zeronic said. He waved his arm around to indicate the large room. "My home when I am in this shape. I can change, you know, but it is not necessary here."

"But why?" Dolner asked.

"He does ask a lot of questions," he said to June. "You will have your hands full, my dear."

June nodded, still too stunned to speak.

"So," Zeronic said. He clapped his hands together and rubbed them. "Why? Why indeed. You are here because you reached out to me, and I have accepted. I have accepted both of you."

Finally, June spoke, "Accepted, my...my Lord?"

"Yes," Zeronic said. "It's time for a little change. Well, a big change, but it's all little in the grand scheme of things, you know. Some things even us gods do not know, right Minokath?"

"Yes," a voice said behind them. "All is part of our Creator's plans."

Dolner and June whirled around to see the Lord of the Seas. He stood before them, his gleaming chainmail dripping, though the drops never made it to the dark wood flooring of Zeronic's home. His green hair and flowing cape dried quickly before their eyes.

"Saint Minokath," June whispered.

"Yes, child," Minokath answered. "I am here."

"So," Zeronic said, getting their attention. "The decision. I have decided to accept both of you. I asked my brother to come because June has followed him her whole life. The last thing I want to do is anger him. After all, June, you prayed to him, while Dolner prayed for my help."

"I understand," Minokath assured him and June. "Our Creator has shown me this. June, you can still follow me *and* be a Rider for Zeronic. It is not the first time someone has followed multiple gods. After all, we all belong to our Creator."

"In uh…in infinite wisdom," Dolner said.

"Well put," Minokath said. "To be honest, my presence was not necessary, but I wanted to meet you two face to face. I am not a jealous god. Only the demons reign jealously over their followers, hoarding them."

He stepped closer to June. "Normally we gods only meet our high clerics. But I made an exception for this occasion. A Rider. And not one of old—they only followed Zeronic."

"A Rider?" June asked.

"Yes," Minokath said. "A Rider. Zeronic will explain. June, I accept you. Here, take this." He held out his hand. In his open palm was a small shell earring. It was a twisted shape ending in a point. She could see it glowing softly.

June slowly reached out and took it. Still looking at him, she reached up, brushed her hair back, and put the earring in. Without a backing, it pulled tight and fit flush against her ear.

"There," Saint Minokath said. "When you wear a helmet, it will not interfere. Can't have that when you are fighting in my name."

The Lord of the Seas stepped back and looked at her. "Now you need a book of prayer spells and a copy of The Book Of The One."

He held out a book. "Here is the spell book. I believe Zeronic will give you a copy of The Book Of The One. I have taken the liberty of writing a few spells in your book myself. I would hate to have you feel compelled while on the back of a Dragon. You might fall.

"I will see you again, my child." Minokath stepped toward the open space.

The Lord of the Seas looked out toward his domain. He called back over his shoulder, "A beautiful view you have, brother. Thank you for the invitation. I will see you again, as well." He stepped out of the window and was gone.

"Wait," Dolner said. "What just happened?"

"Why, the Lord of the Seas accepted June, like I have both of you. Gave her a book of prayer spells, as well. Nice touch. Do you not see her earring?"

"Well, yeah, I see it. It's glowing, I...." He paused and looked at the key in his hand. Like her key, the stone was glowing the same way.

"Yes, my child, you are now a cleric, and a Rider, too," Zeronic said. "Let me explain."

He began pacing, his hands behind his back. "Long ago...long, long ago, I had more followers than I do now. Dragons, Gnomes, Lythons...and Humans. The Humans who followed me were the Riders. Of course, the Riders rode Dragons. The Lythons and Gnomes became followers because they lived where some Dragons frequented. It was only natural."

"Rode Dragons?" June asked. "As in ride them while they fly?"

"Well, yes," Zeronic answered. "There was a time when it was necessary to fight the demons and their Elven followers. You know, for some reason, many Elves have chosen to worship demons. Not all, but many."

He shook his head sadly. "Free will, poor choices. Anyway, the demons twisted and warped creatures to fight alongside the Elves, which encouraged Humans and Dragons to work together and rid the land of them."

"Work together?" Dolner asked.

"It was a big change," Zeronic admitted, "but it was necessary. In time, the Riders died out, and Dragons went on with their own lives, generation after generation."

He stopped pacing and turned back to face them. "Now, our Creator has decided there must be balance. The Elves have Dragons, warped as their minds may be, so I have brought back the Riders."

He started pacing again. "I say *I have*, but you understand, it was your choice to call on me, and it was Wryle and Lyna who allowed you to come close to them. I mean, you could have been eaten, you know."

"What?" June demanded. "I knew it." She elbowed Dolner again.

"There must be free will," Zeronic explained.

Zeronic stopped, turned toward them, and shrugged. "Your choice, their choice."

"Ah, my next guest has arrived. Sister. Welcome to my home," Zeronic said, looking past them. "You just missed Minokath."

Dolner and June whirled again to see yet another of the deities. She was tall for a woman, with striking red hair hanging in ringlets. She wore dark leathers, and a reddish cloak the color of fresh cut cedarwood with its hood down. As she moved, white fur could be seen lining the inside of it and the hood itself.

"Thank you. It is lovely," said Harnette, the Keeper of Flames. She wrapped her arms around herself and nodded toward the empty fireplace set in one of the stone walls. "A little cool, though. Do you mind?"

"Not at all. I suspect the wind chills you some," Zeronic said.

"Thank you," she said and waved her hand. In the blink of an eye, a fire was roaring in the empty spot.

"I saw our brother, and I spoke with him, in passing. You know I rarely see him these days. He would not be comfortable in my cabin, nor would I relish his castle beneath the seas."

She stood facing away from them a moment, holding her hands to the warmth. When she turned, there was a slight glow on the checks of her pale face. It was not as bright as the red lipstick she wore, but it seemed right on her. She nodded at the two mortals.

"Dolner," Harnette said. "Before you ask, yes, I can make flames when there is no source. I am the source of all flame. Yes, Humans and other races make flames. The gift of the knowledge to create fire was given freely when this world was made. I ensure it is never lost."

She paused and answered before he could ask, "No, I cannot simply step in and stop flames from doing what they do. Even fire is free to do what it does. If carelessness causes it to run rampant, it must be allowed. It pains me to see it happen, but all is of our Creator's plan."

"How did you know what I…" Dolner started to ask. June elbowed him and he said, "Right. Deity. Sorry."

"Thank you, June," Harnette said with a twinkle in her eye. "It would be unseemly for me to elbow some sense into a mortal. Especially someone else's man."

June couldn't help the smile on her face. "You're Saint Harnette, the Keeper of Flames. My father's mother spoke of you often."

"Yes, she did," Harnette said. "These days, she speaks *to* me often. She has earned an eternal hearth to keep her warm." She paused and said, "You know, she speaks of you, as well."

"Me?" June said.

"Yes, child," the goddess said. "And I can see that she described your hair accurately. A lovely shade it is. You carry yourself like the warrior she said you would grow to be, full of fire. Tell me, do you still carry the gift she gave you?"

June reached into a small pouch on her sword belt. She pulled out a small, soft leather bundle and unrolled it. Tucked into a piece of wool was an earring. It was unlike the one she had received from Minokath. The small silver earring was of delicately carved flames. When the light reflected from it, it looked both silver and red, and it appeared as if the flames moved on their own.

"She gave it to me in the middle of the night, from her deathbed," June said. The memory, from when she was a child, brought tears to her eyes.

"I am sorry for your loss. But tell me, why do you not wear it?" asked the goddess whose symbol it was.

"I'm afraid I'll lose it," June said. She tilted her head sheepishly. "I wore it once during Midwinter Festival and lost it. It was in the grass where we were all wrestling."

"I know," Harnette said. "You crawled on all fours, looking for it well into the night, until you found it. I was moved."

"I won that year," June said, changing the subject, trying to push the memory of the loss of her grandmother away. "I beat all the boys, too."

"I am aware," Harnette said. "Did you know yours was passed down for four hundred years?"

"I knew it was old," June admitted. "I didn't know it was that old."

"They are worn in pairs, but its mate was lost long ago."

"That's what my grandmother told me," June said. She paused again, lost in thought.

"Will you wear it now?" Harnette asked.

"I can," June said. She took it out of the soft padding and moved it toward the ear opposite the shell earring.

Harnette stepped over, reached out, and took her hand, stopping her from completing the motion. "No child. Not in haste."

The Goddess Harnette looked deep into June's eyes, down into her very soul. When she saw what she was looking for, she said again, "Not in haste. With forethought. Will you wear *my* symbol?"

Dolner realized what she was asking June to do. A deity, one of the immortals, was asking her if she would bear her symbol for all to see, along with everything it could entail in the future. He watched June think for a moment. Resolve came across her face.

June nodded and said, "Yes. I accept, my Lady." Her voice became firmer as she spoke.

The Keeper of Flames smiled once again, the emotion bringing a warmth to the room the fireplace never could. Dolner shivered. She moved her hand. June opened hers, and Dolner could see the earring glow a soft shade of blue, like her other earring and the stones in the keys. June put it in.

"Like your gift from Minokath, it will not come out," Harnette said, "even when you cover your beautiful hair with a helmet."

"Thank you," June said. She dropped to a knee.

"Rise, child," Harnette said. "I foresee you becoming a great Rider for Zeronic with the spells I have added to your book."

Harnette turned to Zeronic. "Changes, indeed. For the first time, *I* asked for acceptance from a mortal, not the other way around. It brings me great joy to tell you she said yes. You now have a Rider who is my cleric *and* our brother's.

"Changes come," Zeronic agreed. "Our Creator wills it so. I but do my part."

"As do I, oldest brother of mine," she said. "As do I."

"Hey!" Zeronic said. "I am only the oldest by mere moments."

"But you are the oldest." She laughed. "And look the part." She indicated his beard.

Zeronic fluffed his beard, then straightened it. He smiled at his sister.

"I must take my leave," Harnette said. "Until next time." She turned to Dolner and her newest cleric. "Call on me, child. I will answer."

The room dimmed as the fire in the fireplace winked out with the disappearance of its maker.

Zeronic clapped his hands together again. "Well, now. There is that. That will be all the guests I receive today. There were a couple more I had planned to talk to. Perhaps in the future."

He turned, walked over to a shelf, and selected two books. "Here are your copies of The Book Of The One. I do not have a book of prayer spells for you, Dolner. Not that it would do any good." He shook his head in dismay. "June, you simply *must* teach him to read."

He ran his hand down his flowing beard, straightening the white curls. "I gave him the language; I'm not doing everything around here, you know."

He patted around the front of his robes until he found the right pocket. "Here, put this on, Dolner. Not only are you a Rider, but you are my first Human cleric in centuries."

"What…what do I do about prayer spells?" Dolner asked as he slipped on the leather band he'd been given. He stared at it, admiring the glow of the stone. "I'll be the only cleric on Kerr with no spells. Great. How am I 'sposed to help people? 'Hey, *trust* me. No, really.' I'll sound like a sneak thief working an angle."

Zeronic smiled. He loved a quick wit. "Wing it, like you did in asking for healing for Lyna. You said you had need, but *you* didn't. You were asking for another. I like that."

"Wing it?" Dolner asked.

"Wing it," came the answer as everything faded.

* * *

Lyna gasped as she felt strength come into her through their hands and into the muscles of her wings. She noticed the soft glow of June's earrings and the familiar stone on the band on Dolner's wrist. She knew her mate saw the bright blue beneath their hands held against her. The gods had answered. One she knew, and others she did not.

*****

Chapter Twenty-One

Three Oaks

The Western Borderlands

Lucas climbed down off the wagon and looked around to see if he knew anyone. The memories were still fresh to him.

Three Oaks was a small town, but, based on the many farms and homes they had passed, he knew most in the area didn't reside in the town itself. The market was much larger than he would have expected. Humans, Orcs, and an occasional Gnome could be seen offering their goods. That explained why the roads were in much better shape than he would have thought.

"Do ye think the hunters are having any luck?" Johan asked.

"I'm to be sure of it," Lucas answered. "We may have only seen the two cabins, but there are many in that stretch o' woods. They'll find them."

Sethon and Marn walked over. "What do we do now?" Sethon asked. "Everyone is looking at us because we didn't bring much to trade. The wagon full of turkeys, they expected. Us, they didn't."

"We just need to find…there!" Lucas said, as he recognized someone. "She's the one to talk to."

He pointed to a woman looking at spices on a small table. The Gnome behind it was talking expressively with his hands. She was scarred and lacked hair on one side of her head, but even at this distance, they could see her radiant smile as she shook her head. The Gnome reached back behind him, opened a box, and took out a bowl with a lid. Her smile grew even brighter.

Lucas waited until her transaction with the Gnome was complete. She put the lid back on the bowl and made sure the small tie strap was pulled tight. She slipped it into a pocket of her cloak and turned to him.

"Sister Katheen," Lucas said. "A word, if ye don't mind."

She studied him for a moment and said, "Certainly. Do I know you? Have we met? Perhaps I have seen you in Waypoint?"

"No," Lucas admitted, "but I have seen ye." He glanced toward a building at the end of the street. "Perhaps we could sit down in your church, and I would be glad to tell ye all."

"We can," she said, "but I would like to know how you knew it was such. The cabin is not marked with any symbol."

"That's because ye are accepted by more than one god, Sister. Saint Minokath, Saint Gonthon, and Saint Lanae, that I know of. There would need to be many symbols."

Katheen pursed her lips in a half smile. She reached up to the side of her head with hair and brushed it back, exposing a dangling earring. Before she could speak, Johan said. "That's to be the claw of Nalcon the Hunter. There are more than I mentioned."

Katheen looked at the grizzled old soldier in his chainmail, the three soldiers standing behind him, and over at the two young men, even larger than the one she was talking to. "What is your name, sir? And why do the ones with you seem ready for a war?"

"Sister, a war is coming. Coming to us all," Lucas said. "My name is Lucas Trant. I have much to tell. Would it be possible for ye to have your father come to the church? I know he doesn't have a castle or even an estate, as such, so his home might not be the place to gather."

"I can. Meet me there in a half an hourglass," she said. "He is with my husband, tending a cow heavy with twins. She should have given birth by now. If all is well, we will meet you there."

She waved to Lucas's daughter, Julia, and to his surprise, the girl smiled and waved back enthusiastically.

* * *

Lord Jynal Narvok and Lur were the last to arrive. Jynal was an old man now, but still moved with a spring in his step. Years of farming and hard work had kept him in exceptional health. Lur, Katheen's husband, was six feet tall, with nearly the build of a normal man, but there was no mistaking his protruding tusks, which labeled him as an Orc. Both wore the plain clothes of a farmer.

After introductions were made, they sat at a large table on the back porch of the cabin that was used as a church and meeting place. Julia, normally shy, insisted on sitting beside Katheen. Katheen smiled in understanding and made room for her on the bench between her and her husband. Without hesitating, Julia slid between them and grinned at Katheen. She even turned and waved slightly at Lur.

Lucas noticed and said, "Sister, my daughter has taken a liking to ye. To be honest, it's the first time I've seen her act this way since she was…Well, since she was burnt. Her mind, that is. Not like…"

"Like me," Katheen said. "It's all right. I knew what you meant."

Katheen reached a hand out and brushed Julia's hair away from one side of her face. When her hand touched Julia's face, she paused and whispered a short prayer. She had to put both hands on the table to steady herself. No fewer than four gods compelled her. Lur stood quickly and moved behind her to support her as she rocked while shaking her head.

"Are you all right?' Jynal asked.

"I have been compelled," Katheen said. Her voice grew stronger. "I must think on it." She waved a hand. "Please, Lucas, tell us why you and the others have come so far to speak to my father."

"I will try," Lucas said, obviously shaken. "Though I have seen you compelled before, and the one time ye healed an ailment from birth." He looked toward Lur. "I don't want to get me hopes up, ye understand."

"How do you know that?" Jynal asked. "Do you know my grandsons? Did they tell you?"

"I do know them, my lord," Lucas said. "Tog gave me this. I was to show it when I went beyond your borders."

Lucas reached into a side pocket of his traveling cloak and took out the piece of leather with the symbol of the Red Fist Tribe on it. He laid it on the table. There was no mistaking it.

"You," Lur said. "You are of Red Fist?"

"Tog said I was…and my family," Lucas answered. "Kryder said, 'It has been said, and it is so.' I'm not sure exactly what that meant, but yes, they insist I am of the Red Fist."

"The son of the son of the chief," Lur said. He nodded once. "If said, is true."

"I will notify the tribal council," Katheen said. "Kryder is unable to right now."

"You are big for a normal man," Jynal said. "Your sons are even bigger. Makes sense. Were you as surprised to find out as I was?"

"No, my lord," Lucas said. "I have known my whole life. My mother's people were originally from the edge o' Minth, when it was much larger, before the Baronies. But to have it acknowledged and to be accepted was a bit o' shock."

"It has been said. It is so," Lur said. He stood and reached across the table. Lucas stood and clasped forearms.

After they sat back down, Katheen asked, "Did you say in old Minth? How many years ago?"

"About a hundred, maybe a little more," Lucas said, "or so I was told when I was a wee lad."

"I see," Katheen said. She paused a moment, thinking. She shook herself out of the thought and said, "Please, tell us of meeting my son and nephew, the piece of leather laying before us, how you saw me before, and…this war you speak of."

"War?" Jynal asked.

* * *

Northern Desert

"War?" Wryle demanded. "Tell me of this war." The Dragon's tail moved back and forth slowly, and he lowered his massive head to eye level with Dolner.

"What did he say?" June asked. She took a step back and moved over beside Dolner. She handed the key she was holding to him.

"He wants to know about the war," Dolner explained.

"Oh," June said. "Well, tell him. Make sure you tell him about the Dragons the Elves may have."

"I will," Dolner said. He looked up the mountainside toward the opening Lyna had entered after she flew up. "I wonder why he didn't go up there with her."

June elbowed him. "How about she needed some privacy? Everyone knows that about birth…or egg laying. Whatever."

Wryle's faced contorted into what Dolner now knew was amusement. "What did you say this time? You are young for a Human, aren't you? There is much you must learn of females, Dolner. Perhaps you should keep some of your thoughts to yourself. I have found it is best. Now, I ask again. Talk to me of this war."

* * *

Kryder lowered the tube and handed it back to Sandwinkle. "You're right. It looks like Dolner is talking to the Dragon. The way his hands are moving, he's talking about the upcoming war. The other still has not come out of the cave it flew up to." He turned to Tog. "I have no idea what he did. One minute the Dragon was laying there, the next it stood, stretched, and flew up to the cavern."

Sylif reached for his bracelet, rubbed the shells, and pursed his lips. "I thought I saw a flash of blue. I cannot be sure, though. May I use the farseeing tube to look?"

Sandwinkle handed him the tube and explained how to focus it by twisting. Sylif looked through at the Dragon. He studied its size, compared to Dolner and June. As he moved the tube over, he inhaled sharply, pulled it away from his eye, rubbed his eye, and looked again.

"What?" Tog asked. "What did you see? Are they all right?" He squinted his own eyes in an attempt to make out more detail.

"Sister," Sylif asked, "will you look and tell me if what I see is correct and not a play of light on the mountainside?" He handed her the tube.

The priestess of Zeronic looked through it. She had the same reaction. "It is not a play of light. I see them, too. One, two, three…no four! I see four."

"Four!" Kryder said. "What? Four Dragons?" He raised a hand, ready to cast a spell to get himself up the cliff. He went through the spells he knew readily, wondering if the shield or rejection spell would hold off the flames from a red Dragon.

"No," she answered before he cast a spell. "I see symbols of deities. One on Dolner's wrist, and something in his other hand, as well. I see the sides of June's face when the wind blows her hair back. Earrings, I suspect."

"Her ears are glowing?" Tog asked. "Wait, does that mean…"

"Yes," Sylif said. "They have both been accepted. Which god has done so remains to be seen. I wonder why they each have two of them. It is unusual, but not unheard of. I have seen matching earrings before on a cleric of Saint Harnette, the Keeper of Flames. She was the High Cleric of their sect."

"Cleric?" Tog asked. "So you're saying Dolner is a cleric? He can't be. He can't read." He grinned, his incisors showing easily. "Dolner a cleric. Oh, he is in big trouble. He hasn't even met my mama, and he's in for it. She'll have him learning to read from early morning until well after dark."

Kryder nodded. "She will. By lamplight or a room full of candles. She doesn't mess around. She taught her husband to read in our language as well as his, and he's not even a shaman."

"Lython shaman learn read etchings," Nifarthan said. He shrugged his shoulders and reached for his necklace without thinking about it. "Not easy. Learn make marks, too." He reached into a bag hung on his shoulder and pulled out a scroll. He opened it and showed them.

Kryder noticed the scroll itself was of the same type used in the school of magic, except this one was only a hand's width wide. The material used and the thin strip of cloth to hold it rolled up was the same.

"I have seen the same writing somewhere," Sylif said. "It looks like the language in the back of Brother Pynon's ancient copy of The Book Of The One. The one no one knows how to read. But I can't be sure. I would need them to be side by side."

"What is it for?" Moonlitdune asked.

The shaman pointed to the first few lines. "This one ease pain, fix broken bone." He pointed to another. "This one help cool body. Some younglings not careful. Get too hot. Can use to warm, too." He nodded as if problems in maintaining body temperature were common among every race.

There were several more, but he pointed to the last one he had. "This one sends fire into sky. Make signal."

"I have the same one written in my book of prayer spells," Moonlitdune said. "I also have several more. Among them is one for dry cough, and another to turn a small amount of water into much more."

"Water?" Nifarthan asked. "Not have that. Maybe teach?"

"I will," she answered. "Will you teach me how to cool the body?"

The Lython chief stepped over to Kryder and spoke at length. The shaman translated. "Chief say, Dragons are back on sacred mountain. He will send warriors to guard caves once again. Those not guarding caves will prepare for war. Will ride south with Gnomes to fight Elves. He say this time, we will fight them before they reach the sands."

Kryder reached out his hand to the Lython chief. "Good. We will need more allies. Any who wish to join us…are welcome."

* * * * *

Chapter Twenty-Two

Minth

King Jondal shook hands with King Nuvalk. "Welcome."

The king of the Dwarves nodded seriously. "The Mountain Kingdom and Minth are allies, it's true. But it is more than that. I have known you your whole life, Jondal. Like a brother you are to me. I could be nowhere else."

"And I would be standing in your cavern awaiting your instructions myself, were invaders at your borders," King Jondal said. "I would not hesitate to swear to this at the foot of my father's grave."

"You would not have to," Nuvalk said, "and every Dwarf alive knows this."

"Let us start this meeting," Jondal suggested.

* * *

King Jondal stood over the map on the largest table in the great hall. With him was King Nuvalk, the Dwarven troop commander Nylon Shieldcrusher, his own knight commander, Sir Markain, Mage Bethany, and Brother Pynon. Dukes, duchesses, a handful of barons, knights representing those too old to lead their own troops, and many minor lords filled the room. Several clerics from other religions were present as well.

He looked down at his map one last time and finalized his decision. He looked up and spoke, "We will meet them on the southern plains. Once all our allies gather, and we finalize the plans, we move. It will be the first of spring."

He walked around the table to stand in front of those seated. "We have no choice but to meet them with all the forces we can gather. To fight several engagements or a running battle will spell doom for us. The information I received tells me they greatly outnumber us."

He let the information sink in. "Lord Koth's cavalry will be coming around the western hills; he can attack their flank and cause them to commit their reserves. We must hold the front lines long enough for that to happen. It is our only chance to even the numbers."

"What of the Dragons, my lord?" a voice called out.

"We must face them, if it comes to it," King Jondal answered. "We will know before the onset of battle. Like the information on the size of their forces, our scouts and spies should bring us more information long before we meet."

Sir Markain spoke up, "Spies, my lord?"

"Yes," the king of Minth said. "These times call for all who wish to remain beyond King Westell's grasp to step forward. I have been contacted by one who offers his guild's services."

"No," Sir Markain said.

"Yes," King Jondal said. "Sneak thieves do not want their way of life changed any more than we do. As of now, there is a kind of truce. If we prevail, and things return to normal, the truce will end."

"So we can lessen the numbers on night watch in our towns and cities?" Duke Rivtarn asked.

"The message came directly from Kelly," King Jondal said. Murmurs could be heard in the room.

"And we are to trust the so-called *Sneak Thief King*?" the duke asked. The doubt was evident in his voice. "If that is really his name. Nobody even knows who he is."

A woman stood up from the back table and walked down the center aisle. When she reached the front, she pushed the hood of her cloak back to reveal dark hair and a tanned face with almond shaped eyes. There was no denying her beauty. The room was silent.

"That," the dark-haired woman said, "is because I did not wish to be known." She turned toward the knight commander. "And it is Sneak Thief *Queen*, if you don't mind."

"Kelly?" King Jondal asked.

She nodded her head slightly. "Jondal."

Sir Markain stepped forward. "How dare you refer to your king by his given name?"

Kelly raised her eyebrow in amusement. "He is not my king. You presume I am from this kingdom. You presume wrong. King Jondal rules in Minth. Sneak thieves are in every town, every city, on Kerr. In Minth, the Baronies, Gar-Noth, and Yaylok. I can neither confirm nor deny their presence in the Mountain Kingdom."

She ignored his open-mouthed stare and looked toward the king of the Dwarves. "We are not only human. Many different races are in the family. Some of us are…mixed.

"This may be the first and last time you ever see me." She stepped in front of King Jondal. "I am here, face to face this once, so you know my word is true. In this, we are allies. I have sent word down to every member of the family. All activities will cease, and we will focus on gathering information for the upcoming war. We will use the coin in our reserves to continue the other things we do."

"I see," King Jondal said. "Why have you come forward; why does your guild, or family as you call it, expose itself?"

"I cannot sit by while a tyrant takes all of Kerr," Kelly answered. "And…I have been compelled." She glanced at the other clergy in the room. "Change comes."

"How will you continue to get the information to me? Especially once we are on the move?"

"We have many ways, none of which I will discuss in front a roomful of others. Know what we learn, we will convey." She turned to go, stopped, turned back, and said, "I may also send you the results of our sabotage and harassment, for your own amusement."

After she walked out of the hall, Sir Markain turned to King Jondal. "Sire, are you going to let her walk away like this? She's a thief. An admitted thief."

"In these times, even the sneak thief is our ally," King Jondal said. He waved an arm, indicating the entire room. "Besides, do you think she would have entered a hall full of armed men, women, and Dwarves…a mage, and several clerics if she was worried about capture?"

"Speaking of clerics," Brother Pynon said, "I did not recognize the symbol of her pendant, but she is accepted by a deity."

"Really," King Jondal said. "Who would have thought it? A sneak thief able to use prayer spells."

"Not only prayer spells, it appears. I do not know if she has the gift, but she did have several magic items on her person," Mage Bethany added.

"Stolen, I'm sure," Sir Markain said with disdain.

"Perhaps," Brother Pynon said, "but perhaps not. Did you not see the shape of her eyes? Her skin may not have been pale, as the paintings and tapestries depict, but I believe she may be Half-Elven."

King Jondal rubbed his chin. "Sabotage. Nice." He paused for a moment in thought. "She said 'other things.' I wonder what other things her guild does besides thieving?"

* * *

Yaylok

Knight Commander Tharyeld threw his mug against the wagon. "What do you mean *all* the water is spoiled?"

The herbalist ducked her head and spoke toward the ground, "My lord, all the water barrels are full of brackish water. It cannot be used. The salt content will make your troops ill."

Tharyeld spoke through gritted teeth, "How did this happen?"

"Some time in the night, all thirty barrels had saltwater added to them. Buckets full of good water were emptied and then replaced." She hesitated and then continued, "Rotted seaweed was found in several. And a starfish…a dead starfish. Several days old, that one was."

"We haven't even begun to move north, and my company has bad water! What will it be like after weeks on the road?" the knight commander shouted. "Fix this! You should be thankful the king himself will not be traveling with us north on winter's end. If he were to taste bad water, heads would roll." He stomped off, spitting to the side occasionally.

* * *

Half an hour glass later, Sir Tharyeld wiped his mouth on his sleeve and shuddered, still tasting the water. "Now, tell me why I was summoned to a blacksmith. Be forewarned, today is not the best of days to try my patience."

"My lord," the head blacksmith said, "we're to be spending the rest o' the week making nails. We cannae shoe horses."

The knight commander gritted his teeth and counted to himself before speaking. He looked at the huge man with arms nearly the size of his thighs. This blacksmith was known to have a short temper and had spent many nights in the local jail for fighting. It didn't matter to him who his opponent was, nobility included.

"Why?" Tharyeld asked. He glanced over at his own mount, waiting in the pen with others.

"Two crates o' nails up and walked away, sure and they did," the man said. He stroked his long mustache. "Sneak thieves, I'm to be thinking. Don't know why they're to be wanting nails, but there it is."

Sir Tharyeld looked down and shook his head. "I'll assign a watch over all the forges." He walked away. "What next?" he mumbled.

* * *

The knight commander looked up. When he saw the head cook and two of his helpers, he sighed. He leaned back on the small stool he was using with his folding desk. "Tell me."

"My lord, how did you know I bring bad news?" the big man asked. He wasn't very tall, but he was large. He looked over his shoulder toward the main camp.

Sir Tharyeld followed his gaze and saw the smoke trailing upward beyond the tree line. It was a much larger and darker plume than normal. Darker by far. "What happened?"

"My lord, four of the kitchen wagons we brought from Gar-Noth are burned beyond repair," the man said. He wiped his hands on his dirty apron nervously. "We may be able to salvage the base and axles on one, but it will need two wagon wheels, I'm sure."

"How?" Sir Tharyeld asked. He was beyond shouting today.

"Someone replaced the cooking oil with a mix of something I've never seen. It didn't even begin to smoke before the pans burst into raging flames. It's a wonder no one was seriously hurt."

"There is that, I suppose," the knight commander agreed. "When we move north, I'll not want inexperienced chefs cooking the soldiers' meals." He grimaced. "Notify the local wainwright and have him build replacement wagons. If not, we resort to cooking over an open fire on the ground, like when I was a page."

He turned to his nearest squire. "Summon the commanders. I want to know if this has been happening to all the units."

As the squire walked away, he said to himself, "We will defeat the Minth armies, but the people themselves? Days like this make me glad I'm not the one trying to rule when it's all said and done."

* * * * *

Chapter Twenty-Three

Three Oaks

Western Borderlands

Lucas folded his large arms across his stomach. "There ye have it, my lord. King Westell aims to rule all."

"Enough of the 'my lord' business. Any friend of my grandsons' is a friend of mine. Call me Jynal."

"Aye. I'll do it. But to be honest with ye, it's more a kinship I feel for the lads than friendship, as the trip we took with Saint Lanae makes it feel as if we spent years together," Lucas said.

Jynal looked to his daughter. She nodded her head in affirmation. When Lucas had told them they'd met the goddess, she'd prayed for confirmation. There was no denying the answer she'd received, and she let all in the room know it. Lucas spoke the truth.

"I, for one, am glad the lord mage met his fate. Knowing now what he did to my family, I would leave on the morn to send him to it if he hadn't," Jynal said. Hearing what had happened to his daughter-in-law at the Halls of Magic—and what had happened to the entire family—had been hard on him. Hard on all in the room, even those who had heard it before.

"I'm to be believing you, good sir," Johan said. "And I would have crossed the world again to be with ye."

"Thank you," Jynal said.

"So what do we do now?" Sethon asked. "Do ye think the Orc tribes will join us in the fight?"

"'Tis a good question," Jynal said. "I will say this. The Western Borderlands will join. You say the mayor in Midpoint is already gathering those he can provision to march east? He is a good man. We will do the same here in Three Oaks." He turned to his daughter's husband. "Call a meeting for noon the day after tomorrow. Send word across the land to all the villages and crossroads."

"By now Zane and Penae will have been contacted by their cousins from Tarlok," Lucas said. "I've no doubt they will head this way to learn more."

"With more hunters in tow, you can be sure," Jynal agreed, "once they gather them."

"I will leave now," Lur said as he stood to leave. He stopped and looked to his wife, the communication between them a look of understanding. "Make a list of the herbs and things you will need." She nodded and smiled.

"What was that all about?" Marn asked after he left.

"I am a shaman of faith," Katheen explained, "and an herbalist healer. My husband knows, as the shaman of Three Oaks, I will go with them and support them in the upcoming fight, to heal the injured with prayer spells and other means. I must."

"I wish I could go with you," Jynal said. He slammed a fist on the table.

"You cannot, Father," Katheen said quietly. "Time rolls on for us all. The Goddess Lan makes no exceptions. War is no place for a grandfather of your age. Nor can Lur. His leg was healed by the gift of the gods many years ago, but he knows he cannot fight on it. He will stay here, with you and the others who will not be going, to help the women and children continue to farm."

* * *

They spent the next two days in Three Oaks, resting and getting the kinks out of their bodies from the long trip they'd taken. Jynal insisted they stay with him. He had a spare cabin on his farm for such occasions. On a walk to stretch his legs, Lucas went to both the waterfall he had seen released on the night of his travels with Kryder, Tog, and the Goddess Saint Lanae, and the spot where Kryder's parents were killed. The images were still fresh in his mind, and it put him in a solemn mood.

"There's to be much on yer mind, old friend," Johan said. "Are ye in need of an ear?"

Lucas gave him a tight smile and said, "No. I'm afraid it is nothing that can be worked out by talking. What bothers me happened nigh on twenty years ago. It's seeing the very places that stirs it up."

"I can imagine," Johan said. "To be honest with ye, there are places I didn't return to in Yaylok. Lost a few o' me friends in battles there, when I was younger and me hair wasn't near this shade."

They both sat in silence for a minute.

"Those are the things that shape a man's life," Lucas added.

"Aye," Johan agreed. "That it does. Speaking of which, Jynal says we are to enter Orcanth in the morning and make our way to the Red Fist Tribe's village. Are ye sure that's what we're needing to be doing?"

"I'm sure," Lucas answered. "We need everyone to fight against King Westell's forces. That includes me distant kin. I have to at least try. Jynal agrees. That's why he's going with us."

"Will we be running?" Johan asked. "That type o' thing is for young men, and the three young men I lead will be staying here in town."

"Sister Katheen says we will walk," Lucas said. "Her father does not need to run such as that. She and her husband, on the other hand, I believe could run the entire morning."

"That's to be a relief," Johan said. "Else Sister Katheen would be praying over my dying body after half an hour's glass or so."

Lucas laughed. "Yer not the only one; me and me boys would be right there with ye, huffing and puffing."

* * *

The next morning, they crossed the creek and stepped into Orcanth. Less than ten minutes later, the closest group on patrol made themselves known. They moved beside them several feet off the trail. They were not only there because they were suspicious of the Human in armor, they were also there to ensure one of their shamans, Jynal, and those traveling with them were safe from the creatures of the forest. Twice they peeled off, only to come back less than a half hour later.

The entire morning, Katheen led the way, holding Julia's hand. They stopped often to ensure Lucas, his daughter, and his sons had plenty of rest. Walking for four hours was not something they normally did. The vast majority of their long trip had been seated. Though he spent his time on horseback these days, the walk didn't bother Johan as much as running might have.

When they finally came into the clearing and could see the cabins ahead, Lucas noticed a welcoming committee waited. In front of them was a large Orc with red leather bracers on his forearms. He had the tip of a huge axe peeking over one shoulder. Lucas recognized him. He was Sar, son of Pon, Tog's other grandfather, and now chief of the Red Fist Tribe. Beside him was a female Orc with grey hair, the head Red Fist shaman.

Jynal reached out and clasped forearms with the big Orc and said, "My chief."

"My lord," Sar replied.

They both grinned at each other. As a member of the Red Fist Tribe, Sar was indeed Jynal's chief. At the same time, Sar was the current Lord of the Axe, a noble in Lord Jynal's barony. This and the fact the two were the best of friends always made them smile when referring to each other's titles.

"A warrior arrived this morning, say you coming with guests," Sar said. "You honor me by coming to our village. Think must be im-por-tant. That big word. I like it."

Jynal turned to Lucas and introduced him to Sar. He then introduced Marn, Sethon, and Julia. He introduced Johan as their friend and traveling companion.

"You are welcome here," Sar said. "Come with Jynal, no problem enter Orcanth."

Katheen stepped up. Sar acknowledged her with a toothy smile. She was not only a member of the Red Fist Tribe, she was the Three Oaks shaman, and the one who had healed his son Lur. As much reverence as he had for her as a shaman, one he would listen to for advice like all shamans, she was also his daughter-in-law and the mother of his oldest grandson. She spoke to him in fluent Orcish.

"Chief of Red Fist, Tog, son of Lur, son of the chief, acknowledges Lucas is of the blood, and proclaimed him of the Red Fist Tribe. Kryder witnessed this. It has been said. It is so. I inform you as shaman to her chief, a member of the Tribal Council. The council must be informed upon the next meeting."

Lucas heard Katheen say Tog's name and understood she was telling him about Tog's claim. He reached into a pouch on his belt and pulled out the piece of leather with the emblem of the Red Fist on it. He waited to hear what came next.

Sar glanced toward the grey-haired shaman. She nodded once in acknowledgement of her sister shaman. Sar turned to Lucas and his family. He held out his hand for the piece of leather and turned it over a few times in his big hands, deep in thought.

"I give this to Tog," he said, "when he become full warrior. He give to you. Tells me much. He say you of the blood. He say you Red Fist Tribe. My grandson great warrior. Smart, like his mother." He nodded his big head toward Katheen. "He say, I accept. Council will know."

Sar reached out and clasped Lucas's forearm in the greeting of Orcs. "You member of tribe. Your family members also of tribe." He handed the piece of leather back. He clasped forearms with Sethon and Marn. When he turned to Julia, she ducked slightly, but allowed Sar to pat her gently on the shoulder as she leaned against Katheen.

He turned to Johan. "You are Human warrior. I see this. Armor, sword, knives. All this you wear in comfort. Is good. Travel many days with Red Fist members. This is good, too. I say you are ally of Red Fist by deed. Will give tribal symbol. Travel Orcanth, no problems other tribes."

"Thank you," Johan said. He hadn't expected to be part of the interaction. "Do I call you chief…or my lord?"

"This good question," Sar said. He reached up and rubbed his chin. "I am Lord Sar to Humans. Is good title, but I think Jynal not like titles. Is his barony. You call me Sar.

"Come," Sar said. He clapped his hands, the sound sharp. "Tribe has new members. We feast."

"There is more," Katheen said. "Lucas has much more to tell you. As we eat, I will translate, so it is fully understood."

Sar stopped and looked at Katheen. The tone of her voice was different. "This you say as shaman. Is im-por-tant. Come. Sit before fire. I will listen as meat is cooked. Not wait until eat."

* * *

Sar stood and paced in front of the large fire pit. "Tog and Kryder kill those who murder Kryder's family. Is good. If not…I go into Human lands and find. Do same. Honor demands."

"Aye," Johan agreed. "Like I told Jynal, I would go with you."

Sar looked at the aged soldier for a long moment, his respect growing for the man. "I believe this. Tells me you strong ally. Live long as warrior makes me believe you good with sword. Would be honored to spar."

While he was standing there, a tall man came running into the village. His face resembled a younger version of Jynal. He was dressed in leather and fur as an Orc warrior, yet he had a Tarlok hunter's antler-handled knife strapped to his thigh, and his leather was colored the browns and greens of hunters. At his sides were two long handled hand axes, and he had a bow and quiver on his back. These weapons were clearly Orcish made.

He stopped and walked around the fire pit several times with his hands behind his head, catching his breath.

"Tired?" Sar asked. "After only a half day's running?"

"Yes, chief," Teel answered in Orcish. "I came from the hunter's lands on the far side of the prairie. I left my horse in Three Oaks with Lur. Too much time on my horse lately, not enough running. I will change that."

Sar laughed, then turned to Lucas and the rest. "Jynal's son, Teel. He is great warrior, skilled with axe and bow, but needs work on running. Tires easy these days."

Jynal introduced Teel to the others. "You look a lot different when you're not chasing chickens and tossing them in the stream," Lucas remarked.

"What? I..." Teel started to say. "How do you know? Did my mom tell you? Great." He looked toward his older sister, Katheen. "Or was it my sister?"

"I watched you," Lucas said.

"I came here as fast as I could...to hear of the coming war," Teel said. "But now I want to know how you could have seen me do that first. That had to be twenty-five, maybe thirty years ago? These days my wife, Gab, keeps our children from chasing chickens in Three Oaks...or here, depending on where we're staying at the time."

A female Orc walked over, leading two Half-Orcs, a girl and a boy. Their mother was smaller than the other females Lucas had seen around the village, but she was still almost six feet tall. Teel ruffled the hair on the boy's head and waited for Lucas to answer.

"Sure and I would be happy to tell ye later," Lucas said. "But I've passed that part o' me story and am now getting to the part about the war and the Elves."

"War?" the chief asked. "Elves?"

*****

Chapter Twenty-Four

Zar

Mraynith looked around in disgust. Even praying to a different demon hadn't brought the Elf the results he wanted. The Dark Prince Slavonne had not answered. He kicked the lifeless body. It did nothing to ease his anger, so he turned to the Elf who had brought the Human child to him. As a lesser Elf, her lot in life was to be a keeper of Humans. The look of horror on her face enraged him even more. It showed him she actually cared for those in her charge.

He raised a hand and spoke. Darts of light shot from his hand and struck the keeper in the chest. They burned through the faded dress, and the Elf fell, screaming until she couldn't as she lost the ability to breathe from damaged lungs. She died, thrashing, as the Elven mage stared without compassion.

"Take them both away," he ordered and tossed his dagger on his desk. The low-level mages scrambled to do his bidding.

Mraynith turned the pages on his partial Book Of The One. "I must find a demon who will aid me," he said out loud. He was now the only one present, so no one heard him…where he was.

* * *

The Fiery Pits

Zargall looked up. Up through the rocks and dirt. Up into the world of mortals. He looked around himself to ensure none of the others had found him. He was tired of it. Tired of the running, of hiding, trying to avoid most other demons. There were those who ridiculed and harassed him unmercifully, until they tired and moved on to do other things.

For an immortal, it was never long enough. They always seemed to find him again to torture him in unspeakable ways. It had always been so. They enjoyed preying on the weak, and he, like the rest of the demons, could not die from it.

He heard Mraynith; he'd been waiting on this. He had heard, from the darkest depths and pits of fire, one who was willing to risk all to surpass the stronger demons. One willing to do anything to become a demon prince…no, the demon king. There were ways he could aid the Elf. Even with the example of Demon Prince Lethrall, he did not care. It took decades before the Creator intervened. There were ways the Elf could aid him to help him grow stronger. Strong enough to throw off his tormentors. He didn't care what the far future held. He wanted it now. He accepted Mraynith. After all, even demons had free will.

* * *

Above the Northern Desert

"So anyway, Zeronic said, like us, they had free will," Dolner said. "They decided not to eat us, and we ended up as Riders."

"Though we don't really know what it entails," June said. "Us, or the Dragons. I mean, besides riding them."

Kryder looked past Dolner as he spoke. Both Dragons waited calmly, their great heads resting on crossed forelimbs as they lay there. He suspected one was translating for the other with a whispering hiss. "Wait, so you can speak their language because it's close to the Lython's, or because the Lython's is close to theirs?"

"I…wait. What?" Dolner asked.

"Never mind," Kryder said. "It's not important. It's probably the same language, and the Lythons have changed it slightly after being away from Dragons for so long. Tell me the rest."

"Well," Dolner said, "my understanding of the language was a gift from Zeronic, like Moonlitdune mentioned. I understand them because I'm accepted as a cleric of Zeronic, and a Rider."

"A cleric!" Tog said. "You are *so* going to have to learn to read.

"And a Rider?" Tog asked after a second or two.

"Well, June is, too," Dolner said. "Only she's accepted by Saint Minokath and Saint Harnette. She's still a Rider for Zeronic, though. It's kind of confusing."

"Riders," Moonlitdune said. "There have been no Riders for many, many years. To most, they were but rumors. Stories told to younglings."

"But you know different, my dear," the Sultan of Sands said. "Tell them."

"There is a scroll, barely legible, which speaks of them," Moonlitdune said. "Human Riders rode upon the backs of Dragons. They fought together. Some of the images show Dragons breathing fire and other things. I do not know what, but it was not flames in the drawings. There are more than Red Dragons depicted. Anyway, some show Riders with bows, others with spears. The images are faint, but you can see them."

"There must be some kind of saddle shown in them," June said, "because we almost fell off Wryle when he carried us back down here."

"You could have ridden me," Lyna called out in the Human language. "I am perfectly fine now."

"I know, Lyna," June admitted, "I was just worried it was too soon. But you're right, I should have." She nodded her head sideways to indicate Dolner and Wryle. "Those two together make me nervous."

"You might as well get used to it," Lyna advised with a rumbling chuckle. "Wryle accepted him as a Rider. They are now a fighting pair, like you and I, when I accepted you."

"Oh, I don't mind fighting," June said. "Actually, I like it. But it's all about precise strikes and angles of attack. It seemed like Wryle went full speed, straight ahead, and Dolner encouraged it when we left the ground."

"Males," Lyna said, as if the word explained all.

"Wait," Kryder said. "Accepted? So you two are the first Riders in hundreds of years? Whatever that entails. We can use all the help we can get, but I don't want you falling off, Dolner."

"The images do depict a saddle," Moonlitdune said. "Perhaps there are some in the caves."

Dolner's knees buckled, so June grabbed him and held him up. "Are you all right?"

"Yes," Dolner said. "I saw an image. There are rows of saddles somewhere. The room was large. It opened to a wide courtyard, I think. Or a rooftop. The walls were an orange color, maybe red."

"The fortress," the Lython shaman said. "You call it the Mage's Library. It has walls of this color. The stone doors are closed and sealed. No one can enter."

"Well," Tog said, "*we* will. We need to get moving. We waited a day for these two to come back down with their new friends. There are more than books and scrolls in that place. I'm glad they brought something to eat but time is passing. Before you know it, Lan will bring the springtime to the world."

"He is right," Sylif agreed. "Saint Lanae waits for no one. We need to go to the fortress. It's not getting any closer as we sit here."

The chief of the Lython nodded his head and jumped to the back of his mount. He had listened closely as Lyna translated for Wryle. He spoke some of the few words he knew in Human, "We go." He turned to one of his warriors and hissed, "Go to the villages. Have others send word. We will join our neighbors in this fight, and we will fight alongside the Gnomes. We will have a war council in three days in the shade of the fortress. "

***

Orcanth

It took three days to reach the location of the tribal council. Johan, Lucas, and his family traveled with Sar, Jynal, Teel, the Red Fist shamans, and a handful of warriors. Other warriors had gone ahead the first morning to the nearest tribes. They, in turn, had sent warriors on to their closest tribes. By the time the group traveled from the Red Fist village, the nine other chiefs were there for the meeting Sar had called. As members of the council, they represented their tribes and their sub-tribes.

There was a stir and murmurs when those gathered noticed those Sar brought with them. The loudest came from Yan, the chief of the Running Boars. "You have brought Humans to the council grounds? This is not right. It is not the first time Red Fist have done this, Sar."

"The last time, my father brought Kryder, a shaman. Human or not, he is a member of Red Fist. Your father voted for it with the others," Sar replied.

"My father is no longer chief of the Running Boar," Yan said. "He runs the trails in the eternal hunting grounds."

"With mine," Sar said. "There is no feud there."

"There is here," Yan said. He turned and walked away.

* * *

Once the meeting began, Sar explained why he'd called it, as was his right as chief of a major tribe. He explained what was happening outside the border of Orcanth. Lucas could not speak and remained outside the ring of seated chiefs with his family and the warriors of Red Fist. As had been explained to them, only chiefs or shamans could speak in the council circle. It was a rule that was sacred. Glances were made their way as the meeting went on.

Several times Katheen helped Sar answer when questions were asked. She was known by all Orcs as one of their most powerful, if not *the* most powerful, shaman of faith. Kryder, though not present, was undoubtedly the most powerful shaman of magic ever known to Orcs. When she spoke, like her nephew, all the chiefs listened intently, even the chief of the Running Boar.

When the news was given and all questions answered about King Westell and the Elves, Sar called for a vote on joining the king of

Minth and his allies, most likely including the Dwarves, in a war against the tyrant. As in all things brought before the council, the vote would have to be unanimous. He voted 'yes' first. He was followed quickly by the chiefs of the Fang, the White Sands, and the Night Stalkers. Several other chiefs talked among themselves and ended up deciding collectively. They all voted yes.

There were eight votes yes, with two chiefs still to decide. The chief of the Long Sticks, Nax, stood up and said, "Sar, you are asking us to send all our warriors to the land of Humans to fight against other Humans. If this were all, I would vote no—but Elves are involved. This fact troubles me, yet I am still hesitant to vote yes.

"My tribe's lands cover the coast north and west of all of Orcanth. The shamans tell me the etchings speak of a time we dealt with Dwarves, but not for many years now. We have not dealt with Humans, or…ever seen Humans, except here, once before today. The one pure Human we have seen is Kryder, the Red Fist shaman of great magic. He gives me hope in the abilities of Humans, but I have not seen one fight. Do they have the skills to stand beside an Orc warrior in battle? Will they fight with honor, or will they admit defeat before they are truly defeated? These are things I must know before I vote."

Sar stood and said, "I believe the Humans we will stand beside will fight with honor. Though too old now to fight, Jynal was once a soldier. This is what they call their warriors. He has great honor. The Humans plan now to go into battle against an enemy with greater numbers than theirs. This takes honor and courage. One of their soldiers is here. He is an ally of Red Fist by deed. He will spar with one of your warriors here…now."

"Now?" Nax asked. "Yes. I would see one spar. Clear the circle. Bring the wooden weapons, and let the warriors choose."

Sar walked out of the circle and over to Johan. "The chief of Long Sticks not vote. Wants see Human warrior fight before voting. I say you spar. Come, pick weapon."

"Wait. What?" Johan asked. "I'm to be sparring here…now?"

"I am afraid so," Katheen said. "Nax wants to see if Humans can stand beside Orcs and fight honorably."

"And just what's that to be meaning?" Johan asked. "Is he saying Humans may be cowards? Is that what ye are telling me?" He started unbuckling his sword belt. He handed it to Lucas. "Some are, I'll grant ye. I'm not to be one o' them."

"No," Katheen reassured him. "He didn't say that. He said he didn't know."

"I'll do it," Marn said. He rolled his shoulders in anticipation.

"No, let me at him," Sethon insisted. He cracked his knuckles. "Who is it?"

"Is good," Sar said. "Both Lucas's sons want fight. This is how Red Fist warrior think. But you are of the blood. Nax want see pure Human fight."

"Boys," Johan said, "settle down, the both of ye. You stay here with yer father. Wooden weapons are to be used, so I don't have to be holding back, like when we spar. And…if I'm to be honest, I'm a bit mad at the moment. I feel as though *my* skills are being questioned, not all Humans. Besides, it's not the first time I've been challenged, to be sure."

* * *

Four warriors brought out wooden weapons from one of the cabins on the edge of the open field. Most were axes. There were several spears, including one with a dull wooden blade on the end. The Long Stick warrior chose it and glanced toward Johan, sizing him up. Johan could tell the young warrior was surprised by his age. Johan looked the weapons over and chose the only longsword in the group. It wasn't actually a longsword to an Orc, but it was nearly the same length as his own.

Still not sure if he was allowed to speak, Johan held his hand up with a motion to show he needed a moment. The Orc nodded. Johan stepped over to Lucas and took a dagger from its sheath on his sword belt. Without asking, he trimmed the handle down quickly until it was the same width as the one on his own sword. When he stepped back in front of the Orc, the warrior nodded his approval at Johan ensuring he was comfortable with his weapon.

They slowly circled, feeling each other's movement out. The Orc spun his bladed spear several times on each side of him, getting the feel of it. Johan rolled his wrist, looping the sword around, checking its balance. Suddenly the Orc struck with a straight thrust toward Johan's chest. With a flick of his wrist, Johan parried the blow and spun inside to slap the arm of the warrior with the flat of his blade, surprising everyone but those who knew his skill with a sword.

Testing his opponent, Johan used several combinations of blows. All were blocked by the shaft of the spear. Johan nodded to the Orc to let him know he was impressed. The young warrior rubbed his sore forearm and grinned, letting Johan know the same. They continued to circle.

The Orc used a series of thrusts and slashes as he attempted to get through Johan's defenses, but even with the longer reach of his bladed spear, he was unable to do so. Johan heard mumbling among those watching. The old sergeant's next series of blows caused his larger opponent to step back several paces as he blocked them. The whispers grew louder.

Several more times their weapons clashed in skilled combinations, with neither touching the other. Johan felt himself tiring, but he kept his breathing even, ensuring his opponent didn't know age was a factor in the sparring session. Realizing he'd better end it soon, Johan waited for his moment. It came sooner than he'd expected.

The Orc feinted with a slashing motion and thrust the spear straight at Johan's face. Johan moved his head in time and struck the ribs under the farthest extended arm. He pulled back and let the tip of the blade travel across the Orc's stomach to his other side. When the Orc flinched and leaned toward the struck side from the pain of the blow, Johan moved his head again to avoid the slower pull back by the Orc as he attempted to slice Johan with the wooden blade.

The Orc grimaced again, and Johan knew he had him confused. In his opponent's hesitation, the old sergeant brought his sword back the other way and struck a blow with the flat side of his blade on the Orc's jaw and ear. Johan hoped the blow would affect the Orc as it would a Human, so he put all he had into it to be sure. The warrior's knees buckled, and he dropped. The spear lay on the ground. There was a collective gasp.

Johan stepped up to the Orc, stuck the tip of his blade in the ground to give himself more leverage with three points of contact, and offered his free hand to help his opponent up. The young Orc's head cleared some. He looked up, showed his full incisors in a wide grin, and took the hand. Once he was standing, he shook his head to clear it all the way, looked down at Johan, and reached out his own hand. It was the forearm grasp of an Orc warrior. Without saying a word, they nodded once to each other again, gathered their weapons, and walked in opposite directions out of the council circle.

"Long Sticks vote yes," Nax said loudly.

* * *

There was one vote left. Yan, chief of the Running Boars. He stood and said, "Long ago, the Running Boars raided Human lands without council approval. The chief who decided this brought dishonor on my tribe. He was killed in the raid. He had no sons, only a daughter mated to my ancestor. Our tribe was moved from the border. The new chief vowed to never leave Orcanth. I honor his vow."

He looked around the circle and his gaze stopped on Sar.

"Running Boar votes…No."

* * * * *

Chapter Twenty-Five

Above the Northern Desert

"No," Kryder answered. "No, I don't."

He glanced up, along with Tog, looking for the two Dragons, but could not see them. Dolner, beside him, noticed and did the same.

"I don't see them either, but I know they're up there," Dolner said. "They really can blend in when they want to."

"Lyna tells me they won't do it if they are in battle or around other Dragons," June said. "They stay their natural color. She said Wryle is especially proud he is... *of the flames*."

"I do not blame him," Sylif said. "Hide not. It is written in The Book Of The One."

"Sometimes it is smart to conceal yourself until more is known," Sandwinkle said. He glanced toward his wife.

"You have a point," Sylif agreed. "Perhaps it is not meant the way I suggested. I mean in battle."

They rounded several hills, traveling along the river. The scattered grasses gave way to more dirt, but this dirt was darker than the sands of the desert they'd first entered. Off in the distance, beside the deeper canyons of the river, was a huge fortress. The sands leading up to it continued to change color like the gorge the water now ran through. It grew from several shades of orange to an almost red color. Kryder knew, deep down, he was looking at the Mage's library.

He pulled up on his reins and stared. The others with him did the same, except Tog, who stopped walking.

"It's big," Dolner remarked.

The Lython continued moving toward the fortress on their lizard mounts. "We need to catch up," Kryder suggested after a moment. "I think it looks closer than it is."

"That's all you had to say," Tog said. He broke into a sprint, his long strides eating up the distance.

* * *

Jonrig's Delight

"Mang pod in the distance! Dead ahead. They're moving a bit starboard," the sailor shouted from the crow's nest high above. "The biggest pod I ever saw! Looks to be at least four hands worth, Cap'n."

"Good eyes, Narvel," Captain Barl Jonrig called up and turned to his first mate. "Close it up, Brother Granby."

"Aye, Cap'n," Granby said. He turned the big wheel slightly and shouted orders for the crew to trim the sails in an attempt to move faster across the rolling swells.

"Do ye think we anger Saint Minokath, taking so many this year?" Barl asked in a low voice. Sailors were a superstitious lot, and he didn't want to start rumors among them.

Granby pursed his lips and reached for his necklace of shells. "No, Cap'n. It's been on my mind of late, so I asked in my prayers last night. It was one of the few times the Lord of the Seas gave me a plain answer. 'The gifts given are part of our Creator's plan, my son. Use them well.'"

The ship's first mate and layman cleric turned to Barl, his eyes glistening, and said, "I may not have a proper church or congregation, but he reminded me that he accepted me long ago."

Barl placed his hand on the man's shoulder. He looked around at the men moving about their business with vigor as the ship gained on the Mang pod, the men entrusting him and his officers to run the ship well. He took in the ship itself, the billowing sails, the freshly scrubbed deck—his pride and joy. He saw the spray of the sea coming up over the wooden rail of the bow. And lastly, he gazed at the sea itself in all its glory.

"This ship is your pulpit. The sea is your church. This crew…this crew, and several others when we're in port, are your congregation. For most of them, yours are the only words they hear of our Creator, Saint Minokath, and from The Book Of The One. Every swaying man aboard this ship has seen your prayer spells work. Just yesterday, we all saw the healing blue glow when young Davey's arm was bent like the lad had an extra elbow."

He turned to look the man in the eye. "There is not a man on this vessel who doubts you have been accepted, Granby. Never doubt it yourself."

* * *

Mage's Library

"I doubt it," Kryder said. "It's too high."

"Well, the entrance is locked," Tog said, "with no locks to be seen. I could work on it with my axe, but it would take forever to cut through the stone. Not to mention what it will do to the blade."

"Don't," Kryder said. "It's not worth destroying your axe. But like I said, there's no way I can levitate that high. It's twice as high as the cliff I sent Dolner and June up."

"I have no prayer spell in my book that will take me up there," Brother Sylif said. "Moonlitdune?"

"I'm afraid I don't, either," the cleric of Zeronic answered. She turned to the Lython shaman.

"Do not," he admitted. "All Lython shaman share prayer spells. The marks not in our scrolls."

"This is ridiculous," June said. She put her hands on her hips and looked straight up. "We know these doors have been opened before." She looked down at her feet. She swept a boot across the stone. "There is a worn line in the stone where both doors swing open. It's plain as day."

"Yeah," Dolner agreed, "but, how do we get it open?"

"We haven't heard from Lyna and Wryle," June said. "Maybe they landed up top somewhere."

"We could get them to fly us up, and maybe come down into the fortress, and open the doors from the inside," Dolner suggested. "Only how do we get their attention?"

"I say we set camp," Tog suggested. "We can start a fire and cook the rest of the big goat Wryle brought us. They'll come back down eventually."

"I'm with you," Dolner agreed. "I bet the rest of the Lythons are, too. It feels good here in the shade."

"It's still hot," June said. "You only think it's cooler because your mind tells you it is. Trust me. In this armor, I'm still hot."

"That's it!" Kryder said. He walked closer to the great doors.

"What?" Tog asked. "Goat droppings, you can be so confusing sometimes."

"We don't *think* we see handles or a lock or anything because our minds tell us there isn't one."

"I think you need to spend more time in the shade," Tog said. "None of that makes sense."

Kryder raised his hand and spoke the words to dispel another caster's spell. A handle appeared on each door. He reached up and pulled. The door he was pulling on wouldn't budge.

"Droppings!" Tog said. "They were there all the time. I wonder if we'd felt for them would we have found them?" He turned to his cousin. "Why couldn't you see the glow or whatever it is you see when something is magic? Let me try."

Tog grabbed the other handle and pulled. The door wouldn't move. He put his foot against the other door and put all his strength into it. Still there was no movement.

"Maybe we should both try," Kryder said.

"No," Tog said. "I put all I had into it. They're not going to open."

"Maybe we could pray about it," Dolner suggested. "I mean, Zeronic told me to wing it. I don't think I need a prayer spell specifically for it."

"You can try," Tog said. "Kryder and I have seen my mama unlock a spring from deep within a hillside."

Dolner stepped up to the doors. When he got close, a section above one of the handles shimmered, and then revealed a keyhole. It matched the end of the keys he had in a pouch on his belt. He looked at Kryder in disbelief. He stepped back, and the keyhole faded. It came back into view when he got close again.

Dolner reached into his pouch and pulled out one of the keys. He inserted it in the keyhole and turned. The key turned easily, and a loud sound inside the doors could be heard. He shrugged, pulled out the key, and put it back in his pouch. Kryder pulled on a handle again, and the door swung outward easily. The only indication that it hadn't opened in a long time was the squeal the hidden rollers made on the stones.

"Why couldn't I see the red glow of magic?" Kryder asked, repeating Tog's question.

"It doesn't make sense," Brother Sylif agreed. "It took a key with the symbol of Zeronic to open it. I see the glow of the stone in the key, but not on the keyhole or the door."

"I didn't either," Moonlitdune added, "and I am Zeronic's high priestess. I suspect the keyhole would not have shown without you dispelling the illusion first. Whoever built this fortress used a spell unknown, perhaps several."

Kryder stepped into a wide hall, followed by the others. He looked up. Near the ceiling were globes of light in groups of three. They hung motionless. *Permanent.* Like the outside, the inside walls and floor were of the same solid rock, reddish in color.

He glanced into the first two openings. Each contained dust-covered tables and chairs, plainly visible due to lights floating in the rooms. The rooms reminded him of those in the Halls of Justice. They passed two more sets of doorways on each side. Up ahead, the passageway met another hall going left and right, and ended at a wall. The light shining from both directions looked to be different than what was emitted from the globes. It looked more like natural light.

"It's kind of…well, it feels strange," Dolner said in a low voice.

"We are the first to walk these halls in hundreds of years," Brother Sylif whispered. "And I agree. It feels odd."

"We not come inside after no more Riders," the Lython shaman said. "The etchings tell us Lython guard for many years. After no see Dragon, still guard."

"If you didn't come inside," Dolner asked in the language of the Lython, "where were your shamans who were...spared the attack of the Elves?"

"There was once a village and temple on the side of fortress," the Lython chief answered. "I have seen the ruins. Once gate was shut and locked, that was where guards stayed, and shamans trained."

"So you never came inside?" Dolner asked. "Lythons, not you yourself, I mean."

The shaman shook his head. "No, not true. Before the gates closed, Lython, Gnomes, and Humans all came inside."

"What are you saying?" June asked. "Nobody else understands them."

"They say before it was locked, everyone could come and go through the doors." Dolner explained. "So it's written, anyway."

"That means we will find some type of barracks, rooms, more classrooms, and the library itself somewhere in here," Kryder said.

"The chief has his warriors guarding the door now," Tog said, "so nothing will follow us in. We're not going to find out anything about this place standing here. I say we go up to the intersection and pick a direction."

"If we see stairs, we should go up," June said. "I want to see how Lyna is doing. It hasn't been many days since she laid eggs."

"We'll make our way there," Kryder agreed, "after we find the actual library."

"We could split up," June suggested.

"What?" Tog asked. "Split up? What's wrong with you? Have you never sat around the fire on a moonless night telling stories? When they split up in an abandoned place or an unknown stretch of forest, someone always goes missing."

"Or worse," Sylif added.

"We're not doing that," Dolner said. "I'm blond. They always get killed in those stories."

"Don't be ridiculous," June said. "They're only stories. The next thing you'll tell me is of haunted castles. I don't believe in those, either."

"If I told you a week ago you would meet Dragons and find out they were thinking, intelligent beings with free will, would you have believed that?" Kryder asked with a straight face.

"You're not helping," Dolner said. "Not at all." He looked around suspiciously. "We are *not* splitting up."

At the end of the hall, the reason for the brighter light was revealed. To the left and right, both halls were lined with windows opening to a large inner courtyard. Kryder could see all the buildings that lined the inner wall of the fortress. The wall making up the rear towered above the roof on the far side. Opposite the windows were several doors like the main hall they'd come from.

On the far ends, both sides ended in a stairwell. "Which way?" Kryder asked.

Tog looked both ways, then turned his attention to the courtyard. "Look. Up on the left. Is that a...yes, I saw red. The Dragons have landed on top of the building."

"Where?" June asked. "I don't see them."

"They're up there," Tog said. "I have almost two feet on you. I could pick you up so you can see. You won't catch a glimpse from down there. No offense."

"I believe you," June said.

"Looks like we go the other way," Kryder said.

They checked doors as they went and discovered bed chambers and large rooms lined with bunks. Kryder led the way up the stairs to a large door. It was locked but had no keyhole. Dolner held one of the keys near it, but no hole revealed itself.

Kryder held a hand out and spoke the words to cancel another's spell. He felt resistance. He kept his hand up and pushed into the spell, harder and harder, then he felt the pressure suddenly stop. "It's unlocked," he said. "Whatever is on the other side was well protected by a powerful spell."

"I don't like it," Tog said. He readied his axe.

"I felt something," Moonlitdune said. "Something not quite right."

"I feel it too, Sister," Sylif said. He reached for his bracelet.

Kryder looked back at Dolner and June. June reached up and rubbed one of her earlobes. Dolner shook his hand as if he'd injured his wrist. A shadow blocked some of the light from the windows lining the stairwell on the courtside. Everyone turned to see what had caused it. Kryder's eyes widened when he saw Lyna hovering with mighty flaps of her wings, her neck stretched toward them, head tilted in puzzlement.

"Don't open it," Kryder said. He reached up and pulled his cousin's hand away from the handle before he could touch it.

"We need to know what's on the other side of this door," Tog countered. "I'm not letting you go through first."

"I was thinking of casting a spell and raising a shield first," Kryder said, "but I don't think it would do any good. We have to let them go first."

"Who?" Tog asked. "Not Dolner...or June. He's not ready for this, and I'm supposed to be teaching her. She's in my charge or whatever."

"Let me go first," Moonlitdune said. "Brother Sylif right behind me."

"That will not be happening," Sandwinkle said. "As the Sultan of Sands, I forbid it."

Hrafarth stepped forward and hissed low. The Lython shaman had been translating as fast as he could, so he understood what was happening. The chief of the Lythons shook his big lizard-like head and motioned for the others to let him pass.

"He says his honor will not allow a female to go first and put herself in danger. Especially not a Speaker for Zeron," Dolner translated.

Moonlitdune placed her hand on Sandwinkle's face, looked into his eyes, and said, without looking Dolner's way, "Tell him that is why I must go first. I am the high priestess of Zeronic. What is beyond this door gives me a sense of unease I have never felt. All of us here who have been accepted feel it, to one degree or another. Even Lyna, there in the courtyard, feels it."

She pursed her lips. "I must go first."

* * * * *

Chapter Twenty-Six

Moonlitdune opened her eyes and said, "Turn the handle and push it open. I am ready. Make sure you step back."

Kryder nodded to his cousin. Tog put his hand on the handle and snatched it back. "It's cold."

"Cold?" she asked. "Here? Even in the halls of this place, the desert lets us know it is near." She placed her hand on the wood of the door. "It is cool. The handle must be cold because it is iron."

"It holds it," Sylif said, "like armor on a cool night."

"Well, I hate the cold," Tog said. "Get ready."

He reached past the two clerics again, turned the handle, and shoved the door open. It swung slowly and came to a stop against the wall inside. The room was dark, the only light streaming from behind them through the doorway. Cold air rolled out of the room down low, near their feet. Moonlitdune stepped into the room, the arm with her bracelet held high. Sylif followed close behind, his hammer in one hand, his other hand held high like hers. Both glowed softly.

Kryder spoke the words to bring light, and eight globes appeared, spread out inside the room near the ceiling. One bounced off an invisible barrier and floated back toward them. At almost the same instant, a snarling beast threw itself against the same barrier and bounced back. It howled in rage and stayed crouched, ready to spring again.

"A demon!" Sylif shouted.

Once again it sprang toward them, only to strike something and fall back. By this time Kryder, Tog, and Hrafarth were in the room. Sandwinkle followed closely behind them, his crossbow in his hands. They eased around the wall to allow themselves room, and to keep the small cleric out of harm's way, should the beast break free from whatever was holding it.

"Stop," Moonlitdune said loudly. "Stay against the walls. Look, there on the floor. Do not cross those lines."

Kryder looked down and could see the outline of a large circle drawn with a brown substance. The solid stone floor had scrape marks from its claws and hooved feet, but all of them were clearly on the inside of the drawn marks.

"Look, there against the wall," Dolner said from behind them.

Kryder looked beyond the circle and the demon. The lord mage's upper body was slumped against it at a strange angle, his legs and most of the hips missing. In front of the mage was an open book.

Kryder eased around the circle, careful not to cross the markings. When he got close, he saw it was a spell book. And not just any spell book—the lord mage's book. He recognized the writing from the pages he'd looked at on the lord mage's desk when they'd first stepped into his office in the Halls of Magic.

"FREE ME!" screamed the demon, his voice gravelly and rough. "Free me NOW!"

"In the name of Zeronic," Moonlitdune said, "you will be silent."

The demon spun toward her and bared his jagged teeth. He rose to his full height, rivaling Tog and Hrafarth's, perhaps even taller. "I…am Slavonne, the Dark Prince. I will not be silenced by one such as you, call upon your deity all you want. He cannot control me. No one controls me!"

"Looks to me like someone has control of you right now," Dolner said. "I mean…" He indicated the circle.

Slavonne screamed in rage and slammed against the barrier in front of Dolner. Dolner didn't flinch. "I've seen wild hogs scarier than you. They smelled better, too."

June giggled and stepped up beside Dolner. Tog looked down and shook his head.

Slavonne stood close to the edge of the ring, his breath coming out as steam in the cool room. It was no longer as cold as it had been, but they all blew smoke when they breathed. "You wear a deity's symbol, too, as does the girl. Do you think your symbols scare me? Think you to slay me with *prayer*? I. Am. IMMORTAL!"

"No," Kryder said, the book in his hands, "but I can make you *wish* you were dead for all eternity. As the sister said, be silent."

Slavonne glared at him and the book in his hands but did not utter another word. Kryder flipped the page he was reading and shut the book. He looked up and said, "He summoned you here, and you answered the call. He died before you could do anything for him." Kryder paused and said, "Answer."

"Yes," Slavonne said in his raspy voice. "I answered his call."

"Why?"

"He has called me before. When we were through with our…business, he released me from the cursed circle to go back to whence I came."

"To go home."

"YES!"

"Only this time he died after you answered," Kryder surmised.

"I do not know," Slavonne said. "He was dead when I materialized here in the world of mortals."

"And now you can't leave," Dolner said. "Serves you right, being a demon and all."

"What and who he is, he cannot help," Moonlitdune said. "Each immortal has their place."

"'As I have created deities, I have created demons,'" Sylif quoted from The Book Of The One.

"Yes," Nifarthan agreed.

"What was your business?" Tog asked. "What would make a man call a demon here?"

Slavonne stayed silent.

"Answer," Kryder said.

"Immortality," the demon said after hesitating almost long enough for Kryder to threaten him again.

"That is not for mortals," Moonlitdune said. "Each is to live the life given them and to answer when our Creator calls for them."

Slavonne shrank back a step when she said 'Creator.' "Don't you think I know this? I was willing to risk it."

"Why?" Kryder asked.

"Do you not know?" Slavonne asked. He narrowed his eyes. "You ask many questions. I am beginning to think you *can't* release me."

"Hey, ugly," Dolner said. "Count the lights. Did the dead mage in the corner ever create that many?"

"He probably can't count," June added. "For those of lesser intelligence in the room, there are eight. That's almost all the fingers on both hands." She looked at his hands. "Oh, never mind, that would be all of yours, stinky."

Tog put a hand on his face and slowly shook it again.

"I've read the spell," Kryder said. "I can release you, or...I can shrink the prison you find yourself in now until you cannot move, and leave you here."

"Fine," Slavonne said. "I gave him time, and he gave me...the blood of innocents."

"I should cut your head off and put it on a log embedded with biting ants," Tog threatened.

"Try it," Slavonne said, stepping back to the line. "Step across and try it, mortal."

Kryder opened the book and flipped back to the page he'd read earlier. When he raised his hand, Slavonne shouted, "No! Do not tighten the boundaries! I swear, if you free me, I will leave this place, never to return."

Kryder looked to Moonlitdune for guidance. Sylif did the same. He was accepted by Saint Minokath, but he had never been face to face with his deity, like she had on more than one occasion. Once again she closed her eyes. Kryder knew she asked for an answer from her god.

When she opened them, she turned to Slavonne. "Swear you to never come to the mortal world again?"

"I swear."

"No. Not good enough," Moonlitdune said. She held her arm up, the jewel on her wrist band glowing brighter for all to see. "Slavonne. Swear you by the One who created all."

Through gritted teeth, Slavonne the Dark Prince said, "I swear by...by our Creator to never come to the world of mortals again."

The jewel flashed a brilliant blue, as did Sylif's bracelet, the shaman's necklace, Dolner's wristband, and June's earrings.

Kryder opened the book, his finger marking the page. He read the short phrase, disgusted at the way several of the words had been torn apart and remixed with others, turning the spell into something it should never have been. *I hope I pronounce them right.*

He raised his hand and spoke the words with absolute conviction. A hole opened in the center of the circle. The orange glow from it changed the lighting, and tremendous heat filled the room. Slavonne stepped over and held his clawed hands out, feeling the warmth as if it was a welcome campfire. With one last look around, the demon stepped off the ledge and dropped into the hole. It closed over his head as he fell, sealing off the burning pits and the ropes of smoke drifting from them.

* * *

Yaylok

Dinky Poore fell. He got up, kicked the fallen branch that had tripped him, turned, and started running again. He ran for his life. They weren't after him yet, but he knew it wouldn't be long. As he ran, he smiled. He couldn't help it, as he looked back occasionally at the glow lighting the treetops from below, revealing ropes of rising smoke.

* * *

"Did you catch him?" Knight Commander Tharyeld demanded.

"No, my lord," his squire answered. "The boy jumped a small creek and scrambled up the bank as we searched for a place to cross. The horses couldn't do it, so we dismounted to continue the chase."

"He's gone," Lord Tharyeld said. He threw his helmet in disgust. "Armored men cannot catch a teenager running through the forest at night. Especially if the boy knows them. Find out if anyone recognizes his description. It's not as if the boy lives a secret life, hidden away from all."

"If he is a sneak thief, he does, my lord."

Tharyeld sat down on his stool and sighed. "How many were we able to save?"

"None…my lord."

"And the rope?"

"Burned, too, my lord."

"So you are telling me we have no catapults and no ballistae left; even the ones under construction have been destroyed. Oh, and lest I forget, no rope to use if we rebuild."

"Yes, my lord."

"Find some," Lord Tharyeld said. "I don't care if it has to come by sea from Gar-Noth; get me some more rope. And have the engineers start building more. How am I to lead an army with no war machines? We will be idiots standing around the outside of the king of Minth's castle."

"My lord, we can build again, but I fear it does us no good. We have no way of knowing who the saboteurs are. They slip in and out of our camps. We only saw this one as he threw a bucket of oil on the last pile of rope in the burn pit. It was already on fire, so it lit the night, and the sentry saw him. We never saw the others."

"Just. Find. More. Rope."

"Yes, my lord."

*****

Chapter Twenty-Seven

Mage's Library

Dolner looked around the large room at all the bookshelves, and the wall with the waist-high rack holding scores of scrolls. There were several items on a table. "Hey, what's this rope?"

"Put it down," Tog said. "You have no idea what it's for."

Dolner shrugged and put it down. "Why isn't it as cold in here as it was where that demon was trapped?"

"Slavonne is from the fiery depths," Moonlitdune explained. "He was slowly freezing here in our world. He was pulling the heat from all around, trying to remain comfortable. From the doors, from the wall facing the court where the sunlight warmed it during the day, and from the very air itself. From the looks of the mage's body, he'd been there for more than a month. It was hard to tell because of the cooler temperatures."

"Lord Mage whatever his name was actually crawled around in a circle and drew it with his own blood?" June asked. "Yuck."

Kryder looked up from the book he was reading. "He did. His own blood was required for the spell. It's almost as if it combined a magic spell with a prayer. One you can be sure I will never use. After I copy any other spells I don't have from his book, I plan to burn it."

"Prayer? To a demon?" Tog asked. "Madness. Is that the book?"

"No, this belonged to another. One who resided here and taught others. I am reading the spell to open a door to other places. I'm pretty sure I can pronounce all the words, though they are in a phrasing I have never used before. It's almost another language with the varying cadences, yet all in mage speak."

"This shelf holds volumes of prayer spells," Sylif said. He stood with Moonlitdune and the Lython shaman as they talked quietly. "Some are of other sects, with other gods, but there is one of Zeronic, and another in my religion."

"Well, if he needs me to scratch anything out in the language of Dragons, I can," Dolner volunteered. "All that other stuff, Human words or whatever, I can't help you with. I'm supposed to wing it."

"Speaking of which," June said, "I would like to go to the other side, where Lyna and Wryle are. From here we can see the open loft. I think we need to use the other stairwell to get there."

Kryder picked up several of the rings he had taken from the lord mage's fingers. He'd discovered a way to determine what spell each ring possessed. "I think it would be safe to split up now."

"I don't have the same feeling I had earlier," Moonlitdune added.

* * *

Dolner and June stepped into the room. One end was open to the roof of the building below. Wryle and Lyna were stretched out, enjoying the warmth radiating from the stone. There was room for a handful of other Dragons, had there been any in this part of Kerr.

"It's about time," Wryle hissed. "I am ready to hunt. Will you hunt with me?"

"With you?" Dolner asked. "As in ride you while you swoop down and drag a big goat off a cliff?"

"Why, yes," Wryle said. "That is a good plan."

"No. Bad plan," Dolner said. He ran his hand through his hair. "I'll fall and die on the rocks below."

"Did you not see the saddles?" Lyna asked. "You walked right by them."

June and Dolner turned around. "*That's* what I saw in my vision," Dolner said. "They *were* saddles."

The saddles were made of leather, with padded seats. They rested on large frames. Dolner looked one over closely. "Hey, look at this."

"A keyhole," June said. "Two."

"Here, get on," Dolner said. "Pretend it's strapped onto her back. Right. Now put your feet in the stirrups. See this piece? It folds over your calf."

June reached down and folded both pieces. "Now what? Do you lock it?"

Dolner inserted a key into a lock. He turned it twice, and they heard a click. He removed the key. "Try to pull your foot out."

"It won't come," June said. "It locks the leather band over my ankle all the way to my knee."

"And that's how we ride without ever having to worry about falling," Dolner said. "I wonder why this leather hasn't rotted after all this time?"

June elbowed him. "Probably because Zeronic made them or had them made. He wouldn't give us the keys to rotten leather saddles."

Wryle hissed in laughter. "I must learn your language, Dolner. Whatever you say to your mate is obviously not thought out ahead of time."

"What? No, I…never mind," Dolner said. He picked up the heavy saddle. "Come closer so I don't have to carry this so far, would you? We need to figure out these straps. I almost tripped on one."

* * *

"If it works, don't trip and fall through," Kryder warned. "I think I know where it will open, but I've only been there a few times. We could be a few steps off the ground."

"I hope you get it right," Tog said. "To be honest, I don't remember much of the baroness's castle, mostly the dining hall and kitchen. I do know the spiced taters were some of the best I've ever had."

"Oh, we're bringing some back," Kryder agreed. "That's the location I picked. Well, let's do this. After a week of studying it, I think I'm ready." He turned to the others. "We shouldn't be gone more than a few hours this first time. Maybe a day, depending on how much it takes out of me. I don't have the jewels the lord mage used. I have to actually cast the spells."

"We will be here," Moonlitdune said. "I'll let Dolner know. He should bring Sandwinkle back before dark. They flew to another of the villages to let the others know to prepare to move south and join the Minth armies. The Lython warriors are also, so when the time comes, we can move together."

"Good," Kryder said. He raised his hand and spoke more words in a single spell than he ever had before. A doorway outlined in red opened before him.

Tog looked over him, through the open door. "Yes! The meal hall. Look at the stares we're getting. Come on. Go, before someone shoots an arrow at us or something." He followed Kryder through.

* * *

Kylin Barony

"Kryder?" Baroness Kylin asked. She lowered her sword.

"Yes, my lady," Kryder said. He stretched; he was stiff and exhausted. "Sorry to intrude on your lunch."

"I'm not," Tog said. He inhaled through his nose, taking in the scent of spiced taters. "I could use a plate of taters and chicken."

She laughed. "I haven't seen you two since the skirmishes. I take it you know we prepare for war?" She sheathed her sword.

"Yes," Kryder answered. "We brought the news to King Jondal and were there when the messengers left to come here to the Baronies West."

The guards and a handful of others followed their baroness's example and sheathed their weapons. Several stayed close to learn how the two of them had simply stepped into the hall. One of them they recognized.

"Mage Kaynald," Kryder said. "It's good to see you made it back here safely."

"You found it," Kaynald said. She stepped closer. "Tell me you found it."

"We did," Kryder said. "We actually came here to bring you to the Mage's Library. I studied the spell to open the door for a week. The library will need someone who knows how to teach so it is easier on others who go there to learn. It was once a learning center for mages and clerics. Well, and one other subject, but we'll save that for another conversation."

"I know one thing," Tog said. "Nobody's *paying* for the right to learn there."

"Agreed," Kaynald said. "Just like no one will have to pay to keep from being burnt." She looked over at her baroness. "I am afraid I must leave again."

"I understand," Kylin said. "From the day you left to go to the Halls of Magic, I knew I would only see my little sister on special occasions."

"Not now," Kaynald said. "Once I learn this spell, I can visit you and my nieces and nephews anytime I choose. I will come back to take others to teach."

The baroness smiled. "Good. I've gotten used to you being around."

"Hey," Tog said, "we missed the noonday meal. We're not going anywhere until I get some taters and chicken in me, so everybody find a seat." Tog grinned at the Baroness. "I mean, please, my lady?"

"Taters!" Baroness Kylin called out. She smiled. "Bring this man lots of taters. He needs to keep his strength up. He grows weak before our very eyes."

* * *

The Fiery Pits

Zargall kicked the weak demon at his feet. "Get out, Slavonne, this is my keep now. Go to the desolate caverns and find somewhere else to live."

Slavonne picked himself up and walked out. As soon as he'd arrived home, Zargall had been waiting. The Dark Prince was surprised at how strong the once ridiculed weakling now was. Whoever Zargall had accepted had provided more than enough innocent blood. The new Prince of Fear was now one to contend with any of his brothers or sisters. It would not be long before the Demon King himself would have to deal with him.

I am not weak, yet he beat me down and threw me from my home. Perhaps I am only weak from my time in captivity. I hope the mortal summoning him does the same to him.

He stumbled over sharp rocks in his haste. *That will never happen to me again. Binding oath or not, I will never go to the mortal world again. Lethrall should have been my example. He is no more. At least I yet live.*

* * *

Kryder and Tog stepped through to the grounds of Lord Korth's estates. "We made it," Tog said. "That's twice we left the library like this and still live."

Several groups of soldiers were startled by their sudden appearance. Lord Korth's knight commander raised a hand before any could react. He stepped over with a puzzled look as Kryder led his horse through behind Tog.

"Kryder, Tog," Sir Brinthder said. "It is good to see you again, but…it is probably not wise to simply walk through a doorway on the archery range when a company of militia is being organized. Twitchy release fingers and all that type of nonsense, you know."

"Brinthder," Tog said in greeting. "You're right. I told him to open it in the meal hall."

"My apologies," Kryder said. "I thought there would be less surprise out in the open, and bringing a horse into Lord Korth's hall would not seem right."

"He would not be pleased, I daresay," Brinthder agreed. "He would hear about it later, as he has made another trip to the king's palace. There was some question about the plan for the cavalry in battle. It is best to have answers now and be able to train for them. Spring is coming, you know."

"It is," Kryder agreed. "We'll go there, too, after we speak with Mage Pelna. Do you know where she is?"

"This time of day, you will find her on the dock at Isle Lake. She waits for her husband's ship after a morning of fishing."

"Speaking of ship," Kryder said, "do you know if Captain Jonrig's ship is still docked?"

"*Jonrig's Delight* set sail a few weeks ago. Barl said he had a hold full of sharpening scales, fowl, and goats. He goes to Orcanth to trade. To the sands, I believe."

"He's going to the shores of the White Sands Tribe," Tog said. "Good. They will trade with Humans."

*****

Chapter Twenty-Eight

Orcanth

"Humans!" Wen cried. "Shaman, Humans come to the shore."

The older shaman stood and walked toward the young Orc and the trail leading through the bushes down to the sandy beach. "Show me."

She stepped onto the sand and watched as a plank was lowered from the large ship to the small narrow dock. She nodded her head in approval. "This is good."

The dock had been built at her suggestion to the chief. Several times a year, a ship anchored offshore and ferried birds and goats to the tribe, in exchange for wood cut and trimmed from the forests an hour's run from the beaches. With the dock in place, she'd believed more ships would come. She'd been right, and when the chief returned from the council meeting, he would see for himself.

Several members of her tribe stood near the end of the pier. One raised his hand toward her. She lengthened her stride to meet the Humans and translate for the chief's youngest son. More trade would be welcome. She wondered what type of wood this Human would bargain for.

* * *

Yaylok

"This is not what I bargained for," King Westell said. "Your emperor said he would send half his forces with mages to join in defeating the Minth forces."

"I'm sorry you misunderstood," Mraynith said. "Half his forces, yes. Half his mages, no. Mages will be on the field of battle, but it will not be half of the mages in Zar."

King Westell glared at the head mage. "Fine. When will they arrive?"

"They will come with the fighters, along with the Dragon masters and five of their beasts," Mraynith answered. "All will arrive in time for the final planning and to move with your forces north. I will arrive on the planned day of battle in the same manner I came here."

"Good," King Westell said, sitting back. "The plans must change, and it will give us time to work around it."

"Change?" Mraynith asked. "How so?"

King Westell waved his hand in dismissal. "It is of little importance in the scheme of things. We will not have the number of catapults and ballistae I first planned on."

"Ah," Mraynith said. "Saboteurs?"

"Those damned sneak thieves. They've destroyed them all again and again. It does me no good to execute those who are supposed to guard them. Like Knight Commander Tharyeld said, it only costs more soldiers. He's right, so I've ordered the engineers to stop building them."

"I see," Mraynith said. "I believe I have a solution. I can arrange for a tribe of Ogres to accompany our forces. Thirty of them, to be precise."

"Ogres?"

"Yes, they inhabit an area of Zar. They are quite loyal to me. You will not need a catapult or battering ram to knock down a castle's door, believe me."

"Yes," King Westell said. He sat up. "Bring them."

"Well, there is the matter of payment, since Ogres were not part of the bargain," Mraynith said. "I can negotiate this, myself." He paused a moment before adding, "For the emperor, of course."

King Westell sat all the way back. He smiled and asked, "Of course. What do *you* need?"

"Children. Young females, to be precise."

* * *

Tarlok

Rannow stood beside his horse, a magnificent red roan. "Hildon, you and the rest of the granders are left with a task I would trust to no other. Watch over the children and those unable to join us."

"We will, Lead Hunter," the older man said. His hair was white now, but he still moved with a silent step through the forests of Tarlok.

Rannow looked over to his wife as she said goodbye one last time to their grandchildren. He looked back to Hildon. "We have always maintained our borders with patrols. We cannot do so now. This once, I want you leave the borders open and gather those remaining to go deeper into our forests. The border can be reclaimed, should any trespass. The children cannot be reclaimed should anything happen to them."

"We will leave in the mists of early morning," Hildon agreed. "We will not be found."

"Good," Rannow said. He put a foot into his stirrup and swung himself up on his horse. He adjusted himself and reached for the lead Hildon was holding. Once his wife was mounted, he followed her and the pack horse she led. The horse was loaded with bundles of arrows and spare bows like his and all the other hunters'.

"We ride for Minth."

* * *

Minth

Jarvis Dapple reached up and drew out his necklace from under his shirt. He pulled a small leather pouch off the emblem it concealed hanging from it. A pendent of swirling fire and ice. They appeared to be at battle with one another, with neither gaining. He held the pendant in his hand, prayed, and tossed a copper into the wooden bowl in front of the cracked mirror. There was a flash of blue, and steam rose from the water. It fogged the mirror in small droplets.

Jarvis waited until the steam stopped rising and grabbed a rag to wipe the mirror. It all came off, except in small places. Those places formed scribbled words, as if written by a finger. *They have stopped building war machines. Forces ready to move north. Time to arrive at planned battle location is two months.* Below the message was another note. *Send a message to the queen. I'm to be leaving the area for fear o' discovery. Taking Dinky with me. -Shayna*

Jarvis wrote down the message to give to King Jondal on a little piece of paper. He slid it in a small wooden tube and fixed it to one of the pigeons in a cage by the window. In a matter of minutes, it would be across the city and on the landing ledge of the king's own pigeon coop, where he'd stolen it three days ago.

The sneak thief reached for another copper and prepared to send a message to the high cleric of his order and the queen of sneak thieves. Things were really moving, and final plans were to be made before the forces allied with Minth came together and started moving south. As a member of the guard, he knew he would be ordered to march with them.

He had enough time to send the message before he had to prepare for his shift guarding the king's messenger pigeons. Maybe one of the others would discover the message. It was always best when they did, but if someone didn't find it, he knew he would.

* * *

"I received the final message," King Jondal said. "King Westell is on the move. We must be in position within two months."

"The army will move slowly, sire, but we will be there in time," Sir Markain said. "We will be ready to begin moving in two days."

"Good," King Jondal said. He looked around the hall. "We go west to meet the armies of the Western Baronies at our border. From there, we go south. We will be outnumbered. Even with our combined forces, we will be outnumbered."

"We have always been outnumbered," the king of the Dwarves said. "Yet we prevail."

"We will this time as well, my friend," King Jondal said. He looked to his leaders and his allies, to the knights representing the Baronies West, the Dwarves with King Nuvalk, to the Sultan of Sands and the chief of the Lython, there with the Gnomes, and to the two Tarlok hunters, with the promise of all the hunters meeting them before they turned south. Lastly, he looked to the two who had brought the initial warning.

"Kryder, do you think there is a chance the Orcs will join us?"

"I can't answer," Kryder said. "Captain Jonrig only met a few of the White Sands Tribe when he traded for the weapons for your fleet. He said they didn't mention it."

"Their chief was gone to a tribal council," Tog added. "It may have been about this."

"Can you cast the doorway spell and find out?" Mage Bethany asked. "Now that I know it, I could, but I have no reference for it to open."

"I can, but I have found the farther one travels, the more it takes out of them," Kryder said. "Going from the Mage's Library to the barony was rough. When I opened the doorway back, it wiped me out. I slept for a day. That's why Tog and I came here from Lord Korth's land. It was closer, and then we came the rest of the way the normal route.

"Once Mage Kaynald creates travel jewels, it will be easy, but right now, the distance is too dangerous, even for me."

"We can count on the Western Borderlands sending archers to Baron Arnwald," Tog said. "That's something."

"Yes it is, and we will take all the help we can get," King Jondal said, "and be thankful for it. Now, about the order of movement…"

*****

Chapter Twenty-Nine

Two Months Later...

A horn sounded. The noise rose from the center of the massive formation of soldiers. King Jondal and his personal company of the King's Own were there, the blue and white colors of their flags and tunics unmistakable. The call by the messengers blowing the long, curved horns of the Mang fish was taken up by others up and down the line in the other armies on both sides of the men and women of Minth.

Minth's allies stood at the ready. Across the massive expanse of open fields, the wall of Goblins in the center of the enemy's formation stirred, driven by their Elven masters. They moved north slowly toward them. Their numbers seemed endless to those waiting for the battle. If it weren't for the Elves behind them and Human armies on each side of the beasts, it would seem they were all they would face.

Though outnumbered, Humans, Dwarves, Gnomes, and the elusive Lythons waited for the next sound of the horns to move toward the oncoming horde, but the notes directing them forward didn't sound. Instead, a series of notes indicated they were to hold fast.

The sound of a large force of cavalry moving from one side of the formation surprised many. They were doubly surprised to see a company of over five hundred Tarlok hunters on their quick horses move to the center in front of their formation.

A cheer rose up when the first flight of arrows arced high from the hunter's bows to land among the moving formation of Goblins. The Goblin horde had groups of archers interspersed among them, but with horn bows, they had no chance of reaching the hunters. Many fell when they were pierced through by the steel-tipped shafts.

Before the Goblins could react, the next flight fell. And the next, and the next, until each man and woman of the hunters had emptied a full quiver of twenty-four arrows. The Goblins who'd managed to protect themselves with their small, misshapen shields were in full flight back toward the Elves, who lashed out at them with their wicked whips. It was mass hysteria on the front lines of the enemy.

The armies and allies of Minth were heartened to see it. They knew the odds were against them, and anything raising them was welcome. They cheered again.

* * *

The cheers of those who came together to defeat the evil across from them faded and grew silent when a sound unheard on the world of Kerr reached their ears. It grew louder. All looked to the hills, as a formation of over two thousand Orcs, running at a speed no man could hope to hold for long, moved in front of the horses of the Tarlok hunters.

For most, it was a surprise. None but the cavalry forces lying in wait beyond the hills knew the warriors of Orcanth had been traveling for days to join in the battle. The best horses in the Baronies West were already here, so messengers from the cities and towns on the road to the battlefield couldn't get ahead and stay ahead of the Orcs to bring the message to the king and his allies. The commander of the cavalry was surprised to find them camped beyond the hills, but she'd assumed it was known and hadn't sent a message to the king.

They were doubly shocked to see the rest of the Orc tribes and their sub-tribes join on the front lines with every kingdom and race. Each tribe had several shamans to translate with the closest commander, and the formations shifted to allow the huge axe- and bladed spear-wielding warriors room to fight with them.

There were no complaints as the Orcs around them studied the bright colors and banners to learn which Humans were their allies. Across the field, the colors and banners tended to be mainly black. Nods and the occasional clasped forearm were exchanged. Their numbers had increased by ten thousand.

* * *

In front of the Tarlok hunters, the best archers from the various tribes readied to launch their arrows. All Orcs fared well with a bow, but these were without peer among the major tribes and sub-tribes. Many of them were the strongest in their tribes, so there were few females, but the Night Stalkers Tribe contributed no fewer than eighteen female warriors.

With the two thousand Orcs out front rode four Tarlok hunters on horseback. Rannow recognized them. Zane pulled up beside Rannow and reached down to pat his horse's neck. "Lead Hunter, it is good to see you again."

"You, as well," Rannow answered. "Ladies." He nodded his head to Penae and the daughters of his old friend, before turning back to Zane. "I wondered where you and our cousins in the Western Borderlands were among the formations. I see you four but know not where the others are. I must admit, I am a bit confused." He indicated the Orcs in two ranks before them.

"The plan is one Sar, chief of the Red Fist, came up with," Zane explained. "We know the Elves will use their shields to protect themselves from arrows raining down. Unlike the Goblins, they will continue to move forward, while hunters use up their supply. When they close with our ranks, the battle will truly begin for them."

"But we have no choice but to try to reduce their numbers," Rannow countered as he spun his horse back around. It was nervous from the proximity of the Orcs. "Some arrows will hit their marks."

"Agreed," Zane said. "Have the hunters rain arrows once again. The Orcs will wait until the first flight lands among them, then they will let loose. With their great bows, they do not have to arc their shots as high as Humans do. The Elves must choose…"

"They can either protect themselves from arrows raining down, or from shots directly at them," the lead hunter of Tarlok interrupted. "They cannot do both. An impressive plan. I would like to meet Sar—a tribal chief, did you say?"

"When the battle is won," Zane answered, "I am sure it can be arranged. He is chief of a major tribe and a member of the tribal council. He is among those in front of us. He will fall back with the others once they exhaust their quivers."

Rannow nodded his appreciation of a leader out front at the onset of battle and the lack of concern about losing this fight. "Let me know when the Elves and Goblins are in range, and we will begin anew." He glanced at the closest Orcs and noticed each had three quivers on their backs, opposite large axes of several types. "We will use two quivers to the Orc's one, and we will see how many panic and leave the field this time."

* * *

The commander of the Elven fighters snarled and snapped his whip. The end wrapped around a fat Goblin's neck as he jerked it to the ground. The time it cost to pull his whip from the thrashing Goblin allowed four more to run by him into the ranks of King Westell's troops.

Captain Traflien shouted at his under-captains as he wrapped the whip around his waist and tied it for later use. "Send the word. We move forward with shields at the ready to thwart the arrows of the cursed hunters. I would have us get close enough to cut the legs out from under the horses they ride. They will face us or flee behind that pathetic army, but either way, the arrows *will* stop."

"Captain," his banner bearer said, "a group has moved in front of the hunters."

"I don't care. They can die with those on horseback." He turned to his messengers. "Send the word, now."

"Yes, Captain Traflien!" the one closest to him answered. He brought his hand to his lips and blew into a small tube of silver.

The shrill whistle sounded several notes, and the formation of Elves moved forward, their bladed shields held in front, ready to be raised overhead. Each was anxious to fight, the lust to maim and kill foremost on their minds.

Behind them, the five Dragon masters and their servants struggled to keep the huge Dragons at bay on chains. Their heads turned left and right, the crazed eyes begging to be allowed to eat, even if it was the Elves in front of them or the Humans behind.

They were restless as they dug deep scars with their claws, but they were not desperate enough to draw the wrath of their masters and the long, sharp-tipped control poles. Each tip was powered with a spell of mild lightning and was able to give the insane beasts a vicious reminder of who was master.

Traflien decided to hold the Dragons back. The arrows would be a hindrance to the great beasts, and enough of them could bring one down, though unlikely. The danger to all was if too many of the masters went down by arrow and a beast had no one controlling it to ensure it only attacked their enemies. The flames erupting from a Dragon's mouth burned whoever it touched, friend and foe alike. A few snapped up fleeing Goblins, but that was ignored by those holding the chains; it was allowed, considering what the snack was.

The formation moved forward, and Captain Traflien smiled to himself as the second arrow hit the shield held over his head. This one glanced off and stuck in the ground. The first had shattered, its tip embedded in his shield. Though one or two had struck his troops, eliciting cries of pain, he knew he would reach the enemy's lines with the vast majority of his own force intact. The battle would be to his liking then.

His smile faded as he dropped to his knees. He looked down. A huge shaft protruded from his stomach after piercing his metal-ringed leather armor. The feeling in his feet faded. He grew cold, and his vision clouded as he heard Goblins scream and Elves cry out. The sound commingled with the clattering of shields to the ground as others fell with him. He would never swing his sword and bladed shield in the upcoming clash of armies.

* * *

"It worked," Tog said as he stood with Kryder. After locating the soldiers of Baron Arnwald, they stood with them, along with the rest of the Red Fist tribe and several of its sub-tribes.

"Did you doubt your grandfather?" Lady Anise asked from astride her horse.

"No," Tog said, his grin showing his incisors, "but I didn't know it would be this effective. I should be out front with them."

"Yeah," Kryder agreed. "Half the Elves are down." He looked over at his cousin. "I know you shoot as strong a bow as any warrior can draw repeatedly, but I'm glad you're here by my side."

"That still leaves plenty," Sir Narthon said. He pulled the hood of his chainmail up over his grey hair and rolled his neck. "We'll get in some sword work after all…or axe, as it were." He nodded at the axe in Tog's hands.

"Sir, by your leave, I'll get back to the cavalry company," his under-captain said. "I've several young pages waiting with my lance and shield ready." She added, "Today, the squires fight."

"I suspect the pages will find a way to get in close, too," Sir Narthon said. "I would when I was their age. Go, Anise, I'm sure you'll swing your axe, too, once there's no room for you and your troops to use lances."

She reined her mount around and leaned into the big black horse's sudden gallop. The commander of the combined armies of the Baronies West watched her ride away with a grin. He glanced at Kryder, looked back at the enemy, and asked, "What will you use when your ability to cast is gone? I know you're powerful, but my sister grows wearier with each spell she casts. Is it not the same with all mages? Surely you cannot last the day?"

"I'll use it until I can't," Kryder confirmed. He flicked his dark hair from in front of an eye with a quick shake of his head, reached down, and placed his hands on both hilts of his sheathed daggers. "Then I'll rely on my daggers."

Sir Narthon shook his head, still observing the enemy as it re-grouped. "Daggers against sword and shield. Madness."

"I don't know," Tog disagreed, "I'm not saying he's right in the head, but they can't hold their swords very well if they lose a finger or three. Besides, he has a hand axe to throw, too."

"Thanks, I think," Kryder said as he reached behind and to one side to shift the aforementioned weapon in his belt.

"Where are the archers from the Western Borderlands?" Tog asked.

"They're formed behind us. They will let fly volleys of arrows right before we meet the enemy. I don't think they will be noticed until it is too late."

"How many came?" Kryder asked.

"I was given the number three hundred," Sir Narthon answered. "An impressive number for a barony of farmers. From what I've seen in the last week, they're all skilled with the bow. I will admit, many are young, hence my decision to place them behind the trained soldiers."

"The Western Borderlands is made up of good people," Kryder said. "I like the idea of surprising the enemy from afar, when they think they have nothing to fear from more archers."

* * *

"There," Tog said suddenly, pointing. "There are three mages. See the red robes? Right in front of the formation with the black flag. What's that on it, a swan?"

"Looks like it. It's kind of far," Kryder said. "Let me see it." He reached for the circle of glass.

"Here," Tog said. "You know, besides the door and the stuff that kills the enemy, that may be one of the best spells you picked up. It's like you're right there when you look through it."

Kryder looked through the farseeing piece of glass. It was about twice the diameter of an eye, and easy to store in a padded pocket. The spell to look through it wasn't especially taxing—for him, anyway. Earlier he had let King Jondal look through it before finalizing his plans with the leaders of the other armies.

"Yeah, that's a swan on the flag," Kryder confirmed.

"That means?" Tog suggested. He knew the answer.

"Yes," Kryder answered. "Those are the troops of the current lord of Marent. Whatever the count's name is. The family of my mother."

"So?" Tog questioned.

"Doesn't matter to me who they are," Kryder said. "The way my mother was treated all those years ago closed that door. They're not my family. I have a family…and a tribe."

Tog put his large hand on his cousin's shoulder as the most powerful shaman to ever claim the title continued to study the enemy across the field. The weight of it let Kryder know his cousin had his back, no matter what. The family and tribe who'd accepted him before he was born was the only one he needed.

Kryder nodded to himself and put the glass away. He raised a hand and spoke the words to bring the clouds together, not enough to block the sun, but enough to generate brief flashes of lightning within them, like the heat lightning of late summer.

Every user of magic on the field took notice. From shamans to magic users to mages, all knew there was someone present with great abilities. They could tell from the red outline of the clouds. Bolts of lightning flashed down among the troops around the swan banner, scattering them. They knew who's side the mage was on. Two of the red robed mages standing there survived, as their shields had overlapped. The third's deflection shield hadn't helped her or the score of armored soldiers near her.

Satisfied, Kryder lowered his hand. The spell was too dangerous to use once the troops intermingled, but he was glad to have been able to use it before the forces met. It wouldn't be the last spell he cast against the enemy this day.

Above them, similar clouds formed. Kryder could see the red edges. Tog looked up and said, "Droppings. Looks exactly like the clouds you made. This is going to hurt."

"No," Kryder said. He raised a hand and spoke the words of the wind spell. A ring on his hand glowed, seen only by those with the gift. The clouds forming above them sheared apart and dissipated.

Kryder knew there was a frustrated mage across the battlefield, probably an Elf, so, for good measure, he raised his hand and sent darts of light across the battlefield in the direction of the largest group of Elves in black robes. That was the farthest distance he'd attempted to use the spell. Four of the eight pierced bodies instead of the deflection shields already in place, through rings or other items. He wasn't sure if he got the spell caster, but he knew the caster would keep his head down for a while, even if he hadn't.

* * *

Mraynith grabbed another mage, spun her in front of him, and ducked behind her. The dart of light struck her, and she screamed. It didn't kill her instantly. The distance had lessened the dart's ability to pierce her completely. She would have a nasty scar from it…if she lived.

Ignoring her, Mraynith stared across the distance, trying to determine who had cast the spell. *Whoever it was, they may rival my own powers. A wind spell. Ingenious defense. A deflection shield wasn't even needed. And to follow it up with darts of light, at this distance?"*

"Did anyone see who cast that?" Mraynith demanded from the mages around him.

"Yes," a voice called out. A mage stepped forward and offered a rounded piece of glass to the head mage. Mraynith recognized Cauthill, a young Elf with promise. He nodded and took the glass.

Mraynith looked through the glass in the direction Cauthill indicated. "There, great one. There beside the Orc. It was the one with the dark hair, dressed in the traveling cloak. They came from his hand."

Mraynith studied his adversary. What he saw did not impress him. The caster wore no robes to indicate a user of the gift. He could see a faint red glow from his hands. *Rings, no doubt.*

"He has stumbled across a powerful ring," Mraynith said. "There are other rings on his fingers, probably from raiding a tomb of some sort. I highly doubt he has the strength of gift to cast a lightning spell or darts of that magnitude himself."

Cauthill nodded as he was handed back the glass. "Will we seek him out, great one?"

"No. If he comes near, I will take care of him, but he will grow weak if he continues to use rings beyond his own ability. He will die in battle long before then." He toyed with the pendant on his necklace.

"We will stay back and cast from a distance," Mraynith said. "Watch for any others so we can disrupt them and destroy them. I have been assured they do not have many with the gift on their side of the battlefield.

"We will also stay back while those arrows fly," Mraynith added.

*****

Chapter Thirty

Jonrig's Delight

"She's burning to the water, Cap'n," the boy in the crow's nest shouted.

"Good eye, Davey! Keep an eye out for others," Captain Jonrig said. He turned to his first mate. "Trying to sneak past us up the coastline. The nerve of them."

"They're not getting past these big arrows and a bucket of pitch, that's for sure, Cap'n."

* * *

Minth

The Orcs emptied two full quivers, and the hunters fired even more. Across the field of battle, the Elves were left staggering, the field littered with bodies, and others too wounded to continue. The Goblins all around them fared even worse. The numbers between the two forces were not yet even, but they were much closer than they had been. The enemy pulled back to regroup.

With a shout from Sar, the Orcs turned and waited. Rannow nodded and put two fingers in his mouth. He whistled the sound of a small bird found among the forests of Tarlok. Like the bird, the sound was surprisingly loud. Almost as one, the hunters turned their horses and rode hard from the field. They disappeared behind several small hills.

Once the horses moved, the Orcs joined their tribes along the front line. Some put their bows on their backs, while others kept them out, depending on the instructions from their chief and the Human unit they were now a part of.

Sar stopped beside his grandsons. He reached out and clasped forearms with both Kryder and Tog. He reached into a small fur pouch on his waist. He pulled out pieces of leather. They both had the emblems of three oak trees and a red fist on them. He handed one to Tog, and the other to Kryder.

"I brought these for you two," Sar said in Orcish. "A shaman and a warrior must show the world who they are."

"The world will know, Chief," Kryder answered back in the same language as he affixed it to a couple of the toggles on his traveling cloak.

"We will make sure of it," Tog agreed.

"Your father and Jynal send their regards. Your mother would not allow them the long run to this battle."

"Aunt Katheen wouldn't," Kryder agreed. "Something tells me she is here, though. Is she in the rear with other shamans and the other races' clerics?"

"She is," Sar said. He grinned, showing his great incisors. "She rode in the wagon with Lucas. I was not going to tell a shaman what she cannot do. That is not my place. She and the others of faith are ready to heal. The shamans of magic are among the tribes, ready to cast until they cannot. They will move back after."

"Right," Tog said. "I bet my dagger some have weapons on them and will fight, too."

"I know of two who are skilled with their bladed spears among the Long Sticks Tribe," Sar said. "I will not take the bet."

"Where are Lucas and Johan...and the brothers?" Tog asked.

"On the edge of our tribe's warriors, between us and the Running Boar Tribe," Sar answered. He tried to conceal a look spreading across his face.

"The Running Boar Tribe?" Tog asked. "What? Why would they fight beside us? Wait. What are you trying to hide?"

"We no longer feud," Sar answered.

"Really?" Kryder asked. "The feud has been going on for decades. Something big must have happened."

"Yeah," Tog agreed. "I didn't think it would ever happen. Wait, what happened?"

"Lucas and his children are of the blood," Sar said. "You said they are members of Red Fist. Kryder was the shaman to hear this. It is so. I accepted this as chief."

"Right," Kryder said. "That's the way it's been done...well, forever. What does that have to do with the Running Boars?"

"After the council meeting, Three Oak's shaman and Red Fist's shaman talked to the Running Boar shaman. She spoke to her chief. At her insistence, he met Lucas and was introduced to Marn, Sethon, and Julia.

"I watched to see what would happen. Yan noticed Julia...was different. You call it *burnt.* I think it was explained to him. We have never seen eye to eye, and have argued many times in council meetings, and almost come to blows, but I have never seen him get that angry. Ever. Chief Yan called another meeting of the council before everyone left. We were all surprised, because the vote wasn't unanimous. Orcs were *not* going to leave Orcanth and join in this battle."

Tog's eyes widened. "Chief Yan voted against it, didn't he? But you're here."

"Yan stood before the council and said, 'Lucas is of the blood. His family is of the blood. Lucas is a member of the Running Boar Tribe. I accept him. I have said it.'"

"Everyone was silent, like you two are now," Sar continued. "The Running Boar shaman said, 'the chief has said it. It is so. I am informing the council of new tribe members.'"

"Wait," Kryder said.

"Yes," Sar interrupted. "Lucas is a member of the Red Fist *and* the Running Boar. His family is, too. Yan walked over to me and said, 'a Running Boar is a Red Fist. There can be no feud among us. The past is the past.' He held his hand out. I stood and clasped forearms."

"Amazing," Kryder said, in Human.

"Yes," Sar said. "That word means good, yes?"

"Yes," Tog confirmed in Orcish. "What about his vote against joining in the battle?"

"The chief of the Running Boars called for a new vote," Sar said. "A member of his tribe was denied something that should have been freely given, and as a result, she is a shell of what she once was and could have been. I never liked him before, but I have to admit, he cares for his tribe and his family. His daughters and his grandchildren are everything to him and his wife."

"I can see why," Tog said. He noticed the looks he was getting. "What? His granddaughter Fay is attractive. That's all I'm saying."

Sar shook his head, showing that he knew this could become an issue in the future. He continued, "A member of his tribe was going to join Minth in a battle against the one who did this to his daughter...or caused it, with his control of the lord mage and the Halls of Magic. Against one who would enslave others. One who fought with Elves and Goblins at his side. Yan declared it was no longer an option to stay within our boundaries when one of his members was going to fight against this. His honor would not allow it. He was the first to vote yes."

"The circumstances changed," Kryder said, again speaking in the Human language.

"That big word," Sar said. "What mean?"

* * *

"The circumstances have changed," King Westell said. "I cannot hold troops in reserve. Their cavalry is waiting to come from those hills. I have to send mine to meet them, or they may begin rolling us up. The reserves will go into the line where the cavalry was."

"What does that have to do with me?" Mraynith demanded. "The remainder of the Elven fighters are more than enough to break through, even with an under-captain leading them."

"I want you to call the Ogres forward to take on the opposite flank," King Westell answered. "Thirty of them will tear through the soldiers on the far flank, and they can do what the cavalry is denied now. It will simply happen on the opposite end of the formations."

Mraynith turned to the Elf now leading the fighters. He raised an eyebrow and was answered with a nod. He turned back. "Give them time to move forward and swing around. An hourglass should be sufficient."

"Done," King Westell said. Mraynith walked away.

When he was out of sight, King Westell said, "Then we move on their pathetic army. Surely by now they run low on arrows. If not, the numbers are still with us. I should have never agreed to let the Elves lead the attack."

"I would rather they take the brunt of those arrows, sir," Knight Commander Tharyeld said. "Better their soldiers than ours."

"True," his king agreed.

"Sire, you must move back with your guards," Tharyeld said. "Once we win the field, it will be safe for you to claim victory."

"Nonsense," King Westell said dismissively. "I have my guards and two mages. Besides, I can still swing a sword with the best of them. Go. Lead my forces. In less than an hour, sound the advance for everyone."

* * *

An hour later, King Jondal turned to his right and said, "Signal the advance. They've committed everything. Their cavalry moves. Notify ours now."

The horns sounded the advance. A series of notes followed after. On the right flank, the two massive formations of cavalry met first in a clash of lance on shield, and sword on sword. It didn't take long for the dust kicked up to create a cloud floating over and among those riding within it.

The advantage in numbers the Gar-Noth forces had was countered by the larger, stronger horses their opponents rode. Like their riders, the Minth warhorses were skilled fighters. Not only did they respond swiftly to commands given by their riders' knees and shifting weight, they attacked and kicked out when the opportunity was given them. Many of the enemy troops found themselves striking the ground hard when their horse's leg was shattered by a well-placed kick.

Lady Anise threw the remainder of her lance to the ground and grabbed her axe. She slipped her hand into the leather loop and used it one handed. If the battle lasted too long, she would have to hang her shield on one side and use two hands. Her horse collided with another, turning sideways as it was trained. She ducked her enemy's sword and slashed her axe into his side. It didn't cut deep through the chain mail, but several ribs shattered. She jerked it free as the man slid from his horse. Her horse wheeled and kicked out, striking another unhorsed swordsman.

When five hundred Tarlok hunters came around the hill behind the dust cloud, it was over for the enemy cavalry. They were hit by well-placed arrows from behind and the side as they attempted to fight with sword and axe. Those who found themselves dismounted fared worse. A man in armor cannot reach a fast horse with a skilled archer riding it.

* * *

Arrows flew overhead before the Elves and Goblins reached the forces under command of the Baronies causing the Goblins to panic and slow once again. Two more flights of over three hundred arrows each made them panic. The Elves cursed and kicked at the fleeing Goblins but continued to advance. They were met by Humans and Orcs. The former they expected, but the latter was a nasty surprise they realized as they got closer.

Kryder and Tog fought side by side. Tog's axe smashed shields aside and buried deep in the Elves' metal-ringed leather armor. Darts of light sped from Kryder's outstretched hands and burned through the same leather. Tog was holding his own against a snarling Elf with a sword and his slashing shield. That gave Kryder time to look to his other side. He threw his hand up and stopped an Elf in mid-swing. His hand shook slightly as he held him long enough for Sir Narthon to get to his feet and strike a killing blow.

All around, the battle raged as they fought side by side. Neither was able to see how their tribe and those of Three Oaks fared. Four Elves fought their way to them with the intention of taking out the mage who had killed so many. Kryder was surprised when an arrow flew past his head and buried in the face of the closest. Three more arrows followed, taking down the others.

Teel stepped up and pulled his bloodied hand axes off his hips. "That was my last four," he said as he stepped forward to fight a handful of Goblins brave enough to turn back around and finally catch up to the Elves.

"Thanks," Kryder called out as he drew his daggers. More Goblins were running toward them. "Have you seen Lucas?"

"Not in a while," Teel answered as he buried both axes in a large Goblin. He spun and struck another. Kryder lost sight of him.

* * *

Lucas stood between his sons as they swung their hammers in bone-crushing blows and countered attacks with the long handles. They stayed close to their father to protect him, but he was still able to kill Goblins as they slipped below those fighting above and around them. He smashed arms holding odd-shaped short swords and crushed skulls with his studded club. He was no longer a young man, and he realized it shortly into the fight. He glanced over to see if he could find Johan.

* * *

Johan fought like a man possessed. His longsword was a silver blur as he fought two Elves at once; neither was able to get past his defenses. His sword smashed aside the bladed shields. Anyone watching would have sworn a young man was dealing death to the Elves, but his grey hair and moustache gave him away. One of his soldiers was down and unmoving, while the other two with him fought back-to-back.

The last of the Elves dropped when his head went flying. Breathing heavily, Johan turned to find three more advancing on him. Without hesitation, his body took control, and his sword flashed yet again. The fight slowed for those around him as the Elves were nearly all defeated. Many stood in awe as he fought. Before those not engaged could move to help him, the last Elf fell victim to his sword.

Johan put the tip of his sword in the ground and breathed heavily. The air would not come fast enough. He saw spots of light, then darkness tunneled his vision. His chest ached, and his left hand lost feeling. Everything went dark. The sword fell. Johan followed it.

* * * * *

Chapter Thirty-One

Down the line, companies met companies and fought to gain ground. The battle raged on, with neither side giving way. For a while, the numbers seemed to give King Westell's forces the advantage, even with the devastation the Elves took before the battle began. The Orcs were the turn of the tide.

When Humans fought Humans, it was nearly even, with a few notable exceptions. When the forces of Gar-Noth met a unit with Orcs fighting with them, it was far from even, and little by little, the Minth forces pushed forward.

Across the battlefield, fireballs blossomed, and darts of light struck. Wind raged, and tangled webs held groups of three and four. Many times spells were cast in twos and threes, as mages and magic users from both sides cast until they were exhausted. Most moved back to help with the wounded and give the clerics whatever help they could afterward.

Katheen knelt beside a young man she could no longer help and looked up to see if others needed to be placed on the wagon as it moved the fallen back behind the lines. The battle moved away from her in its ebbs and flows but was still close. She saw a familiar figure topple. Without thinking, she ran past others to him.

Johan lay next to his sword, breathing shallow and fast. His skin was a pale grey. She feared she was too late. She looked for a wound but found none. Katheen reached down the neck of his chainmail and pressed hard against his chest. She could feel his erratic heartbeat weakening. She ran the shells of her necklace between the fingers of her other hand and closed her eyes. *Saint Minokath, will you hear me?*

* * *

Katheen found herself elsewhere.

Saint Minokath stood with some of his brothers and sisters. Lan smiled at her, giving her hope. Saint Gonthon took off his brimmed hat and wiped his forehead before putting it back on. Even Nalkon the Hunter stood among them, in leathers of greens and browns, with a beautiful owl resting on his shoulder. She knew who they were, though she had only seen one of them in her lifetime, many years ago when she was but a child.

"We all hear you," Saint Minokath said, "as you are accepted by us all."

"We brought you here to see the one who was so strong in her faith, and with a belief and willpower nearly rivaling ours," Lan said gently.

"You have asked us to save one who deserves to live," Nalkon said. "A good man."

"Like the seeds you once planted in my name, his heart will grow stronger," Saint Gonthon said.

"You mean?" Katheen asked.

"Yes, Katheen," Minokath said. "Our Creator has answered all our prayers. Go, now. We will all see you again. When, I cannot say. Like in all things, we are but part of our Creator's plan."

* * *

"In infinite wisdom," Katheen whispered and opened her eyes.

She felt Johan's heart grow stronger and beat more steadily beneath her palm. She moved her hand when his legs stirred. She looked up to see the Red Fist shaman kneeling on the other side of Johan with her hand on his shoulder. The shaman's eyes were wide.

"I saw them," she said. "I saw them all."

"You will need more jewelry," Katheen said with a smile on her face. "Come, there are others in need."

* * *

"We need to do something," Sandwinkle said.

He handed his viewing tube to Hrafarth. The Lython shaman translated as the Gnome explained how to use it. He knew the chief had understood when he inhaled sharply.

"If those Ogres get to the line and take out the company on the flank, it won't be good," Sandwinkle said. "King Jondal and his forces are engaged. We're the only ones left to help on this side. Everything is moving the other way."

Hrafarth spoke to his warriors, "We must fight them. Each of you, take one of our brothers of the sand with you."

Before Nifarthan could translate what the chief had said, Sandwinkle found himself swept up by Hrafarth. The remaining Lythons did the same with others. In minutes, they confronted thirty Ogres who were late to the fight, but eager to kill.

Sandwinkle readied his crossbow as soon as the Lython chief put him down. He cocked it and aimed it at the huge monster fighting

Hrafarth. The Ogre towered over the Lython by more than three or four feet, but Hrafarth was faster, and he dodged the swing.

The Ogre's bone club buried itself in the dirt from the mighty blow, so Hrafarth took advantage and slammed his club down on its hand. The Ogre howled in pain and kicked out. Another Lython struck the extended leg with his own stone club. All three of the knife blades from Sandwinkle's crossbow buried themselves in its shoulder.

Sandwinkle reloaded as the Ogres tried to contend with more than twice their number in Lythons. The sharp blades of the small Gnomes running everywhere and the remainder of the Human company confused them as they tried to fight the quick Lythons. When more Humans arrived to help them, the Ogres died one by one. Many Humans, Lythons, and Gnomes died to accomplish it, but the threat of the flank attack was ended.

"Look," the shaman said, "the Dragons fight." He said the same thing in his own language, and everyone turned to see a sight unseen in hundreds of years.

* * *

"There!" Dolner shouted. "Down there."

"I see them," Wryle hissed. "They are of the Flame, but they cannot fly. Their wings have been cut. Look how they move and how they act."

"They are insane," Lyna said. "I have seen it. We must put an end to their suffering."

"And the ones who did it," June shouted. "The Elves on the ends of those chains."

"Wait," Wryle said. "We will go first. They may not fly, but they may still have flames. Let us see how they will fight."

Before Lyna or June could argue, Wryle folded his wings and dove. Dolner, secure in his saddle, ducked low and stayed close to the Dragon's neck. They had practiced this move many times hunting goats on the mountainside. Dolner reached down and felt for the three spears strapped to the saddle. Though he couldn't shoot a bow very well, they had discovered he was good with the spears he'd found on a rack in the saddle room.

Before they struck the ground, Wryle pulled up and flew low and fast, straight at the first Dragon. He inhaled deeply, tightened the muscles in his throat, and squeezed the glands holding the combustible liquid only a Red Dragon could produce. When he exhaled, the mist coming from him met the air and ignited two feet from his mouth.

His flames met the flames from the crazed Dragon straining at the chains held by the Elves all around him. Several were lifted from the ground and torn loose from them. The flames met each other and blossomed. The blossom moved toward the chained one as Wryle beat his wings hard to slow his flight. He pulled up in time to fly over his opponent. By the time he banked around, Dolner had a spear in hand.

Wryle felt the movements in the saddle and knew Dolner was ready. He looped around so the Dragon on the ground couldn't use his flames against them. Dolner threw the spear, and it flew straight and embedded in the side of the disfigured one. Wryle rolled to escape a plume of flames from the next of the five Dragons. Dolner felt heat but not actual fire as they flew upward.

Seconds later, Dolner watched in awe as Lyna hovered, nearly still in flight, as her wings beat steadily. June readied her bow. The tip of her arrow ignited. She took careful aim and sent the flaming arrow down the throat of the Dragon closest to them as it inhaled. The explosion tore its head from its neck, and it toppled over on several of its handlers.

"I wonder how she did that?" Dolner asked as Wryle circled and prepared to dive again.

"Don't ask her," the Dragon advised. "You may get another elbow in your ribs."

Dolner readied another spear. Wryle rolled and dove. There were three left to put out of their misery, and a wounded one busy eating its handlers.

* * *

Kryder was exhausted, both physically and mentally. He put his hands on his hips and took a deep breath. He bent down and pulled the hatchet from the chest of the man in front of him. It left a jagged, bloody hole in the black tunic of the man, dead center in the white swan. He turned around and watched as Tog wiped the blood from his axe. Both of them were too tired to notice the arrival of several Elves through a door spell. Tog shouted, and he turned.

An Elf stood in robes with two others in front of him. The Elven mage stared long and hard. He turned his head left and right and took in the devastation of the battlefield, of the dead and wounded, and the large groups surrendering to the forces of Minth.

"I see you have many rings Human," the Elf said. "I have also watched you use them over and over. Oh, I suspect you cast a few spells yourself, but you cannot now. An idiot could see you are exhausted."

Tog stepped up beside his cousin with his axe ready. Kryder reached for his hatchet. Both the mages in front of the one speaking raised a hand.

"I wouldn't," the Elf advised. "It would be easy to fill you both full of darts of light."

Kryder paused. He knew it was useless. They were too far away to reach in time. He might be able to cast a shield, but it wouldn't protect Tog. He doubted he even had the strength to complete the spell.

"I have another plan. One for you, and for everyone here. *Everyone.*"

Kryder watched the Elf slide a small dagger from his sleeve. The Elf cut the tip of his finger. He bent down and drew a wide circle in the dirt. He spoke the words of a spell Kryder recognized. It was the one he had burned, along with others in the lord mage's spellbook.

A demon rose up in the circle. It was bigger than the last they had encountered. It stood tall and strong, not weak like the one in the Mage's Library. Kryder noticed Tog shifting his weight beside him in anticipation.

"Why do you bring me here with no sacrifice, Mraynith?" the demon asked. "This is not our bargain. Where is my blood?"

"Oh, I have a sacrifice for you, Zargall," Mraynith answered. "Many sacrifices."

Mraynith looked at Kryder and Tog. "My apologies. I am being rude. Meet Zargall, Prince of Fear. Zargall, meet two of your sacrifices. The rest are here on this battlefield."

The two mages lowered their hands and backed around the circle holding Zargall imprisoned. One threw a red jewel down and stomped it. A doorway appeared. Both went through. Mraynith stepped over to it and turned. He smiled, reached out with his foot, and brushed the bloody dirt away, breaking the barrier. He jumped back through the door, and it shrank quickly and disappeared.

Zargall threw his head back and roared. "I am free! Free in the world of mortals!"

The demon leapt at Kryder with his clawed hands extended. Kryder had never seen anything move so fast. Tog's axe struck the hands and knocked them away before the claws could impale him. Zargall kicked Tog and sent him flying with a sharp hoof. Tog didn't move.

Kryder looked up from where he'd been knocked to the ground. Zargall stared at his hands as they dripped black blood. Kryder saw the deep cuts slowly closing. While the demon was distracted, he ran to Tog's side and dropped to his knees. Zargall ignored them.

The side of Tog's chest was caved in, and he struggled to breathe. Kryder knew if he'd been conscious, the pain would have been unbearable. He stared and was unsure of what he should do. He heard his Aunt Katheen's voice from a sermon she'd once taught. 'Mortals have free will to choose. Of good and evil, only one can save you.'

Only one can save you. Only one. One. Only One. The Book Of The One. Kryder closed his eyes and prayed. *Creator…will you hear me?*

* * *

Kryder appeared in a bright room. Seated on a throne was something—or someone. He could not describe the image, though his mind desperately tried.

"Kryder Narvok. In you, I am pleased. You have chosen to ask your Creator to answer your prayer. You have bypassed all the deities I have given to the world of Kerr. Tell me why."

"I..." Kryder answered. "The Book Of The One tells us only One can save us. You are the One."

"I am," the Creator said.

Kryder felt a strength flow through him. It was as if he had slept well all night long. He also felt the pressure of his gift yearning to be released. It was stronger than he'd ever felt before.

"I have known you before you were born. I know you now, and I know you for eternity. You will bring balance to Kerr. With free will, you have made decisions leading you here. I know all possibilities. All. In this one, I am pleased."

Kryder felt a slight weight on his chest. He looked down and saw he was wearing a necklace. On it was a symbol. A wooden cross.

"Kryder Narvok, I accept you. I have given you a symbol, one unknown in this reality. In others, it is well known. Those places do not concern you. Wear my symbol and know your prayers will be answered."

Kryder was speechless. He looked around the room and saw the faces of all the deities he knew, and many he didn't. All looked pleased.

"You have the gift given to those in this world who are to protect the weak and the innocent. This is part of my plan, and has been since time began in your reality. Use it with prayer. Together, the balance will be restored."

"Go," the Creator said. "An immortal is loosed upon Kerr. I would have it sent back to its place."

As the room faded, Kryder heard, "Know your place."

* * *

Kryder watched as Tog's chest reshaped itself, and his cousin's breath came easier. Below his hands, a bright purple light shone. It was not the blue he had seen before from prayer spells.

He stood and turned toward the demon. The blood had stopped dripping from its hands. Zargall looked up and snarled, showing sharp fangs. Its mouth slowly closed as it stared at the cross on Kryder's chest. When the Prince of Fear's eyes rose to meet his, Kryder saw the fear in *them.*

Kryder raised his hand. *Please?* His mother's ring glowed purple as Kryder spoke the words. His hand held steady as Zargall's arms were pinned to his sides. The demon could not move.

"How?" Zargall asked. His raspy voice was barely a whisper. "There is no circle. How am I bound?"

"You are bound because our Creator wills it so. I will send you to your home, but only if you swear to never enter the world of mortals again. Or I will simply leave you here for the forest to grow up around you in time."

"I swear," Zargall said.

"No, that won't work," Tog said. He stepped up beside Kryder and tapped the side of his axe in his palm. "We've seen this. Do it right."

"I swear by the Creator, I will never return to the mortal world."

Kryder's cross flashed a brilliant purple.

Kryder spoke the words he'd memorized weeks ago. A hole opened below the demon. Kryder released him, and he fell. The hole closed over it.

* * * * *

Chapter Thirty-Two

"What do ye mean, King Jondal wants to see me?" Johan asked the squire in front of him.

"More than three thousand Yaylok prisoners surrendered without fighting yesterday," June said. "A handful of companies. Several of them were mercenary companies. Maybe it has something to do with that."

"I heard two mages never cast a spell and are with them," Dolner added.

"All I know is, he sent me to get you, my lord," the squire answered.

"Lord?" Lucas asked. "I've never known ye to be of noble blood, but it fits ye."

"I'm no noble, to be sure," Johan said. "Fine, take me to him." Johan mounted Kryder's horse.

An hour later, Johan was back. He was pale as a ghost. Katheen rose from beside the young soldier she was tending. "Are you all right? Is it your chest? I don't know how it can be your heart. You were healed."

"No, sister," Johan said. "It's not me heart hurting. It's me head. I…I."

"What happened?" Kryder asked.

"Those men," Johan said. "The prisoners. I know many o' them. I've known some for years. They…I."

"Look," Tog said. He pointed with the chicken leg in his big hand. "You need to start making sense. Kryder confuses me enough."

"It would seem a message was sent to King Jondal from someone named Kelly. The king of Yaylok abdicated his throne. Up and walked away from it, he did. This Kelly says he left it to me."

"What?" Dolner asked. "Well, what do you know? King Johan."

"What now?" Sylif asked.

"Now I pack my things. I've over three thousand o' me soldiers ready to march home, with me leading the lot o' them."

* * *

The next day, the same squire came looking for Kryder.

"Why does he need to see me?" Kryder asked.

"Maybe you get a kingdom, too," Tog teased. "I mean, the chief of the Running Boars did kill King Westell and two of his guards."

"They deserved it," Kryder said. He turned back to the squire. "I'm not getting a kingdom, right?"

"He did mention something about the Marent family being next in line to the throne in Gar-Noth," the squire answered. "Whatever that means."

* * * * *

About Kevin Steverson

Kevin Steverson is a retired veteran of the U.S. Army. He is the author of the Amazon best selling science fiction novels, the Salvage Title Trilogy, which are now optioned for feature film. He is a published songwriter as well as an author. When he is not on the road as the Tour Manager for the band Cypress Spring, he can be found in the foothills of the NE Georgia mountains, writing in one fashion or another.

Website: www.kevinsteverson.com

Instagram: kevin.steverson

Facebook: https://www.facebook.com/kevin.steverson.9

Twitter: @CallMeCatHead

* * * * *

About Tyler Ackerman

Tyler Ackerman is a singer/songwriter and an international touring artist. He is one half of the duo Cypress Spring. He lives in Ohio, where he and Melissa are raising their two boys. A fan of the fantasy genre, his first foray into writing stories as opposed to songs is a collaboration with the novel Burnt.

* * * * *

Get the free Four Horsemen prelude story "Shattered Crucible"

and discover other New Mythology titles at:

http://chriskennedypublishing.com/

* * * * *

The following is an

Excerpt from Book One of Forge and Sword:

Keep of Glass

Steven G. Johnson

Available Now from New Mythology Press

eBook, Paperback, and (soon) Audio Book

Excerpt from "Keep of Glass:"

Trinadan peered at the spot Forge was examining. She thought she saw a bit of movement.

A second later, the wildlife burst into squawking, scrambling motion all around them. A family of rabbits rushed across the trail in a close grouping, making for the distance with great, stammering hops. Birds exploded from every tree and bush in the vicinity, fleeing upward like ashes from a drenched fire. She heard the bleat of red deer and saw a bluish-green lizard leap from tree to tree on fans of skin under its arms.

Forge was off his horse and on the ground in one step, as smoothly as if his horse were still. In another instant, he unslung and strung his bow, nocking an arrow as he knelt behind a blackberry tangle along the trailside. His gray eyes had not left the bend in the trail behind them.

"Forge, what—"

But then she heard it, the thunder of hoofbeats. Several horses, driven hard, had panicked the animals as they crashed toward the spot on the trail where Trinadan's little convoy stood idle. She barely had time to turn her charger around.

And they were upon her. Three horses, swathed in yellow and blue, rounded the bend at speed, weapons held high. They saw her and pointed, the leader in half-plate and a high bucket helm as he spurred into a full-tilt gallop, taking the lead from his two companions. She saw his lance drop to fighting trim, its head growing enormously as it arrowed toward her at the speed of a maddened horse. The head was not the basket-cup of a jousting lance, but real iron, forged and worked to a cruel point.

* * * * *

Get "Keep of Glass" now at:
https://www.amazon.com/dp/B08RMVLWXV.

Find out more about Steven G. Johnson and "Keep of Glass" at:
https://chriskennedypublishing.com

****

The following is an

Excerpt from Book One of The Watchers of Moniah:

The Watchers of Moniah

Barbara V. Evers

Now Available from New Mythology Press

eBook, Paperback, and (soon) Audio Book

Excerpt from "The Watchers of Moniah:"

The queen focused on the gentle bubbling and ignored the stream of sweat trickling between her shoulder blades. "Send in the champions."

The assemblage shouted their approval as two foreigners walked forward to accept the accolades they deserved. The men's lighter coloring no longer startled Chiora unlike the day she and a squad of Watchers found them at the bottom of a muddy cliff. The man on the right, Micah, saved her life during the war with Maligon. Her gaze ran over his tall, lithe build in appreciation. Light hair, bleached white from the sun, glowed against his Monian-kissed suntan like bones on the prairie. Clear blue eyes gazed at her with startling familiarity, stuttering the pulse in her neck.

She drew another calming breath as his companion knelt before her. Unlike Micah, this man's fair skin had blistered and burned in the harsh sun of their land, a point that favored the reward she would grant him.

Micah maintained his focus on her and nodded in acknowledgement before kneeling. Chiora breathed deeper to suppress the shiver of excitement prompted by his forthright behavior.

"Our dear champions." Her low-pitched voice echoed throughout the huge open hall. She thanked the Creator that it came out strong and clear, with no hint of the emotions tumbling her soul. "Your journey from beyond the northern mountains came at a fortuitous time. Your courage in the face of our recent struggles brought peace to our lands. As reward, the kingdoms have decided to grant you titles and property." She turned to Micah's companion. "Donel, you will be known as Sir Donel and receive land as a vassal to Queen Roassa of Elwar."

A glimmer of a smile ghosted his face. She suspected his pleasure stemmed from admiration for Roassa rather than the title and cooler climate. Her sister queen shared this interest and had suggested his placement in Elwar rather than Moniah.

Whereas, Chiora could not stop thinking about the other man before her. Micah.

She stood and approached him, placing her hand on his shoulder in the formal greeting reserved for one of her subjects. "As for you, Micah—"

As her fingers settled on his rough, leather vest, the bond with Ju'latti surged into her mind in a flash of light. She gasped, closing her eyes. An image appeared. Micah stood by her side. Between them stood a young girl, her skin a blending of Chiora's amber-colored skin and Micah's pale complexion. The child's hair was twisted into a Watcher's braid the shades of a lion's mane. In the image, the girl walked away from her parents. With each step, they faded from view, first Chiora, and then Micah. The girl continued to walk forward, alone.

The landscape around the child changed, first the flat plains of Moniah, then the mountains and forests of Elwar. With each step, the girl matured. She halted at the top of a hill, now a young woman dressed in leathers, a quiver of arrows strung over her back, a sword at her side. The shadow of a man emerged from the forests and stood beside her. A divided path lay before them, one route blocked by a monstrous blazing fire, the other by a wall taller than the eye could see. The young woman raised her head, blue eyes blazing, and stepped forward, aiming for the point where the two paths merged together in a wall of conflagration. The man's shadow followed.

Chiora bent over, gasping for air, as the vision faded. Two Teachers of the Faith rushed to her side, their green robes swaying in their urgency to support their queen, but Chiora remained upright, her fingers digging into Micah's shoulder. He rose to steady her, a look of concern in his eyes. She gazed back at him, the warmth of his touch flooding her veins.

The Creator had not only sent her a champion to help defeat Maligon, he had sent her a partner. They would make a strong child together, an heir to Moniah's Seat of Authority. A child who would face insurmountable struggles.

*****

****

The following is an

Excerpt from Book One of The Milesian Accords:

A Reluctant Druid

Jon R. Osborne

Available Now from Blood Moon Press

eBook, Audio, and Paperback

Excerpt from "A Reluctant Druid:"

"Don't crank on it; you'll strip it."

Liam paused from trying to loosen the stubborn bolt holding the oil filter housing on his Yamaha motorcycle, looking for the source of the unsolicited advice. The voice was gruff, with an accent and cadence that made Liam think of the Swedish Chef from the Muppets. The garage door was open for air circulation, and two figures were standing in the driveway, illuminated by the setting sun. As they approached and stepped into the shadows of the house, Liam could see they were Pixel and a short, stout man with a greying beard that would do ZZ Top proud. The breeze blowing into the garage carried a hint of flowers.

Liam experienced a moment of double vision as he looked at the pair. Pixel's eyes took on the violet glow he thought he'd seen before, while her companion lost six inches in height, until he was only as tall as Pixel. What the short man lacked in height, he made up for in physique; he was built like a fireplug. He was packed into blue jeans and a biker's leather jacket, and goggles were perched over the bandana covering his salt and pepper hair. Leather biker boots crunched the gravel as he walked toward the garage. Pixel followed him, having traded her workout clothes for black jeans and a pink t-shirt that left her midriff exposed. A pair of sunglasses dangled from the neckline of her t-shirt.

"He's seeing through the glamour," the short, bearded man grumbled to Pixel, his bushy eyebrows furrowing.

"Well duh. We're on his home turf, and this is his place of power" Pixel replied nonchalantly. "He was pushing back against my glamour yesterday, and I'm not adding two hands to my height."

Liam set down the socket wrench and ran through the mental inventory of items in the garage that were weapons or could be used as them. The back half of the garage was a workshop, which included the results of his dabbling with blacksmithing and sword-crafting, so the list was considerable. But the most suitable were also the farthest away.

"Can I help you?" Liam stood and brushed off his jeans; a crowbar was three steps away. Where had they come from? Liam hadn't heard a car or motorcycle outside, and the house was a mile and a half outside of town.

"Ja, you can." The stout man stopped at the threshold of the garage. His steel-grey eyes flicked from Liam to the workbench and back. He held his hands out, palms down. The hands were larger than his and weren't strangers to hard work and possibly violence. "And there's no need to be unhospitable; we come as friends. My name is Einar, and you've already met Pixel."

"Hi, Liam." Pixel was as bubbly as yesterday. While she didn't seem to be making the same connection as Einar regarding the workbench, her eyes darted about the cluttered garage and the dim workshop behind it. "Wow, you have a lot of junk."

"What's this about?" Liam sidled a half step toward the workbench, regretting he hadn't kept up on his martial arts. He had three brown belts, a year of kendo, and some miscellaneous weapons training scattered over two decades but not much experience in the way of real fighting. He could probably hold his own in a brawl as long as his opponent didn't have serious skills. He suspected Einar was more than a Friday night brawler in the local watering hole. "Is she your daughter?"

Einar turned to the purple-haired girl, his caterpillar-like eyebrows gathering. "What did you do?"

"What? I only asked him a few questions and checked him out," Pixel protested, her hands going to her hips as she squared off with

Einar. "It's not as if I tried to jump his bones right there in the store or something."

"Look mister, if you think something untoward happened between me and your daughter –" Liam began.

"She's not my pocking daughter, and I don't give a troll's ass if you diddled her," Einar interrupted, his accent thickening with his agitation. He took a deep breath, his barrel chest heaving. "Now, will you hear me out without you trying to brain me with that tire iron you've been eyeing?"

"You said diddle." Pixel giggled.

"Can you be serious for five minutes, you pocking faerie?" Einar glowered, his leather jacket creaking as he crossed his arms.

"Remember 'dwarf,' you're here as an 'advisor.'" Pixel included air quotes with the last word, her eyes turning magenta. "The Nine Realms are only involved out of politeness."

"Politeness! If you pocking Tuatha and Tylwyth Teg hadn't folded up when the Milesians came at you, maybe we wouldn't be here to begin with!" Spittle accompanied Einar's protest. "Tylwyth? More like Toothless!"

"Like your jarls didn't roll over and show their bellies when the Avramites showed up with their One God and their gold!" Pixel rose up on her toes. "Your people took their god and took their gold and then attacked our ancestral lands!"

"Guys!" Liam had stepped over to the workbench but hadn't picked up the crowbar. "Are you playing one of those live-action role playing games or something? Because if you are, I'm calling my garage out of bounds. Take your LARP somewhere else."

"We've come a long way to speak to you," Einar replied, looking away from Pixel. "I'm from Asgard."

"Asgard? You mean like Thor and Odin? What kind of game are you playing?" Liam hadn't moved from the workbench, but he'd mapped in his mind the steps he'd need to take to reach a stout pole which would serve as a staff while he back-pedaled to his workshop, where a half-dozen half-finished sword prototypes rested. From where he stood, though, he didn't feel as threatened. He knew a bit about gamers because there were a fair number of them among the pagan community, and he'd absorbed bits and pieces of it. Maybe someone had pointed Liam out to Pixel as research about druids for one of these games—an over-enthusiastic player who wanted to more convincingly roleplay one.

"Gods I hate those pocking things," Einar grumbled, rubbing his forehead while Pixel stifled another giggle. "Look, can we sit down and talk to you? This is much more serious than some pocking games you folk play with your costumes and your toy weapons."

"This isn't a game, and we aren't hippies with New Age books and a need for self-validation." Pixel added. Her eyes had faded to a lavender color. "Liam, we need your help."

*****

Get "A Reluctant Druid" at
https://www.amazon.com/dp/B07716V2RN.

Find out more about Jon R. Osborne and "A Reluctant Druid" at:
https://chriskennedypublishing.com/imprints-authors/jon-r-osborne/

*****

Made in the USA
Middletown, DE
21 May 2022